GIRL A

DAN SCOTTOW

To David,

Thanks so much for your
support. You're a star.
Enjoy, and keep
reading!

BLOODHOUND
— BOOKS —

Print ISBN 978-1-913942-38-0

ALSO BY DAN SCOTTOW

Damaged

For my Dad. Trying every day to make you proud.

PROLOGUE

JULY 1985, PERRY BARR, BIRMINGHAM, ENGLAND.

Meandering through the crowd, Wendy Noakes has a broad smile on her face, and Billy's tiny hand in her own. The warm early-evening sun beats down on her bare shoulders. People are out in droves for a visiting summer fair. Billy is too young for the rides, but he wanted to come. Wendy's husband is at home. He couldn't be bothered with it all. Noisy crowds and screaming teenagers are not his thing. But Wendy doesn't care. These are the memories that Billy will look back fondly on when he's older. It's a shame that Doug isn't here, but at least Billy will remember his mother at the fair, in the sunshine. Perhaps he will recall her backless white linen sundress, with the three large wooden buttons on the front, or the pink plastic slides in her long sandy-blonde hair. Maybe not. But hopefully he *will* remember tonight.

Brightly coloured balloons are tied up in bunches all around them. The ghost train rattles on its tracks, cutting over the rest of the noise. Laughter and the odd scream bellow out from all directions, as kids and adults alike scare themselves silly on the rides. There is a clatter as a pile of cans is knocked over somewhere close by.

Billy giggles.

Wendy looks down at her beautiful son. His blond, almost white, hair curling at the ends. Doug says Billy needs a haircut, but Wendy wants to let it grow. He looks so adorable in his blue-and-white stripy T-shirt, and denim shorts with turn-ups, finished with a little pair of brown sandals. Her heart melts as she looks at him, and he beams back at her. The sickly-sweet smell of sugar and popcorn drifts into Wendy's nostrils, and she smiles again, crouching down beside Billy.

'Would you like to try some candyfloss?' Wendy asks him.

Billy looks confused. He doesn't know what Wendy means, so she points to the pink fluffy mass that a child nearby is gobbling up greedily. Billy smiles and nods. Wendy straightens up, and they walk hand in hand to the food stall. A spotty teenager behind the counter looks towards Wendy and she holds up two fingers, nodding at the candyfloss maker. Billy giggles again as the girl winds the sugary strands around a wooden stick. Wendy can't stop grinning as her son sees the joy of candyfloss for the first time in his life. As she watches, she hears a voice from her left-hand side.

'Wendy?'

She turns her head and sees an old classmate from school approaching. Becky, or Brenda, she can't remember, and bites her lip in embarrassment. They were never particularly close. The woman grins as she marches towards the food stall.

'Wendy Boyce? I thought it was you. How the devil *are* you?'

'I'm good, thanks. It's Wendy Noakes now. How are you? I've not seen you since...' She trails off, hoping the woman will fill in the blanks.

She obliges instantly.

'Leavers' dance! Can you believe it's been twelve years? I didn't know you were still living around here. I never see you about.'

Wendy blushes and smiles as she thinks about that night, a long time ago.

The awful bubblegum-pink dress she wore.

She looks down at the grass.

From behind the counter, the server holds out the two sticks of candyfloss, breaking the awkward silence that has ensued.

'That'll be three quid, please,' the girl shouts over the noise of the fair. Wendy lets go of Billy's hand, rummaging around in her purse for the change. She hands it over and takes the treats, turning back to Becky, or Brenda. Or is it Bella?

'No. I moved away for a little while, into London. My mother was unwell last year, so my husband and I came back to be closer to her.'

'Oh, what a shame. How is your mum now?'

'Yes, she's much better, thanks. So... what about you?'

Wendy doesn't care, but she was raised to be polite.

The woman reaches up and fans out her hand, wiggling her fingers excitedly to show a plain gold wedding band.

'Chris and I got married... no surprises there, I suppose. He's over on that horrible ride.' She points at a huge machine, spinning carriages of people around, high into the air. 'No, thank you! So me and Chris Junior here are getting some treats, aren't we, hun?' A plump boy a few years older than Billy stands near her, and nods impatiently. He's more interested in the food than the conversation.

'Have you got kids?' the woman asks, and Wendy smiles.

'Just the one for now. This is Billy.' She glances down behind her, but Billy is not there. She spins round in confusion, looking for her son, but she can't spot him among all the people. Her heart pounds. The noise seems to dissipate, and all she can hear is her own heavy breathing, her heart thumping in her chest. Everything seems to slow down.

'Billy?' she shouts as confusion turns to panic. People turn around, hearing fear in her voice.

The woman takes a step closer to her. 'Is everything okay, hun?'

'It's my son. He was right here... next to me. I only let go of his hand for a second...' She turns towards the girl who had served her. 'Did you see my son? Do you know where he went?'

The teenager stares blankly at Wendy and shakes her head. 'He was *right* here, we ordered the candyfloss together, remember?' The girl seems embarrassed. She's not used to dealing with uptight mothers.

Becky, or Brenda, or whatever her name is, places a hand on Wendy's shoulder. 'Why don't you try to calm down, hun. He's probably wandered off to look at something. He can't have gone very far now, can he?'

Wendy shrugs her hand off. 'Don't tell me to calm down. My son is gone. He's only two.' She drops the candyfloss onto the grass by her feet and runs a few paces into the throng of people.

'Billy! Billy, where are you?' She's screaming now. People turn and stare, Wendy doesn't care. She glances around, but she can't see his stripy T-shirt anywhere. Everything is blurry. Tears distort her vision.

'BILLY!'

People are milling around her, asking what's wrong.

She can hear the murmur of the crowd.

'My son. He's two. Blond hair!' she shouts. 'He's wearing a stripy blue-and-white top and denim shorts. Has anybody seen him?'

But the people around her shake their heads.

Wendy wants it all to stop.

She runs from stall to stall demanding if anyone has seen her son, but nobody has been paying attention. They are all enjoying themselves, and there are lots of small children wandering around. Wendy searches desperately, but she can't find him.

As the red sun sets on the horizon, across the park at the edge of the field, three tiny figures walk away from the fair. Their elongated shadows trail across the grass behind them. A little blond boy in a stripy T-shirt holds the hand of a young girl, as she and an older boy lead him into the woods, away from his mother.

Away from his life.

1

Two little words.

That was all it took. Eight letters scribbled on a scrap of paper, and one family's world was about to come crashing down around them. When you imagine things that might alter the course of your life, you think of major catastrophic events.

A car crash. An illness. Hard-hitting, a punch in the face.

In reality, sometimes it's not like that at all. As Charlie Carter sat watching the television with his wife Beth on a Friday evening, neither of them had any idea that everything they knew was about to change.

A quiet existence was all they wanted. And so they made one for themselves. Two great kids. A nice secluded farmhouse with no neighbours. The Carters kept themselves to themselves and they were happy that way.

As Charlie watched Beth struggling to stay awake, two fictional detectives on the telly argued about who the killer may or may not be. The security light at the front of the house flicked on suddenly, streaming through the bay window. This was not so unusual in their remote location; often triggered by a cat or a fox, sometimes maybe even a bat.

But tonight the loud and unmistakable chime of the doorbell closely followed, echoing through their home.

The dog barked excitedly. Charlie and Beth glanced up from the television and their eyes met across the living room. Charlie frowned, the unspoken question between them, *who could that be?*

Beth glanced at the clock on the wall opposite, as did Charlie. Ten thirty. Bit late for a house call, with their closest neighbours being a five-minute drive away.

Cooper the spaniel ran out to the hallway, still yapping.

'I'll go,' Charlie said as he pulled himself up from his armchair. He made his way to the front door, but it surprised Beth that he didn't open it. She stood up and walked to the doorway, leaning against the frame as she watched her husband. He straightened, having crouched to pick something up, and now stood with his back to her, shoulders hunched. From the angle, it looked like he was holding something. His body obscured her view. Charlie turned around scratching his head, a puzzled look on his face. In his hand, a small sheet of paper.

'What's that?' Beth asked through a yawn, tucking a strand of blonde hair behind her ear.

Charlie held up the paper. 'It's a note.'

'Who for?'

Charlie turned it over in his hands. 'Not sure. It doesn't say.' He held it out, and Beth walked over to his side, taking it from him. He waited as his wife read it. She pulled a face and handed it back to him.

'Must be one of Peter's mates having a laugh or something,' she said dismissively.

Charlie opened the front door and stepped out into the darkness, the timer on the security light having turned it off by now. The beam clicked back on as he took a few paces out onto the driveway, gravel crunching under his feet.

'Hello?' he called out. 'Anybody there?'

Beth moved forwards, but lingered in the doorway.

Nothing. The calm of night. No retreating footsteps. No roar of a car engine, or screech of tyres speeding away from the road at the end of the drive. Only eerie silence.

Charlie came back into the house, shutting the door behind him and sliding the security chain into place. He turned and walked along the hall into the kitchen, tossing the note onto the worktop. He filled the kettle at the sink and flicked it on to boil. Beth switched off the TV and joined her husband.

He was staring at the note, the words scrawled in scratchy black ink on the small scrap of paper.

FOUND YOU.

'Bit weird, though, isn't it?' Charlie said, holding it towards his wife. 'And it's late. Plus all Peter's mates will be out with him tonight at that party.'

Beth took it and folded it in half along the creases, placing it back down in front of her. 'You know what teenagers are like. Probably a game.'

'If it doesn't involve his phone, I doubt that very much,' Charlie retorted, with a sneer.

The sound of soft footsteps on carpet drew their attention out to the hallway. Daisy, their six-year-old daughter came padding barefoot down the stairs, in her pink unicorn pyjamas, rubbing her eyes.

Charlie turned, scooping her up in his arms. 'What are you doing out of bed, you little rascal?' he whispered into her ear, before kissing her softly on top of her head.

'I heard the doorbell,' Daisy replied. She wasn't fully awake yet. Her hair, dark brown, the same as her father's, matted from slumber.

'Yep, you did. But don't you worry about that. You should be asleep! It's *very* late.' Charlie spun around with Daisy in his arms, and she giggled.

'I *was* asleep. The bell woke me up,' Daisy protested.

'That was very naughty of someone ringing the doorbell at this time of night and waking you up. Why don't I take you back up to bed and tuck you in?' Charlie said playfully.

'Okay,' Daisy replied.

Charlie carried her over to Beth, who gave her a kiss on the forehead. 'Night. Sweet dreams, love,' she said.

As Charlie turned and walked up the stairs with their daughter in his arms, Beth fingered the note on the worktop, pushing it around as if it were dirty. As if touching it might transfer something foul to her skin. She flicked it open and looked down at the words again.

Cooper yapped at the back door. Beth shushed him. He sat staring at her, whining. The kettle clicked and Beth poured two coffees. She listened as Charlie's footsteps plodded down the stairs, and she folded the note back over, crossing the kitchen. She opened the fridge, taking out the milk, before returning to the cups. Charlie leaned on the worktop, picking up the paper again.

Beth watched his brow knit, as his dark eyes read it once more.

'I'll ask Peter in the morning when he's home,' she said. 'I'm sure it's nothing to worry about.'

Charlie dropped the note on the worktop and Beth joined him at his side, handing him a cup of coffee. He took it, turning to go up the stairs. 'Bed.'

'You go. I'll let the dog out. Be up in a minute.'

She reached her hand around the back of Charlie's head, ruffling his short, thinning hair, then pulled his face towards hers. His rough stubble rubbed against her cheek.

Charlie trudged up the stairs, pulling off his T-shirt as he went. As he entered the bedroom, he threw the top towards the laundry basket in the corner, missing. He walked into the en suite, picking up his electric toothbrush. Cooper was barking from downstairs, followed by the sound of the door closing as Beth let him back in from the garden. Charlie rinsed his mouth, expecting Beth to come join him in the bedroom but frowned when she didn't appear. He stepped out of the bathroom and walked out onto the landing, standing at the top of the stairs for a moment. The lights were extinguished below, but Beth was still down there. He stood, listening.

Silence.

Descending the stairs, he rounded the corner into the kitchen, where he found his wife in darkness, gazing out through the patio windows.

'What are you doing?' Charlie asked.

Beth didn't turn around. She continued to stare.

'Beth, are you okay?'

Charlie crossed the kitchen to his wife's side. She looked at him as if in a daze.

'Beth?'

'Sorry, love, I was daydreaming there.'

'You coming up to bed?'

'Yep,' she replied. And then she did something strange. She drew the curtains.

In seven years living in the farmhouse, Charlie had never seen Beth do this. There was no need. They lived in the middle of nowhere with a long driveway. A dense hedge and tall trees shielded their property from the road. Few people came out this way unless visiting the family. Charlie frowned again and watched with slight bewilderment as his wife meandered through the entire ground floor of the property closing every blind and curtain. She blocked out all the windows before heading up the stairs.

2

———

Bacon and coffee.

The smells filled the house as Charlie cooked breakfast in the Saturday morning sunlight.

He looked up as Beth appeared in the kitchen doorway. She hadn't slept much last night. Charlie heard her up a few times to go to the toilet. She wasn't looking her best now.

'Look what the cat dragged in,' Charlie joked as Beth stood in the doorway. He motioned with his head towards their sixteen-year-old son sitting at the island unit, his elbows on the worktop, and his thumbs jabbing away frantically at his phone.

'Hello, love,' Beth said, stifling a yawn. 'Good party?'

'Was all right,' he mumbled without looking at her.

The bacon sizzled in a pan on the hob. Cooper sat at Charlie's feet waiting for something to fall.

'Hungry?' Charlie asked, pouring Beth a cup of coffee and sliding it across the counter towards her.

'A little,' she replied. But Charlie thought she looked like she wanted to vomit.

'You were tossing most of the night so I thought I'd let you sleep.'

'Thanks,' Beth replied, turning to her son. 'Zoe not here?' she asked.

'Obviously not,' he retorted, still not glancing up from his phone, already mastering the art of sarcasm. He was his father's son in that respect.

'You two okay?' Beth questioned.

'Yeah, Mum, we're fine. We're not joined at the hip. She's got this thing with her parents today. She's coming over later.'

'Good,' Beth replied. Charlie and Beth liked their son's girlfriend.

Peter was a likeable boy, as far as teenagers go. The being permanently glued to his phone, and usually not being able to hold a conversation of over three words with his parents aside, he was a nice lad. Not a dick. No parent *really* knows what their child is like. But Zoe seemed pleasant enough. She didn't have those ridiculous painted-on eyebrows for a start, and that, in Charlie's books, gave her an immense head start over most girls her age. He failed to understand the thing with teenaged girls and eyebrows. But also, unlike their son, Zoe was always happy to chat to them, and she was a nice girl. And nice girls don't date total dicks. So Charlie was pretty sure that his son was *okay*. Some of his friends not so much. But you can't choose them any more than you can choose your kids.

Charlie shovelled the breakfast onto a plate, plonking it down with a clatter in front of Beth, who sat beside her son. Picking up a fork, she began to push food around the plate, unable to bring herself to eat it. She speared a small button mushroom from the edge of the dish. As she lifted it, a drop of fat ran from its edge and dripped onto the scrambled eggs below. Again, Beth looked like she might vomit. She placed the fork back on her plate, opting for a mouthful of coffee instead.

'The note wasn't Peter,' Charlie said, suddenly.

Beth froze, her mug halfway to her mouth.

'I can't believe you thought I'd actually have anything to do with some weird note through the door.'

Daisy skipped across the kitchen from where she had been sitting on the floor talking to Cooper.

'What note?' she asked inquisitively.

Charlie looked at Beth. She shook her head.

'Never you mind!' she said playfully, giving her daughter a fake punch on the shoulder.

Peter slammed his phone onto the worktop with an exaggerated, overdramatic sigh.

'Careful, Pete! If you break that screen again you'll be paying for it yourself this time!' Charlie shouted.

'Yeah, yeah. Whatever,' he grumbled, almost unintelligibly. 'Anyway, why would my mates put a note through the door saying, *found you*? That's just weird,' Peter continued.

'Peter, can we *not*.' Beth rolled her eyes towards Daisy.

Daisy climbed up on a stool opposite her brother and leaned on her fists with her bony elbows on the worktop. 'What note?' she shouted.

'I said never you mind, nosey!'

Beth shovelled a forkful of scrambled egg into her mouth. She chewed, but didn't swallow. She gulped a mouthful of hot coffee, washing down the food, then slid her plate away from her, placing her fork on the counter. Charlie eyed her curiously, and then the plate, a mock sad expression on his face. He stuck out his bottom lip in protest, folding his arms across his chest.

'Oi!'

'Sorry. I've... lost my appetite.'

Beth shot her husband a weak smile.

Charlie picked up the plate. 'Suit yourself.'

He offered the food to Peter, who shook his head, pushing it away.

'Why do I bother?' Charlie crossed the kitchen, bending over and scraping the food into Cooper's red plastic bowl by the back door. Cooper scurried over to it, gobbling up the bacon and eggs.

'I knew *you* wouldn't disappoint me, buddy.'

Charlie crouched, stroking the spaniel on his head. Cooper wagged his tail and trotted off to his bed in the corner.

Peter slid off his stool and strolled to the fridge. He opened it, taking a bottle of lemonade out, before removing the lid and gulping it straight down.

'Oi! Glass!' Charlie shouted.

Peter burped, wiping his mouth with the back of his hand. 'Why were the curtains drawn this morning when I got home?' he asked from across the kitchen.

Charlie looked towards his wife. All eyes in the room were on Beth

'Because I wanted them shut,' Beth replied, rather unconvincingly.

Charlie frowned. Something about Beth's behaviour was off.

'*So* weird,' Peter said, shaking his head. 'I'm going to bed. I'm knackered.'

He sauntered out of the kitchen and up the stairs, dropping his denim jacket on the hall floor at the bottom. An aroma of stale beer and cigarettes followed behind him as he left. Beth stood up, picking up the jacket from the floor, and opened the cupboard. She hung the coat up on the rail inside.

'He's been smoking.'

'He's sixteen,' Charlie replied. 'Didn't you ever do anything wrong when you were a teenager?'

Beth shrugged and walked to the sink, filling her mug with water. Draining the cup, she filled it again, sitting on a stool at the island.

Charlie pulled at the doors, opening up the kitchen to the patio. Daisy skipped outside, followed by an excited spaniel. She picked up a tennis ball and threw it into the field beyond the garden. Cooper chased after it, bounding over the low fence and out after the ball.

'What the hell was that about?' Charlie asked as soon as Daisy was out of earshot.

'What?'

'The curtains. We *never* draw the curtains. There's nobody around for miles. Why would you close them? Are you okay?' Charlie sat down on the stool beside Beth.

'I thought it was a bit strange, that was all. Somebody had obviously been at the house to put that note through the door. I was worried they might be out there. I didn't like the idea of them looking at us. It gave me the creeps. That's all.'

Charlie wrapped his muscular arm around Beth's shoulder, and pulled her to his chest.

'Come here you wally,' he said with a laugh. 'It's like you thought last night. Probably someone having a laugh.'

'Yeah, you're probably right. I spooked myself. And then Cooper was growling. I felt... strange.'

'That's fair enough. It is odd, us getting a visitor at that time, I admit. But I really don't think it's anything to worry about.'

Charlie hopped up, grabbing his car keys from a bowl on the kitchen counter. He crossed to the hall cupboard and opened it, taking out his leather jacket, sliding it on.

'Right,' he said chirpily, 'I'm off to work. You going to be okay?'

Beth hugged her husband. 'Yeah. I'll be fine. I wish you weren't working on a Saturday though.'

'It's only for a few hours. I'll be back after lunch. I've got to tie a couple of things up at the office before Monday.'

He kissed her and walked towards the front door. Without another look he was away.

Daisy was playing with Cooper in the garden; aside from that the house was quiet. Beth headed upstairs for a shower.

17

∼

Peter lay on his bed in a pair of grubby white Calvin Klein pants. Unable to get to sleep, he listened to the sound of the shower running from his parent's en suite. A few minutes later the noise of footsteps padding down the stairs. He jumped up, opening the door and hurrying out onto the landing. 'Are you going out, Mum?' he shouted.

'Yeah, I'm popping into town for a bit,' Beth replied.

'Can you hold on? I'll grab a lift with you. Just need to throw some clothes on.'

He hurried back into his room, without waiting for a reply, pulling on a plain, black T-shirt, and a pair of baggy jeans with large rips in both knees. He rushed down the stairs into the kitchen.

'Have you had a shower?' Beth nagged, sniffing her son as he passed her.

'Nah, don't need one,' he replied, heading out of the front door.

Beth shook her head, following behind him.

They drove into town with Daisy and Peter arguing for most of the thirty-minute journey. Beth pulled up in a parking bay and the kids jumped out onto the pavement.

'How long you going to be, Mum? I've got to pop to the record shop. There's some new vinyl I want.'

'Don't know, Peter, call me when you're done.' She pulled her phone out of her bag, checking her battery.

'Can I go with Peter?' Daisy asked.

'No!' Peter protested. Beth shot him a scolding look.

'Please, Petey?' Daisy's tone indicated a tantrum was imminent. Beth mouthed *please* to her son.

'Fine,' Peter said sulkily.

'Don't let her out of your sight,' Beth shouted as the kids

walked away from her. She watched them turn the corner, then she sighed and glanced around. Town was busy. Saturday morning shoppers lined the streets, and Beth felt a little more relaxed.

She'd felt a sudden need to be around people. She didn't need anything in town. It was just nice to be out of the house.

She crossed the street and headed into a small coffee shop. As she was standing staring blankly at the menu, someone tapped her on the shoulder.

Beth pivoted, still a little on edge, and found herself looking up at a tall woman.

'Margot! Hello,' Beth said, relieved to see someone she recognised. Margot was a lawyer at the small publishers in town where Beth worked. Crossing paths most days, she was probably as close to a friend as Beth had.

Margot was in her early-forties, at a guess, about five feet eleven and eternally stylish. She had deep auburn hair, dyed, Beth had always assumed, but impeccably styled. Being single and having no children, she had all her money to spend on herself. And money was something she had in abundance. She was independently wealthy from a successful career in law, but as Beth understood it, when Margot's husband found out that she couldn't conceive children, he had left her. And Margot had taken him to the cleaners. This morning Margot was wearing an ankle-length cashmere jumper dress, in varying shades of blue. She had a white silk scarf with royal-blue doves printed on it, draped over her shoulders, and an enormous pair of designer sunglasses covering her eyes. Reddish-brown hair fell in loose curls around her shoulders. She pulled the glasses off, revealing her expertly applied make-up, and gave Beth a tight smile.

'Beth, hi!' she said, with a loud air-kiss on each cheek. 'What a surprise! It's so lovely to see a friendly face, darling! I absolutely abhor these Saturday morning shoppers. Try to avoid them whenever I can but needs must.' Margot's perfect received pronunciation stank of an exceedingly expensive education. When she had first started at Greys a few years earlier, Beth had been terrified of her. But the first time they'd chatted, side by side at a mirror in the toilets, they had clicked. Margot had been touching up her flawless make-up. Beth had been fiddling with her hair, tucking it behind her ears, then tying it back in a loose ponytail. Margot had given her a sideways look in the mirror and said, 'You should wear it down. It's fabulous,' before offering Beth her Christian Louboutin lipstick to try.

Margot had spent the majority of her career in London, working in family law. She also devoted most of her free time and a *lot* of her money volunteering with underprivileged children. She had once claimed rather flippantly to Beth that as she couldn't have any of the little buggers herself, she thought she would help the ones that other people didn't want.

'How are you? I didn't see you at work this week, were you off?' Beth asked, still half reading the coffee-shop menu on the wall behind the counter.

'Indeed I was, my dear. Helping out with some kids. They needed a chaperone on a camping trip, so I thought what the hell, why not?'

Beth smiled briefly at the idea of Margot camping but refrained from commenting.

A young lad turned to Beth from behind the till. *Camp* was an understatement. Tall, and slim, wearing far too much make-up; she couldn't help thinking he could do with some lessons from Margot on how to apply it properly.

'What can I get you?' he asked.

With one last glance up at the menu, Beth ordered a tall, skinny Americano. 'And whatever she's having.' She motioned towards Margot.

'Not at all, darling. These are on me. I'll get a vanilla oat latte, please,' she said.

'Really, I'll get these,' Beth objected, taking out a crisp ten-pound note from her purse.

'Put it away, darling, I insist.' She gave *Kyle*, as his badge informed them was his name, a huge stage wink. The boy didn't crack a smile. He stared at Margot, holding out his hand for the money.

She handed him some cash and turned to Beth, shaking her head. 'Honestly, I don't know what's wrong with young people these days. No humour.'

Kyle handed them their drinks and they grabbed a table in the corner by the window.

As they sat down Margot smoothed out the creases from her dress. She saw Beth staring at her and smiled. 'You like? It's Prada, darling. I got it in Paris at fashion week.'

'It's beautiful. Really suits you,' Beth said. Margot swatted her hand, with a smile on her face.

'So...' Beth started. 'Camping?' She raised an eyebrow.

'It was an absolute bloody nightmare, darling! I tell you. If I ever think about doing anything like that again, you have my permission to slap me, please. You should have *seen* the lavatories. I didn't urinate for five entire days.'

Beth laughed, pleased for the distraction. 'What on earth were you thinking?'

Margot took a sip from her oat latte, then dabbed at the corner of her mouth with a paper napkin.

'The trip was on the verge of being cancelled if they couldn't find another chaperone. These kids, they don't have good lives. It's rare they look forward to anything. So to cancel something like this trip... for them it would be absolutely devastating. I couldn't do that to them. As awful as it was... it was worth it to see them enjoying themselves.'

Beth took a sip from her own drink, slightly in awe of Margot. The woman was a machine. She worked long hours, sometimes seven days a week. When she wasn't working, she seemed to be off somewhere helping out for some good cause or another. Beth felt so tired after her Monday to Friday, nine-to-five, that she could barely manage a conversation with her husband at the weekends, let alone keep her *own* children entertained.

Margot finished her coffee, then pulled a compact mirror from her small Chanel handbag. She opened the case and reapplied her lipstick, as quick as a flash. The edges perfect and precise. She snapped the mirror closed, popping it back in her bag.

'Anyway, darling, I've got to go. I have an appointment with my accountant. Was lovely to see you though. Let's do lunch one day this week. I'm back in the office on Monday.' She stood up from her chair, and glided gracefully out of the coffee shop, leaving a trail of perfume in her wake.

Beth stared after her for a few moments. Two short beeps from her purse told her a text message had arrived. She pulled her mobile from the bag, glancing at the screen. It was from Peter.

At the car. Where are you?

Beth drained her mug of what was left of her drink and then left the café, making her way back towards the shops.

Peter stood leaning against his mother's car. Two girls from school, Melissa and Jodie approached him, and started chatting.

'Can't believe the holidays are nearly finished,' Jodie said, smiling at Peter, twiddling her hair. 'Have you had a good summer?'

'Yeah, it wasn't bad,' Peter replied nonchalantly, doing his best to sound mysterious and sexy. He saw his mother come around the corner on the high street and head towards the car, and he hoped to God that she wouldn't embarrass him. As she got closer, he saw her expression change, and she picked up her pace a little.

'Where's your sister?' she called to him. Peter looked back towards his mother, then down by his side where he thought Daisy was standing.

But she wasn't there.

Peter shrugged and turned back towards his conversation.

'Where is Daisy?' Beth stormed up to Peter and stood in between him and the two girls.

Peter looked at his mother. The girls did too. 'We'd best get off,' Melissa said with a smirk on her face.

'Yes, you best had,' Beth said sternly, as they turned and walked away. Peter cringed.

'She was right here, Mum, honest. She can't be far away.'

'You were supposed to be watching her!'

Peter scanned the crowds of people. What was Daisy wearing? He couldn't even remember.

'Daisy!' Beth shouted. 'Daisy, where are you?'

Peter thought she was overreacting, but nevertheless, he began calling out Daisy's name too. People were looking, the panic in Beth's voice causing a stir.

'Excuse me...' came a voice from behind Peter. He saw his mother spin round to face an elderly woman walking towards them, holding Daisy's hand.

'Daisy!' Beth shouted. 'Where the hell have you been?' She snatched Daisy's hand from the old lady.

'She was looking in the window of the toy shop,' the woman said.

'Don't you do that! What have I told you about wandering off? Don't ever, *ever* wander away!'

Daisy looked scared. 'I'm sorry, Mummy. The man said he wanted to show me something cool. I was only over there.' Daisy pulled her hand away from Beth, turning and pointing towards the shops across the road.

'What man?' Beth demanded.

Peter watched dumbfounded as his mother shouted at his poor sister.

Daisy was fine. Peter couldn't understand what all the fuss was about.

'I don't know,' Daisy continued. 'He said his name was Billy.'

The colour drained from Beth's face.

'He said that he knows you. He knew your name. That's why I thought it would be okay.'

Peter frowned, guilty that this had happened while he was meant to be watching his sister. He didn't recall seeing a man approach them, but admittedly his eyes had been on fixed on Melissa's low-cut top.

He chided himself for not paying more attention to Daisy, but he hadn't wanted her to tag along with him in the first place.

'Daisy, what man? Where is he? Is he still here?' Beth sounded calmer now, but Peter could tell she was still angry.

'Daisy, where is the man?'

Daisy looked around, crying now.

'He's gone. He said he was your friend. I thought it was okay,' she repeated.

Peter looked at his sister, noticing she was holding something.

'Daisy, did the man give you *that*?' Peter asked, an edge of concern in his voice now. It was a large, brightly coloured lollipop. Concentric circles in alternating colours, getting smaller into the middle.

Peter saw his mother's gaze turn towards Daisy's hand. Her eyes widened.

Peter watched in shock as his mother snatched the lollipop from Daisy. 'Did the man give this to you?' she asked, less stern, but deadly serious.

Daisy nodded.

'*Never* take sweeties from strangers. I've told you that so many times. Never! Understand?'

Beth threw the confectionary down onto the pavement. It hit the ground and shattered into tiny splinters. People were gawping now, but she didn't seem to care. Peter was mortified.

Daisy's eyes filled with tears.

'Mum, you're scaring her! What the hell? It's a lollipop... she didn't eat it. It's fine.'

'Get in the car!' Beth shouted.

Beth unlocked the Range Rover, opening the back door. Daisy crawled in, fastening her seat belt sheepishly, tears streaming over her cheeks. Peter climbed into the front. He tried not to look at the two girls he had been talking to, who now stood a few metres away staring at him with bemused expressions on their faces. They were whispering and laughing.

Beth pulled herself into the driver's seat, slamming the door with a thud. The kind old lady was shaking her head.

Peter sat in silence as his mother started the engine and sped off towards home.

3

'I still don't understand why you haven't called the police,' Charlie grunted, standing in the doorway.

'What would I tell them? That somebody gave our daughter a lollipop?' Beth replied.

'She could have been abducted!' Charlie slammed his fist against the door frame, making Beth jump in her seat. He rarely got angry.

Beth stood up from her armchair, ushering Charlie into the living room and closing the door.

'Can you keep your voice down. I've not long got her calmed. We don't want to set her off again.' She sat on the sofa in front of the bay window and patted the cushion next to her. Charlie sat obediently, still holding his leather jacket and car keys. He felt pissed off but was also aware that Beth had had a scare, so he was trying to keep his cool.

'Let's put this in perspective. She wasn't abducted. Somebody gave her a sweet and took her over the road to show her something in the window of the toy shop. And yes, that's creepy, and *definitely* not okay for a stranger to do that. But in the grand scheme of things, he didn't *do* anything illegal, and Daisy is fine. I upset her more with my meltdown. I had a scare and I overreacted.' Beth's voice, calm and matter of fact, bugged Charlie.

'I don't like it at all. And why the hell is she taking sweets and walking off with a stranger anyway? I hoped we'd brought our kids up to be much smarter than that.' Charlie's eyes, red and tired after a Saturday morning at work, bore into Beth's, as he tried to make sense of the situation.

Beth ran her hands through her hair, holding them on the back of her head. 'He said he knew me. He used my name. So Daisy assumed it would be okay. She's six.'

Charlie stood up. 'But that's even freakier. Why would somebody say that? And how would he have known your name?'

'I don't have the answer to either of those questions, Charlie, I'm sorry.'

Beth put her hand on his inner thigh and stroked his leg. 'The crucial thing is she is okay. She's upstairs, and she's fine.'

'And you're sure it's not someone from work?'

Beth put her fingers against her temples, sighing. 'One hundred per cent positive, Charlie. I don't work with anyone called Billy. And anyway, why wouldn't he have stuck around to speak to me? Rather than disappearing?'

'I guess,' Charlie mumbled. He walked to the door, opening it and leaning out into the hallway. 'Daisy! Can you come down here a minute please?' he shouted in the general direction of the stairs, his voice loud and authoritative. A few seconds later, they heard the sound of Daisy's bare feet on the stair carpet. She came into the living room sheepishly. Her eyes were still red from crying. Charlie sat back down next to Beth on the sofa.

'Sit down, love, will you?' Charlie said softly, motioning

towards the armchair with his head. Daisy crossed to the chair, plonking herself down.

'Your mum told me what happened in town.'

Daisy looked down at her hands and started fidgeting. For a second Charlie was worried she would bawl.

'It's okay, sweetheart. You're not in trouble. We just want to talk to you.'

'Okay,' Daisy replied quietly.

'So you remember that your mummy lost her parents when she was young?' Charlie asked.

'Yes. In a fire.' Daisy's eyes darted towards Beth.

'That's right.'

Beth sat staring at Daisy. Charlie hated having to bring back the memories for Beth, but this was important.

'And you know that Mummy doesn't have anyone from her childhood, any friends or anything, who you wouldn't recognise, right?'

Daisy looked at Beth for reassurance. Beth smiled, nodding. Daisy nodded too.

'Because she moved around a lot when she was little,' Daisy said, more assured this time, well versed in the story of Beth's upbringing.

Beth's father had been in the army. Beth and her parents had never settled in one place. She didn't remain in any school long enough to make any lasting friendships. She had been a very lonely child. Her parents were killed in a house fire when Beth was eighteen. When Charlie met her in the first year at university, she had still been grieving. She had been aloof with their peers and had struggled to bond with anyone. It took months for Charlie to get her to open up about her family. Charlie was one of the few people she told. Their friendship grew at a fast pace after she confided in him, and soon blossomed into a romance. They had been inseparable ever since. Beth had no friends. She didn't form any other relationships. She was guarded and private, except with Charlie. He had once asked her why she didn't have any friends. She looked sad a moment, and replied she had never learned how.

Charlie looked at his wife, then back towards his daughter. 'So if anyone you don't recognise tries to speak to you, if they tell you they are a friend of Mummy or Daddy, and you don't know who they are, then you don't talk to them, okay?'

Daisy nodded again.

'You don't talk to them. You don't take anything from them. You don't go anywhere with them. Not even if they tell you it's okay. Do you understand, darling?' Charlie whispered. Daisy's head bobbed up and down slowly. 'I need you to tell me you understand what I'm saying.'

'Yes. I understand, Daddy,' Daisy breathed.

'Good girl. Now come here.' Charlie opened up his arms for a hug. Daisy stood up, unsure at first, but crossed the room for a cuddle. He enveloped her, kissing her on the top of her head, then ruffled her hair with his left hand.

'Okay. That's it. Off you go and play.'

Daisy didn't need telling twice and ran back up the stairs.

'Do you think this has something to do with that note?' Charlie asked when he was sure Daisy couldn't hear them.

Beth shook her head.

'I wouldn't have thought so.'

'I don't understand who it could have been,' Charlie said.

'No. I don't either. Can we drop this please? We're going around in circles now and not achieving anything, apart from giving me a headache. We'll need to keep a closer eye on her from now on.'

Charlie frowned, but something about Beth's tone told him to leave it there. He stood up, taking his jacket to the hall cupboard. He heard the front door opening and turned to see Beth slipping through it with Cooper at her heels.

'Where are you going, Beth?' he shouted after her.

'Taking the dog for a walk.'

The door slammed shut behind her. Gravel crunched as she walked down the driveway, away from the house.

4

Kitty Briscoe skulked along the path. It hadn't been dark for long, but that didn't mean she wouldn't be in trouble when she got home. She smoothed her hands down the front of her yellow dress, trying to rub some deep crimson marks away, but it was no use. The stains weren't going anywhere.

Kieran gave her a sideways glance. She looked in his direction, and his eyes darted from her.

'What?' she shouted.

Kieran continued walking along the dusty path but didn't reply.

'What, Kieran? Stop watching me like that!'

Kieran turned to her, his face serious, eyes dark.

'We're agreed, right? We won't say anything to anyone. Not a word.'

'Agreed,' Kitty replied. She walked on, but Kieran grabbed her wrist.

'Ouch! Let go, you're hurting me!' she cried.

The older boy held her in a vice-like grip. Her flesh went pale beneath his fingers.

'Kitty. This is important. We could get in a lot of trouble. We need to make sure we say the same thing.'

Kieran was eleven, and Kitty realised that he knew things. Things that she didn't understand yet.

'We agreed, okay. I won't tell.'

'Promise?'

'Promise.'

They resumed their journey, Kieran a few paces in front. Now and then he would peek over his shoulder. Each time he looked, Kitty stared straight back at him. Her expression blank.

They walked for a few minutes in silence. The sound of their small feet dragging through the dry soil and gravel, the only noise. Kitty couldn't bear it.

She held the skirt of her dress in her tiny hands, twisting the lacy hem between them. The stains appeared almost black in the moonlight.

Her eyes flicked to the blood on Kieran's bare arms, and she shivered.

She eventually spoke, more to break the silence than for any other reason.

'Kieran?' she whispered.

'What?' Kieran didn't turn around. He shoved his hands in the pockets of his shorts and continued along the path.

'It's not very far. Billy will find his way home, won't he?'

Kieran couldn't tell if it was a statement or a question. It was one of the small social nuances that he sometimes struggled with.

'Course he will. Like you said. It ain't that far, is it.'

Kitty skipped a few steps to catch up with Kieran. She took his hand in her own. Kieran looked down at her and smiled.

'Everything will be okay,' Kitty said in a matter-of-fact way that made her sound much older than her seven years.

5

Taking a mug from the cupboard, Charlie spooned two heaps of instant coffee into the bottom. Flicking the switch on the kettle, he heard a cough behind him, turning to find Peter skulking in the doorway.

'I'm sorry about Daisy, Dad. Honestly, I only took my eyes off of her for like a minute or two, she *literally* disappeared.'

Charlie rolled his eyes at Peter's use of the word. He once told his parents he was *literally boiling*. Charlie had replied that he hoped not, getting a laugh from Beth. It had been lost on their son.

'She was right next to me,' Peter continued. 'These girls from school came over to say hi and I only took my eyes off her briefly, but I thought she was standing beside me.'

The kettle clicked to a boil, and Charlie poured his drink, sliding onto one of the bar stools at the island unit.

'Pete, it's fine. It's not your fault, mate. We don't blame you at all. But remember, when you're responsible for a child, you can't take your eyes off them for a second. A guy I work with took his toddler to the park, glanced down at his phone quickly to read a text message from his Mrs. When he looked back up, the kid had fallen in the duck pond. Almost drowned. He's never really got over it.'

Charlie held a mug up to his son, offering him a drink. Peter shook his head and ran his hand through his messy brown mane, making Charlie wish he still had all his hair.

'Is Mum all right?' Peter asked, sitting down opposite his father at the island.

'She's a bit shaken, that's all.'

'Yeah, I know. But... how she reacted... Dad, the way she flipped out. It wasn't normal. Totally over the top. I've never seen her like that before. She was manic. A different person. Like that time we were in town a few years ago and that news crew filmed us. She went mental because the cameraman hadn't asked her permission first. Remember that?'

Charlie nodded as he recalled the day.

'Like that...' Peter continued, 'But literally a *million* times worse. I wondered if there was... something going on with her.'

Charlie frowned. His wife was usually quite a calm person. He often marvelled at her ability to remain composed in a crisis. When Peter had fallen off a climbing frame when he was three, and split his forehead open, Beth had been like a machine. She sprang into action without panicking, while Charlie had been useless, the sight of all the blood making him feel a little faint. He looked at the pale scar on Peter's brow, shaking his head.

'I don't think so. She hasn't said anything to me. I'm sure she was just scared for Daisy. You won't realise this yet, but when you have kids of your own, there is nothing quite like the fear when you think harm has come to them. It's... awful.'

'You're not getting divorced, then?'

Charlie laughed. 'Of course not! Why would you say that?'

'Russell's mum and dad got divorced and his mum went a bit psycho while it was all going on.'

'No, we are *definitely* not getting a divorce.'

Peter nodded, then paused for a second. 'It freaked me out. Not only what happened to Daisy, but Mum. She was *really* scary. Her eyes were wild. She looked ready to kill someone.'

'I'll keep an eye on her, but don't you worry yourself about it too much.'

The sound of the doorbell ended the conversation, as Peter sprang up from his stool. 'That'll be Zoe,' he said, hurrying out to welcome her. Charlie watched with a smile on his face as his son greeted his girlfriend. The pair started their usual hugging and kissing, as if they hadn't seen each other for days, rather than hours. They walked down the hallway holding hands and Zoe smiled, waving at Charlie as they stood in the kitchen door. Her long ginger curls in a loose plait hanging down over her shoulder. She wore a short green sundress, and white trainers.

'Hey, Mr Carter,' she said, polite as ever. As she smiled, her freckles seemed to dance around her cheeks.

'Hi, Zoe, how are you?' Charlie asked.

'Yeah, I'm okay, thanks.'

Peter pulled her by the hand, dragging her up the stairs.

'See you later,' Charlie said as they made their way up to Peter's bedroom. 'Pete. Door open!' he shouted towards their backs.

'I know,' Peter replied, his voice laced with sarcasm.

He heard a key in the front door and looked up to see Cooper scurry in. Beth entered more slowly behind the spaniel.

'Nice walk?' Charlie asked.

Beth took a mug from the cupboard and poured herself a coffee. Nodding before sitting beside her husband.

'Are you all right?' Charlie continued, a concerned tone to his voice.

'Not really. I thought someone had taken her. It was terrifying.'

'Yeah, I bet it was horrible. Is that all? You've been a bit *off* today.'

Beth shrugged. 'Yeah. I also didn't sleep that well last night. I'm tired, that's all.'

'Okay,' Charlie said. 'But you'd tell me if anything was wrong, wouldn't you?'

'Yes, Charlie. I would definitely tell you. Like I said, I'm exhausted.'

'Okay. Zoe's upstairs.' Charlie changed the subject casually.

Beth stood and leaned into Charlie. 'I'm sorry. I'm aware I've been a little grouchy today. I'm shattered. And then all that with Daisy in town didn't help. The whole situation was awful. Made me feel like a terrible mother. I felt sick. And then it really pissed me off that she'd taken something from a stranger. I was... disappointed, I suppose. I thought she was smarter than that. I'm sure tomorrow everything will be back to normal.' She gave her husband a reassuring smile.

Charlie didn't feel too convinced.

'Okay. I'm going to have a shower. I need to wash today away. You can join me if you like?' He winked mischievously at Beth from the doorway.

'You go ahead, Romeo. I'll pass.'

Charlie walked out into the hall, pausing at the bottom of the stairs. He looked back towards Beth, sitting in the kitchen, holding her coffee in her hands, staring through the patio doors. Completely unaware that she was being watched. Lost in her thoughts. Charlie followed her gaze, but she was looking out into space.

6
———

Sunday passed, uneventfully. Beth felt pleased about that. Things between herself and Charlie were tense. Despite her best efforts to convince him not to worry, he wasn't buying it. Both her children gave her a wide berth for the rest of the weekend after the episode in the town. She couldn't blame them. She'd totally lost it. They both eyed her with caution and avoided talking to her where possible. If she looked up from what she was doing, their eyes would dart away speedily, as if Beth had caught them doing something they shouldn't. Even Zoe acted strangely towards her. Peter had clearly told her his version of events; his deranged mother flipping out and showing him up. Beth wondered if he'd mentioned the two pretty girls from school, twiddling their hair, while he leaned up against his mother's Range Rover trying to act cool.

As Beth drove to work on Monday morning, she recalled a brief conversation with Zoe the night before. Beth had been watching TV with Charlie, when she heard Zoe come down into the kitchen to get a drink. Charlie, as usual, had been snoring on the sofa, so Beth slipped out to make a coffee. She enjoyed her chats with her son's girlfriend. Zoe smiled and turned to leave the kitchen without saying anything, which was odd. Beth asked her if everything was okay.

'Yes, thanks,' she replied, stopping in the doorway as if she felt guilty about rushing off.

'Peter told me about Daisy. He's really sorry, you know. He feels awful.'

'Yes, I know. I shouldn't have lost it with him the way I did. I also feel terrible.'

Zoe raised a hand and dismissed the comment with a wave. 'He'll get over it. Anyway, I should go back up. We're watching a film and I need to be home by ten.' Zoe turned and trotted up the stairs. She'd been so eager to get away, she had left two glasses of Coke sitting on the worktop. Beth frowned. Zoe was usually so happy to chat to her. Although she had been her usual, polite self, there had been something in the way she looked at Beth. That same worried caution that her son assessed her with. God knows what Peter had said about her.

Beth pulled into a parking space and made her daily jaunt through town to the offices of Greys. Beeping her pass card against the reader, the door clicked, allowing her in. She made her way to her office, waving hello to a few people as she passed them, the usual Monday morning conversations playing out around the water cooler. As she neared Margot's office, she saw her on the phone, deep in conversation. Margot glanced up and gave her a wave. Beth smiled, returning the gesture, then walked down to the end of the corridor, unlocking her office door. As she hung her jacket on the coat stand, a knock at her door resonated through the room. She called for her visitor to come in. A guy from accounts who she knew only as Tim entered with a young, awkward-looking girl.

'This is Beth Carter. She's in charge of all the submissions. She filters out the crap before they go to Chloe for more careful scrutiny.' Tim sounded bored. Nobody liked showing new staff members around.

Beth crossed the office to greet them. The girl, small and mousy, looked about twelve. Long, dirty-blonde, straight hair hung unstyled halfway down her back. Large, thick, tortoiseshell-framed glasses covered most of the top half of her small, almond-shaped face. She wore a knee-length grey polka-dot dress, and no make-up. Small white pimples decorated her skin, from her chin up past her mouth and onto both cheeks. Beth tried not to stare at them. The girl had a thick, woolly, brown cardigan over the top of her dress and finished off her *look* with a pair of grubby pink converse boots. She stared at Beth with an odd expression on her face, which Beth couldn't figure out.

'This is Vicky. She's starting with us today in accounts,' offered Tim, through forced chirpiness.

'I'm sure you'll love it here. It's a really friendly place to work.'

'Hello. Pleased to meet you.' She raised an eyebrow. 'Have we met before?' A northern lilt played on her voice. She smiled, exposing a mouthful of overcrowded teeth.

'No, I don't think so,' Beth replied.

'You look *really* familiar.' Vicky eyed Beth from behind her glasses, the dense lenses causing her eyes to look abnormally large. She was not letting this go.

'Nope, I'm pretty sure we've never met. Sorry. Maybe I've just got one of those faces.'

'Hmm,' Vicky muttered, in a sceptical tone that suggested she may still be pondering it.

Beth made an overdramatic show of looking at her watch, and Tim and Vicky took the hint. They said their goodbyes and left Beth to continue with her work.

Beth shut her door and returned to her desk. She turned on

her computer and it whirred to life. She logged in to her emails and began making her way through hundreds of submissions that had arrived in her inbox since she left on Friday evening.

After she'd read a few of them, a chime told her a new message had arrived. A small window popped up on her screen saying, *email from Vicky Kershaw*, with Vicky's mousey face next to it.

```
Hi Beth. Great to meet you. Your face is so
familiar. Racking my brains as to why! I'm
sure it will come to me. :)
```

She finished it with a little smile made from a colon and a bracket, which made Beth want to punch her. Beth sighed, clicked delete, and didn't bother replying.

She skim-read a few further submissions, marking some for a more detailed look, dumping the rubbish. After an hour or so of staring at the computer, she needed a break. Grabbing her mug, she walked out into the main office heading for the kitchen. The new break-out areas had been erected recently, slap bang in the middle of each floor. The directors said it encouraged a more sociable atmosphere. In reality, Beth and a few of her colleagues thought it might be so people spent less time in the kitchen gassing. Beth spooned some instant coffee into a mug full of boiling water, then stood stirring it for a second.

Feeling uneasy, like she was being watched, she glanced up, scanning the office.

Her skin prickled as her eyes came to rest on Vicky. She stood behind someone at a desk right over the other side of the room. Vicky paid no attention to whatever the girl was saying. She was staring straight at Beth.

Beth frowned, looking away, embarrassed. She glanced back

up a few moments later, surprised to see the girl still regarding her. Instead of averting her eyes, as any normal person would do when caught staring, Vicky smiled and held up her hand, giving Beth a wave. Beth didn't wave back. She returned to her office, closing the door behind her.

At about one o'clock, Margot knocked on Beth's door, offering to grab her a sandwich, as she was popping out.

'I'll come with you. I need a walk,' Beth said, grabbing her jacket from the coat stand.

As they walked, Beth relayed the story about the stranger approaching Daisy at the weekend.

'Oh my God, that's terrible!' Margot exclaimed. 'And it definitely wasn't a friend?' she asked.

'No. I'm sure.' Beth shook her head.

'Is Daisy okay?'

Beth shrugged, shaking her head again. 'She was upset, but probably more because I totally flipped out. I'm so embarrassed. And you should have seen Peter. He hates me now, I'm sure.'

Margot placed a hand gently on Beth's arm. 'It's understandable, darling. Children are precious. The little ones I care for, they're not even mine, and I get so anxious if I lose sight of one of them for a moment. It really is an awful emotion. God knows, there are terrible people out there, you never know what might happen. I think your reaction is completely justified. Don't worry, Peter will get over it. He's a teenager. He's probably forgotten about it already.'

They walked into a deli and perused the daily selection.

'And how about Charlie?' Margot asked, her voice dripping with concern. 'Is he all right?'

Margot made no secret of the fact she thought Charlie was *a dish*. Beth found it hilarious. Charlie found it terrifying.

Beth picked up a ham and pickle sandwich and shrugged. 'I

think we're both a little shaken. He wants to get the police involved, but I'm really not sure.'

'Oh, darling, you must! Daisy may be okay, but what if the next child isn't so fortunate?' Margot picked up a quinoa and pine nut salad, and they both joined the queue.

'I really don't know what I'd say to them. I'm pretty sure they would tell me that nothing illegal has happened. There's probably nothing they can do.'

'That's not the point, my dear. At least you would have reported it so they would be aware.' She gripped Beth's arm. 'Think about how terrible you would feel if a child were to be abducted.'

'I suppose you're right.'

Margot smiled. 'Good girl.'

They walked back to the office, chatting about the rest of Margot's weekend, with Beth only really half listening. Other things were on her mind...

7

The late evening sun bled into a beautiful bruise across the sky as Charlie stared out of the window. His office had a magnificent view out over the rooftops of Brighton and further afield towards the remains of the fire-ravaged West Pier in Hove. What once had been a stunning example of Victorian engineering was now little more than a skeletal silhouette. A blot on the horizon.

An orange glow fell onto Charlie's desk, hitting his keyboard and dancing off the edges of the keys. He usually loved this time of the evening towards the end of the summer. Everyone else had gone home for the night and he had the peace and quiet he needed to concentrate on his work. More and more frequently these days, Charlie was starting to feel that his job in advertising was no longer for him; that he was too old for it all now.

A team of noisy twenty-somethings sat at the bank of desks behind him. Painfully close. They didn't stop talking all day. It was a constant stream of verbal diarrhoea. Usually about *Love Island*, or *Made in Chelsea*, or some other nonsensical reality TV show that Charlie had never seen. From the moment they arrived at nine each morning, to the minute they shut down their computers just before five every evening. You could set your watch by them. Youngsters nowadays did not understand hard work, Charlie thought. He saw it in his own son regularly. They seemed to do the bare minimum to get by. The idea of working a second past their contracted time filled them with horror.

These few precious hours after they were all gone. These were Charlie's golden moments.

Tonight, though, he was distracted. He gleaned no pleasure from watching the sun set over the city he'd loved and called home since meeting Beth here at university over twenty years ago. Things at the house were still tense. Charlie was able to count on one hand the occasions he'd felt like this during his time with Beth.

They had a *great* relationship. Generally they put their differences aside quickly. Although they chatted for a short while yesterday evening, things were far from normal.

He powered down his computer and packed his belongings into a rucksack. Pulling his phone out of his pocket, he typed a message to Beth.

Heading to the gym. Don't wait for me for dinner.

Reading it back, he added an x at the end before sending it.

He grabbed his bag and moved to the lift at the opposite end of the floor, taking it down to the basement. He knew he was avoiding going home, but exercise was an excellent excuse. He could work off some pent-up frustration at the same time.

He changed into his running gear, threw his stuff into a locker, and headed down the corridor towards the gym.

The motion-activated lights came on one at a time as he made his way along the narrow walkway. He swiped his access card and pushed the door open. He stepped into pitch darkness briefly, before the sensors picked up his movement and the white lights flickered on. He filled his bottle at the water cooler, then walked around the corner towards the treadmills. The lights came on in the far corner of the room. The basement of the building was predominantly storage, but an odd, compact space in one corner had been converted into a gym. It was an L shape, made up from two isosceles triangles, with large cubic pillars dotted around the room, holding up the rest of the vast building above it. The cardio equipment was housed in the smaller of the two triangles, with the weights and other machines in the larger main area.

Charlie pushed his wireless headphones into his ears and started his *running* playlist on his phone. The loud repetitive beat thumped, getting him in the mood for a long run. He hopped onto the treadmill, pushing up the speed to a comfortably paced jog.

After a short while the lights around the corner switched off, throwing half the space into total darkness. The sensors in that area couldn't pick up movement from this side due to the pillars and the odd shape of the room.

The sweat formed on Charlie's brow as he increased his speed. He tried not to think about Daisy walking off with a stranger while his son flirted with some girls from school.

He tried not to think about his wife's dismissive attitude about the entire incident.

And he tried not to think about his son's words describing the way Beth behaved when she arrived back at the car.

I've never seen her like that before. She was manic. A different person.

It took a lot to get any sort of reaction from their teenaged son. He was usually unfazed by anything. He was so laid-back Charlie and Beth often wondered and discussed if he might be smoking dope. But they never smelled it on him, and Beth even searched his room a few times, to no avail. Charlie surmised that their son inherited the calmness he had always seen in his wife. The calmness that had deserted her at the weekend, if what Peter described to him was accurate. Peter seemed genuinely worried about her.

That was enough to make Charlie concerned. He glanced down at the timer display. He'd been going for twenty minutes, and the sweat was dripping from every pore now.

The light flickered on around the corner, shaking Charlie from his thoughts. He turned his head, waiting to see if someone came into view, but when they didn't, he shrugged and resumed his run.

After a while the light turned off. Damn building was always going wrong. Music continued to throb in his ears, the beat working in time with his feet as they pounded away.

The lights came on again.

Charlie stopped the treadmill and paused the music on his phone. He stepped down, removing his earbuds.

'Hello?' he called out.

Silence.

He walked down to the corner, peering round into the bigger part of the gym. Three large pillars blocked most of his view but looking at the wall of mirrors running down one entire side of the room, nobody appeared to be present. Charlie threw his towel from his shoulders down onto the floor, marching around the corner.

'Hello, is someone there?' he shouted.

No reply.

'Derek, is that you? This isn't funny,' he called out.

Silence.

He moved to one side to see around a pillar and as he did, he heard the door click shut.

Stepping forward, something on the floor in the middle of the room caught his eye.

A small red box, tied with a gold ribbon, and a bow on top. Charlie frowned, wiping perspiration from his face with the back of his hand. He peered through the glass-panelled door. There was nobody there.

He trudged back to the box, picking it up. It was extremely light. A handwritten tag was tied to the box.

One word. Scratchy black ink.

Charlie.

He carried the parcel, walking back towards the door. Pressing the release button, he opened it and stepped out into the corridor.

'Hello!' he shouted again, heading towards the stairs. The lights were all on, showing someone passed this way moments earlier.

He threw open the door, stepping out into the stairwell. He looked up through the gap in the centre but saw nobody ascending them. Whoever deposited the box left in a hurry.

Charlie returned to the changing room and sat on a bench. He untied the ribbon, opening the package.

Inside was a small piece of paper.

With trembling hands, he unfolded it, revealing a handwritten note. He swallowed hard as he read the words, then shivered, despite his body temperature being raised.

He dressed without showering, folded the note up, placing it into his pocket, and headed quickly out to his car.

8

The words from the note kept circling through Charlie's mind during the entire drive home. He drove angrily, dangerously at times. Usually an exemplary motorist, tonight he didn't care. Wanting, instead, to get home as quickly as possible to speak to Beth about the note.

As he walked in through the door, he heard the familiar sound of the telly blaring out from the lounge. He stepped into the room, pulling off his leather jacket, and slung it onto the armchair. Beth looked up. Charlie picked up the remote and turned off the TV.

'Oi, I was watching that!' Beth protested.

'Where are the kids?'

'Peter's out with Zoe. I told him to be home by ten. Daisy's in bed.'

Charlie pulled the note out of his pocket, fiddling with it between his thumb and fingers. He didn't take his eyes off Beth. He threw the note at her.

'Charlie, what the hell are you doing?'

'Read it.'

Beth leaned forward from her armchair, picking the piece of

paper up from the floor. She unfolded it and read the words. Charlie regarded her intently. He watched her face change, a fleeting look of... what was it? Fear, panic maybe? Whatever it was, was replaced quickly by anger.

'What's this?' she asked.

'I was hoping *you* could tell me that.'

Beth frowned. 'I haven't got a clue.' She passed the note back to him.

'Bullshit, Beth.'

Charlie read the words aloud.

'*How well do you know your wife?* Seems like a fairly straightforward question to me.'

'Where did this come from?'

Charlie sat down on the sofa, letting out a long breath before answering. 'Somebody left it for me at work this evening.'

'What? What do you mean?'

'I was jogging, and someone came into the gym and left that on the floor.'

'How do you know it was meant for you?'

'Because it was in a pretty little gift box with my name written on it!' Charlie bellowed.

Beth stood up, crossing to the living room door, closing it softly. 'Shh, you'll wake Daisy!' she hissed.

'Right now I don't actually give a shit, Beth! I want to know what the hell is going on.'

'How do you mean?'

'Something weird is happening here. It started on Friday night with that note through the door. I thought nothing of it at first. But then with what happened to Daisy, and now this... I think there's more to it, and it seems apparent that it's something to do with you. You've been acting strangely since that first note, and I think you know more than you're letting on.'

Beth laughed, a loud, almost hysterical laugh. 'Charlie, calm down. You're letting your imagination run away with you. I agree, this situation is odd, but I can assure you I *honestly* don't have a clue what it's all about.'

Charlie stared into Beth's eyes.

'Swear,' Charlie said through gritted teeth.

'Excuse me?'

'Swear. On your parents' graves.'

She didn't flinch. She didn't blink. 'I swear. On my parents' graves. Okay?'

Nobody said anything for a while. Charlie sat fidgeting, staring down at his hands. Beth stood up and crossed to the settee, sitting down next to Charlie, and lacing her fingers into his.

'Charlie, I get that you are spooked by all this. I admit, it's a worry, but we should stick together. Are you going to doubt me over some random note left for you by God-knows-who in the gym? We can't turn on each other right now. There's obviously something going on. We need to figure it out. *Together.*'

'Why would somebody write that? And the other one. It's all so strange. I think we should talk to the police.'

'And tell them what exactly? Some weirdo has been leaving us notes? Charlie, they would laugh at us.'

'No, they wouldn't. This seems a little sinister to me. And if you factor in what happened to Daisy–'

'That's assuming the two things are connected.'

'Even if they aren't, I still think we should *tell* someone.'

Charlie took the note from his wife's hands and focused on the words.

How well do you know your wife?

Something told Charlie there was more to this than Beth was

making out, but he didn't want to fight with her. She was right in one respect, they needed to stick together.

'Give me that,' Beth said, reaching for the paper in Charlie's hands. 'I'll put it in the bin.'

Charlie snatched his hand back, shaking his head. 'No. We should keep it. Where's the other one?'

'I threw it away.'

Charlie jumped up from the couch and rushed out to the kitchen. 'What the hell did you do that for?'

Beth followed behind him. 'I thought it was a prank. Why wouldn't I?'

Charlie started riffling through the bin, pulling rubbish out onto the tiles around his feet. Beth placed a hand on his back. 'The bin's been emptied, love. I wouldn't bother.'

Charlie sat down on the floor, surrounded by empty cans and food packets. 'We should have kept it. What if–'

Beth sat next to him, pushing a stinking, half-empty packet of bacon out of the way with her toe first. She draped an arm around his shoulder, and stroked the back of his neck, fiddling with his hair between her fingers.

'But we didn't. What's done is done. We have the new one. Let's not worry about it for now. Cuppa?'

Charlie nodded. 'I'll make them. You go and sit down.'

Beth heaved herself up from the floor, and traipsed out of the kitchen, into the lounge. Charlie stood up, filled the kettle and flicked it on. He took two mugs from the cupboard, opening a drawer to get a teaspoon. As he went to shut the drawer, he noticed something peeking out from beneath the plastic divider. A small scrap of white.

Charlie reached down, lifting out the tray and fished the folded piece of paper from underneath.

He knew in his gut what it was immediately, but he unfolded it anyway.

FOUND YOU.

Friday night's note. Where this all began.

The one Beth had, moments earlier, repeatedly said she had thrown away. And yet here it was, tucked into a drawer, hidden.

So why would she lie?

9

Charlie opened his eyes. The bedroom was pitch black. For a moment he didn't know where he was. He resisted the urge to look at the clock beside the bed, in case it was almost time to get up. He wanted to relish this time, before the reality of having to prepare for work hit home. But it didn't *feel* like the morning. It felt like the middle of the night. He gave in and looked. It was 2am.

He rolled over, but found Beth wasn't beside him. He reached his arm across the covers, as if his eyes were deceiving him, but the mattress was cold. Sitting up, he glanced around the room. His vision had not adjusted to the darkness, and he couldn't see much. He flung back the duvet from his legs, slowly stepping onto the carpet. The light in the en suite wasn't on. He whispered Beth's name through the door to be sure. No reply. He made his way to the landing. The entire house lay in darkness. He stood at the top of the stairs, listening.

Not a sound. No movement. Nothing.

Making his way down the stairs, he felt apprehensive, but he didn't know why. He couldn't put his finger on it, but something niggled at him. He inched along the hallway, stubbing his toe on the hairpin legs of a narrow console table against the wall. Swearing under his breath, he continued towards the kitchen. Cooper leapt up and excitedly scurried across the floor towards Charlie. Circling repeatedly in front of him.

'No, Cooper, back to bed, it's not time yet,' he hissed at the dog. Cooper continued to wag his tail and look at Charlie expectantly. Charlie tried the back door, which was firmly locked, with the key in it. So Beth couldn't have gone into the garden. He flicked the light switch on the wall next to the door anyway. The lights came on, but the garden appeared empty.

Charlie patrolled the rest of the ground floor, but Beth wasn't in the house. He opened the front door. It was unlocked, suggesting that Beth had gone out this way. Standing on the doorstep, he stared out into the darkness. The cars were both in the driveway, so she hadn't driven anywhere. But there was no sign of her outside. He stepped out onto the path, wincing as his bare feet touched the gravel. The security light clicked on, illuminating the Range Rover and glinting off the roof of his Audi beside it. As the light dissipated in the distance, it scarcely highlighted the tips of the hedgerows beyond, before fading into black. Charlie retreated into the comfort of the farmhouse, brushing some loose stones from the soles of his feet.

His sense of unease was growing. Why on earth would Beth leave the house in the middle of the night?

He returned to the bedroom, retrieving his mobile phone. He dialled Beth's number, and immediately it started to vibrate from her bedside table. Ending the call, he climbed into bed, pulling the duvet up around his shoulders. He lay on his side, staring at the glowing red numbers on the clock radio.

Wide awake.

Eventually at 2.45, Charlie heard the front door quietly open. He listened as Beth tiptoed up the stairs and into the bedroom. He closed his eyes, pretending to be asleep, as she undressed silently, folding her clothes over the back of a chair where they had been before. She climbed into bed, turning her back to him.

Charlie lay with his eyes wide open, listening to the sound of Beth's breathing.

He could tell she was awake.

He resisted the urge to speak to her, to ask her where she had been. This was not the time for that conversation.

He would wait until the morning.

Beth's behaviour was odd. Worrying even. And as Charlie lay drifting off to sleep, one sentence ran through his mind on loop.

How well do you know your wife?

10

The following morning, Beth left for work before Charlie had a chance to talk to her. So he had to wait until they were both home in the evening, after Daisy had gone to bed. As usual, Peter had shut himself away in his room with his video games and phone, so there was no fear of him interrupting them.

Beth was standing at the kitchen sink, cleaning the dishes after dinner. Scrubbing baked-on lasagne from a Pyrex dish. Charlie sat himself down at the island unit, drumming his fingers on the worktop. Beth didn't turn around. She just stood with her back to him, humming a familiar tune that Charlie couldn't place.

'I spoke to the security officer at work today. He checked the footage to see who left that note.'

Beth paused for a second, then continued to clean the dish. 'Oh. And?' she said, inquisitively.

'Nothing. He was wearing bike leathers, helmet and all. Couldn't see the guy's face. He didn't lift his visor up.'

'Right,' Beth muttered. 'Oh well.' She sounded disappointed.

'Funny thing is, the entire building is locked down. You can't get through a single door without a staff card.'

'Same as our place. How did he get in, then?'

'They checked the security log. He swiped a visitor pass. Sure enough, when they counted the passes at reception, there was one missing. So basically it could have been anyone. No way of knowing.' Charlie let out a long breath and ran both his hands through his thinning hair. Beth carried on with the dishes without a word. She simply shrugged.

'Where did you go last night?' Charlie asked casually. Beth froze.

'What do you mean? I was here with you all night,' she said assertively.

'No. I woke up. You weren't in bed. Try again.'

Beth stopped washing up and peeled off her bright yellow Marigolds, slinging them into the sink with a satisfying wet slap. She turned to face Charlie.

'I couldn't sleep. I came down and made a drink. Sat on the sofa, read for a few hours, then when I finally felt tired, came back to bed.'

Charlie slammed his fists down on the worktop so hard that Beth flinched.

'No, Beth, you didn't. I looked round the entire house for you. You weren't here. And the front door was unlocked. The cars were in the driveway. So I'll ask you again. Where did you go?'

Beth's face coloured, and a panicked expression flashed across it, but only fleetingly.

'I went for a walk, okay?' She stormed past Charlie obstinately, towards the kitchen door.

'Then why lie about it?'

'Sorry?'

'Why lie? You told me you came down for a drink and to

read, which was an outright lie. I don't understand why you wouldn't just say you went for a walk, if that's what you were doing.'

Beth stopped in the doorway and turned back towards Charlie. 'I was embarrassed. It's not exactly *normal* behaviour to go walking in the middle of the night. And on top of what happened when I freaked out with Daisy at the weekend, I didn't want people *judging* me. I'm aware that my son already thinks I'm a total psycho, I don't need to add fuel to that fire.'

Charlie stood up. 'But you're not talking to your son! You're talking to *me*. And I would hope that you know me well enough to realise that I would *never* judge you. And while we're at it, why did you lie about the note?'

Beth frowned, confused.

'What do you mean? How did I lie about the note?'

'You told me you threw it away. But I found it in there.' Charlie tilted his head towards the drawer opposite him.'

'Oh for Christ's sake, Charlie, I didn't *lie*. I was mistaken. I *thought* I had thrown the note away. It was late, and I was tired, and I *thought* I threw it in the bin, okay? But obviously I didn't. *Obviously*, I put it in the kitchen drawer, and I made a mistake when you asked me. Like the time you lost your car keys, and you said I had tidied them away somewhere. You were *adamant* that you had put them in the bowl on the kitchen side. And then *where* did you find them?'

Charlie didn't say a word.

'Well?' Beth bellowed.

'I found them in my jacket pocket, hanging in the hall cupboard,' Charlie replied quietly.

'Exactly. Because when we are tired and we have had a hard day, and it's late, we sometimes misremember things. But because you've received some mysterious fucking note saying you don't know me, you think that I'm lying to you. That's right, isn't it? That stupid note has spooked you. It's made you *doubt* me.' Tears welled up in the corners of Beth's eyes.

Charlie's face sank. Angry, and wrapped up in what the note had said, he had jumped to conclusions. Beth was right. He *had* doubted her. The one person he should *never* doubt. He nodded, afraid to look her in the eye.

'That hurts, Charlie. I have *never* lied to you. I've always got your back. I will always fight your corner. And I deserve the same level of loyalty from you.'

Charlie took a step towards his wife and reached his hand out to her arm. She shrugged it off.

'Don't!' she snapped.

'I'm sorry. Beth, I'm so, so sorry. You're right. I owe you more than that, and I apologise. I'm such a dick.'

'Yeah, you are,' she said churlishly.

In that moment, Charlie felt an overwhelming surge of affection for his wife, and he hated himself for upsetting her.

'Can we draw a line under this?' he pleaded softly. Beth stood with her arms folded.

'Come here.' Beth didn't budge, so Charlie took another step towards her, wrapping his arms around her. She tried to push him away at first, but eventually she relaxed into the hug.

They walked into the living room, and Beth flicked on the telly. As she sat surfing through the channels trying to find something to watch, Charlie stared at her. He was able to count on one hand the number of times he had seen his wife cry. She rarely showed this level of emotion.

'Beth, are you okay?' Charlie asked.

She continued to flick, pointing the remote at the telly. 'I'm annoyed. I don't understand why we are receiving these notes. It's screwing with my life, and I don't like it. This has been an odd week.'

Beth muted the telly for a moment, turning towards Charlie.

'I want things back to normal. It's been one thing after another since Friday night, and I'm exhausted. I've got loads of submissions to get through at work before the weekend, and I've fallen behind. I should be working late, but I don't have the energy. On top of all this, I've hardly spoken to my kids this week. I'm sure Peter hates me.'

'He'll get over it. Let's face it, he's a teenager. He talks to us as little as possible anyway.' Charlie smiled. Beth didn't smile back. She unmuted the telly and continued searching for something to watch.

Charlie sat observing his wife. He trusted her, he always had. She'd never given him any reason not to, and so he should have believed her when she said she had made an honest mistake.

So why was there still a niggling doubt in his mind?

11
_____

The smell of strong coffee filled Beth's nostrils as Margot topped up her cafetière with boiling water from the tap.

'I simply couldn't face any more of that free instant rubbish they give you here, darling,' she was saying. 'I remembered I had this little thing in a cupboard somewhere at home, so I thought I may as well put it to some use.' She placed the lid onto the cafetière, picked up two cups and trotted back towards her office. Beth followed, trying to avoid the disturbingly intense stare from Vicky as she passed her desk. Vicky smiled, waving. Margot lifted the hand holding the mugs and wiggled it around. Beth was worried Vicky might take it as an invitation and closed the door to Margot's office firmly behind her as she entered.

Margot sat down on a plush, grey fabric sofa, placing the coffee and the cups down on the small table, motioning for Beth to sit in the chair opposite. She sank down, letting out an audible sigh. As Margot pushed the plunger on the coffee, Beth eyed her.

'Not sure about that new girl. She's a little... peculiar,' Beth said nervously.

Margot poured two coffees, sliding one towards Beth.

'Vicky?' Margot sounded confused. 'Oh no, she's a sweetheart. She's just a little gauche.'

'You like her?'

'I don't *like* anyone, darling. But I don't dislike her. That's the fundamental thing. We were having a brief chat in the lift the other morning. She's a media studies graduate. Says she has always dreamed of working for Greys. All total nonsense, of course. I think she thought I would find it flattering. Little does she realise I don't actually give a hoot. Her heart's in the right place. We've all been there, haven't we? New job, new people to impress.' Margot took a long sip from her steaming hot coffee. 'Oh now that is just *divine*, darling.'

'Every time I look up she's staring at me. I thought I was imagining it at first, but as the week has gone on, I've noticed it more and more. I bet if I were to turn round now...' Beth swivelled in her chair to see through the wall-to-wall glass of Margot's office. 'Yes! See, I knew it. She's doing it *right* now!'

Margot peered over Beth's shoulder, catching Vicky's eye. She gave her a delicate wave and a smile, and Vicky looked away.

'Yes, now you come to mention it, she did seem *extremely* interested in you the other morning when we were chatting,' Margot said, staring at Beth over the rim of her coffee cup.

'What do you mean? What was she saying?'

'Oh, she was asking all sorts of questions. *How long had I known you? Where are you from? What's your background?* That kind of thing, you know?' As Margot spoke her hand gave a dramatic flourish in the air. Beth couldn't help think Margot should have gone into theatre rather than law.

'My God! I think she's obsessed with me. She behaved bizarrely when we were introduced.'

'Maybe she fancies you?' A wry smile spread across Margot's face, followed by a wink.

Beth stood up from her chair, walking to the window. She held her coffee cup to her lips, watching Vicky, whose eyes darted up from her screen, meeting Beth's and staying there.

'And she never looks away when I catch her staring either. She's weird. I don't like it.'

'Come on, Beth, don't be mean. Perhaps she's got a crush on you or something. Who can blame her? You're a looker.'

'Oh *please*!' Beth retorted, stifling a laugh.

'You need to learn to take a compliment, my dear. Trust me when I say, I certainly don't dish them out willy-nilly.'

'Seriously, though, I hate it. It makes me feel uncomfortable. I'm quite a private person, you know that. I don't like people I'm unfamiliar with digging around asking questions about me. Especially with what's been going on at home...' Beth trailed off as she realised she had said too much. She sat back down in the chair, facing Margot, who stared intently at her.

'What do you mean? What's happening at home? Is everything okay?'

Beth felt her cheeks flush. 'Oh, you know. With Daisy at the weekend,' she backtracked, hoping that Margot would let it go.

Margot pursed her lips and frowned, clearly not buying what Beth had said. But she asked nothing further. That was one thing Beth loved about Margot. She never pushed for personal information. She waited for you to offer it up. And if you didn't, she wouldn't ask.

'Anyway, darling, what are you and that *gorgeous* hubby of yours up to this weekend?' she asked, changing the subject expertly.

'Actually, that reminds me. I have a favour to ask you.'

'Shoot.'

'I'd forgotten we've got this dinner party tonight at Charlie's boss's house. Would you mind looking after the kids while we're out? I don't feel comfortable leaving Daisy with Peter at the moment, after, you know, the weekend. I'd rather there was an adult in the house.'

'Oh, of course I will. I'd only be staying in with a book and a bottle of red tonight anyway. I suppose this saves me from being a terribly dull singleton, sitting in my house alone on a Friday night.'

'No. You can spend it with a teenager who won't come out of his room, and Daisy, who will probably be desperate to redo your make-up and hair for you. I warn you now. You'll need to be firm with her, else she'll have you looking like Coco the Clown by the time you get home.' Beth paused, smiling at Margot. 'Thanks. I appreciate it.'

Margot swatted her hand towards Beth dismissively. 'Darling, this is what I *live* for most weekends.'

Beth felt she could do without the whole social circuit tonight. She wasn't in the mood. But Charlie hadn't reacted well when Beth suggested they make an excuse. It was his boss, after all. It wouldn't look great. Plus, it had been on the calendar for months.

'Will it be a late one?' Margot asked, cocking an eyebrow.

'God, I hope not. It's up at that big fancy house in Hove. I think some celebrity used to live there or something.'

'Sounds stunning.'

'Yes, it's very nice. I'm sure it will be a lovely night. But I can't really be bothered.'

'You'll be fine once you get a glass or two of champagne down you.'

'Hmmm,' Beth murmured unconvincingly.

Margot glanced at a dainty gold watch on her left wrist. 'It's as good as five now, why don't you shoot off early and get yourself in the mood?'

Beth shook her head. 'No, I can't. Shouldn't even be in here now. I'm behind on submissions. I've got so much to do.'

'Nonsense. Those budding bestsellers can wait another few days to hear your verdict. Let's face it, most of them will go straight in the bin.'

Beth laughed, and Margot joined in.

'Yeah, you're right. I doubt I'll get any more done tonight anyway.'

Margot shooed Beth with both hands.

'Off you go. I won't tell anyone.' She winked again. 'What time do you need me?'

'We're supposed to be there at eight, so if you can make it round for seven fifteen that would be wonderful.'

'See you then.' Margot waved Beth out the door. She headed to her office to grab her bag, then out towards the lift. As she turned around, she saw Vicky's eyes locked on her. She was chewing the corner of her bottom lip and scratching her head with a pencil. As the doors closed, Vicky didn't look away.

She smiled. *Knowingly*, Beth thought.

But what does she *think* she knows?

12

————

Beth stepped out of the shower, wrapping a soft white towel around her body, and picked up her glass of champagne from beside the sink. She reached her other hand up to the back of her head and massaged it softly. It felt good.

As she sauntered out of the en suite, Daisy came scurrying into the room, Cooper hot on her tail. They both hopped up onto the bed. Beth looked on in horror as the spaniel sprawled out on her garments.

'No, no, no!' Beth shouted. 'Dog off, please!'

Cooper jumped obediently down onto the floor, looking crestfallen.

'Are you and Daddy going out tonight?' Daisy asked as she fingered the dresses.

'Yep. We're having dinner with Daddy's boss. I hope your hands are clean.'

Daisy pulled her fingers back from the fabric sheepishly.

Although technically Derek *was* Charlie's boss, he was more than that. They were friends.

'Does that mean I'll be here alone with Petey all night?' Daisy pouted, folding her arms across her chest.

Beth sat down at her dressing table, picking up her hairdryer.

'No. Aunty Margot is coming over to babysit. Do you remember her?'

Daisy shrugged, but smiled. Beth flicked on the dryer and blow-dried her hair. Daisy perched on the edge of the mattress, watching Beth's every move.

She turned off the dryer and placed it down on the dressing table.

'Which one are you going to wear?' Daisy asked, motioning towards the gowns laid out in front of her.

'Not sure yet. Which do *you* think I should wear?'

Daisy looked down at the dresses. Her eyes darted from a red lacy number with long sleeves, to a black velvet off-the-shoulder dress, a little shorter, a little tighter.

'I like the red one! I can't wait till I'm big enough to wear it.'

Beth laughed. 'Oh yeah? You think you'll be borrowing my dresses, do you?'

'Yes!' Daisy shouted.

Cooper's ears pricked up at the sound of Charlie's key in the door and he scurried out of the room. Daisy ran after him. They both scrambled down the stairs.

'I'm up here getting ready!' Beth shouted. 'Fancy popping those nuggets and chips in the oven for the kids?'

'No problem!'

Beth stood up, dropping her towel in a heap on the floor.

She crossed to the bed, picking up both the dresses, holding each in front of her as she glanced at herself.

Climbing into what passed for her best underwear, she pulled on the red dress, pushing one foot into a red stiletto. She turned to each side, assessing herself. With one hand, she piled her hair up, sucking in her tummy. Shaking her head, she slid the dress off, draping it over the back of a chair before performing the whole act again with the black one. She sat down at the dressing table and pulled her hair up into a French twist, fixing it in place neatly.

As she was applying her make-up, her phone sprang to life, dancing about noisily on the bedside table. She crossed the room to retrieve it, assuming it would be Margot running late.

Beth frowned as she glanced at the digits on the screen.

She unlocked her phone, opening up the message.

I liked the red one better.

Beth spun around to face the large dual-aspect windows in the corner of the room. Running towards them, she stood, staring out across the driveway, into the fields and the trees beyond. Her eyes frantically scanned the landscape for any movement.

There was nobody there. At least, nobody she could *see*.

The phone chimed again.

Holding her breath, Beth's eyes shot down towards the screen.

Can you see me?

Her heart pounded.

A bead of sweat formed on her hairline, slowly trickling down her neck. A prickling sensation made its way from the top of her head and through her entire body, down towards her fingers and toes. For a moment she thought she might pass out.

She pulled the curtains shut, turning her back to the window. Feeling faint, she placed one hand against the sill to steady herself, staring at the phone.

A new message flashed up.

Spoilsport. Don't be shy. You never used to be.

With trembling fingers, Beth typed out a reply. *Who is this?*

She bit down on her bottom lip, nervously waiting.

Three dots appeared on her screen. Her stalker was replying. The device vibrated in Beth's shaky hands.

A friend.

She was about to respond when she heard heavy footsteps ascending the stairs.

Charlie.

She quickly flicked her phone to silent, tucking it under her make-up bag as Charlie entered the room. He whistled as he walked towards her, a huge bunch of white roses in his hand.

'You look stunning,' he said, offering them to Beth.

She smiled, hoping it didn't appear forced. 'They're beautiful. You shouldn't have!'

Her voice trembled.

'I wanted to.'

From beneath the make-up bag, the phone buzzed. The sound seemed to fill the room. Charlie's eyes drifted to the dressing table.

'Thanks. They really are lovely,' Beth said, trying to distract him.

The phone buzzed again. And then a third time. Beth ignored it. Her eyes not leaving Charlie's face.

'You not gonna get that?' he asked, sounding confused.

'It's probably work emails coming in. I'm ignoring them until Monday.' It was weak, but she prayed he bought it. 'Would you be a love and pop these in a vase for me downstairs while I finish doing my make-up?'

Charlie leaned down to give her a peck on the cheek.

'I know you said this morning you weren't in the mood. But I couldn't cancel. It would be odd if you were missing, this has been arranged for so long.'

'It's fine. I'm sure it'll be fun.'

'Thanks.'

Charlie turned to leave. He stopped as he reached the bed, looking at the drawn curtains, and glanced over his shoulder towards his wife. Without saying a word, he left the room. Beth heard him head back downstairs.

She grabbed her phone.

Three new messages were on her screen. She opened them with trepidation.

I enjoyed the show.

Loved it when you dropped the towel.

Come on. Open the curtains!

Bile rose into her mouth as she read the words.

Whoever was messing with her and her family was sitting outside the house right now.

Watching.

They had seen her naked through her bedroom window. They had watched her in her private, intimate moments.

What else had they witnessed?

13

Beth felt sick. Her head was spinning, partly from the champagne, mostly from fear.

Was somebody watching Charlie and Daisy downstairs now? Or Peter in his bedroom next door?

She applied the rest of her make-up in a rush, grabbed a jacket from the wardrobe and made her way down the stairs.

Daisy was sitting at the dining table, chatting to Charlie while he took her dinner out of the oven, and plated it up. He smiled at Beth across the room as she hurried into the kitchen.

Ignoring him, she headed straight to the French doors, turned the key in the lock and closed the curtains. Her family stared at her in bewilderment.

She covered every window. For only the second time in the seven years they had owned the house.

Beth came back into the kitchen, pouring herself a second glass, before taking a large gulp.

'Are you okay?' Charlie said, placing the plate of food down in front of their daughter. He crossed the room, standing next to Beth. 'You look a little pale.'

'Yes, I'm fine,' Beth lied.

'What's with the curtains again? It's still broad daylight.'

'Margot's coming over to babysit, I don't want her to feel like she's on display.'

'Are you kidding? Margot loves to be on display!'

Charlie reached a hand up to Beth's forehead, and she flinched.

'You're shaking. What's wrong?'

'I'm cold. Maybe I should change. It's not as warm as I thought.'

'Up to you. You look amazing though.'

Daisy was still staring at Beth, while shovelling a chicken nugget into her mouth.

'I thought you were going to wear the *red* one!' Daisy shouted obstinately, mouth full of food.

'I changed my mind,' Beth said. 'And don't speak with your mouth full!'

Beth heard raucous rock music as Peter's bedroom door opened and he came bowling down the stairs.

'Woah, Mum, you look *hot*,' he said, a cheeky smile on his face.

Charlie laughed. 'What do you want, Peter?'

'Can't I pay my *beautiful* mother a compliment without you thinking I have an ulterior motive? That hurts, Dad, really.' Peter clasped his hands to his heart and pulled a sad face.

Beth didn't say a word. Charlie wasn't sure she was even listening. She stared towards the back door, a distant look in her eyes.

'Really, Pete. What do you want?' Charlie joked.

'Can Zoe come over tonight?'

Charlie looked at his wife, waiting for her to decide. But she didn't say anything.

'Beth?' Charlie said.

'Sorry, I was a million miles away.'

'Your son was asking if his girlfriend can come over tonight while we're out.'

Beth looked at Peter, then back towards Charlie.

'Yes, I suppose so.'

Charlie frowned.

'*Really*?' Peter couldn't hide the surprise from his voice.

'Yeah, *really*?' Charlie echoed.

'Yes. Margot is coming over so it's not like they'll be unsupervised.'

'Great!' Peter exclaimed, bounding up to his room and shutting the door.

The doorbell rang.

Beth stood petrified. The hairs on her neck tingled. She glanced nervously out into the hall.

Charlie raised an eyebrow, then walked past her and opened the door.

Margot stood on the doorstep.

Beth didn't realise she had been holding her breath until she let it out again. A long, relieved sigh.

'Margot!' Beth pushed by, opening the door fully to let Margot in.

'Am I too early?' Margot asked, checking her watch.

'No, not at all. Come in.' Beth stood aside and Margot breezed into the hallway wearing an all-in-one black playsuit, a fuchsia cashmere pashmina draped loosely over her shoulders. She gave Charlie a large, exaggerated kiss on each cheek.

'Hello, you gorgeous hunk of a man!' she said flirtatiously.

'Right back at you!' Charlie replied.

'God. I need to up my HRT dosage if you think I look like a man!' she retorted.

Charlie blushed. 'No, what I meant was–'

'Oh shush, I'm teasing you, darling.' She dismissed him with a flick of her wrist.

Daisy stood at the kitchen doorway, looking shyly out.

'My dear... look how big you've got!'

Daisy didn't reply. Beth crouched down to Daisy's level.

'You remember Margot, don't you?'

Daisy stuffed her thumb in her mouth and fiddled with her skirt with the other hand.

'I've got something you might like to play with,' Margot said in a sing-song voice, while rummaging frantically in her small handbag. She pulled out an expensive-looking lipstick, holding it out in front of her.

Daisy's eyes flicked to her mother's face. Beth smiled and Daisy took the lipstick, beaming.

Beth placed her hand on her daughter's shoulder. 'What do you say, Daisy?'

'Thank you,' she muttered.

'Don't open that unless Aunty Margot is supervising, okay?'

Daisy ran off into the kitchen. Charlie opened the hall cupboard, fishing out his jacket and pulling it on. The familiar smell of his aftershave drifted into Beth's nostrils and almost made her feel safe. Almost made her forget about the terrifying prospect of someone waiting outside her house. *Almost.*

Beth's head began to spin. She wobbled, steadying herself against the wall. Sweat began to form on her brow again.

'Are you okay?' Margot cocked an eyebrow.

'Actually, I'm not sure I'm feeling that well.'

'Oh nonsense. You look fabulous.'

'Thanks. But I really don't feel it.'

Charlie approached the front door with his car keys in one hand, and a bottle of red wine in the other.

'It's too late to cancel now. Derek would be so pissed off. You're gonna have to suck it up.'

'Really, Charlie, maybe you should go by yourself.' Beth looked at her husband.

'Beth.' The tone of Charlie's voice, the look on his face... Beth knew this wasn't up for discussion. And for a moment she resented him.

Perhaps she should tell him about the text messages?

But then he would insist on calling the police. And Beth didn't want that. Too much hassle.

'Okay.' She turned to Margot. 'I'm sure we won't be late. Thanks again for this. You're a lifesaver.'

'Be as late as you like. I'll be fine.'

'Daisy's bedtime is eight thirty. She'll kid on that she's not tired, but you have to be firm. You won't see much of Peter. His girlfriend is coming over so they'll be upstairs all night. Make sure the door is open.'

Margot nodded, then ushered Charlie and Beth out.

As an engine started outside, Margot glided into the kitchen. Daisy was sitting by the back door, trying to apply lipstick to a small toffee-coloured spaniel, who wore a pale-blue-and-white polka-dot bandana.

'Right, my darling. That lipstick is *far* too expensive for a dog to wear,' she said, as Daisy looked up, grinning.

'Cooper is a boy, but I don't care.'

Margot raised her eyebrows. 'I can tell we're going to have fun tonight.'

A knock drew her away from the kitchen. She opened the front door to reveal a young, pretty redhead standing in the driveway. She looked confused as she eyed Margot up and down.

'Oh... hi,' she said. 'I'm here to see Peter.' The inflection in her voice made it sound more like a question than a statement.

'You must be Zoe. Come in, dear, come in.' Margot stood aside, and the girl stepped into the hallway, closing the door behind her. She wore a yellow top with spaghetti straps that should have clashed with her hair but somehow worked. She stood with her phone in one hand.

'I'm Margot, I'm sitting with the kids tonight while Beth and Charlie are out.'

Zoe's face instantly relaxed, and she smiled, making her appear even more attractive. Peter has done well for himself, Margot thought. She could see why Beth liked this one.

'Go on up, you know where you're going, I'm sure.'

'Nice to meet you,' Zoe shouted as she skipped up the stairs.

Margot stood on the bottom step and craned her neck to hear. 'Door open, please!'

Hearing the latch click gently shut, she sighed. Teenagers will be teenagers. She walked back into the kitchen, deciding to let it go. Let them have some fun.

'Right, Daisy, my darling. What would you like to do first?' she asked in the poshest voice that Daisy had ever heard.

14

Beth placed a pile of plates next to the sink in Derek and Anna's immaculate kitchen, turning on the tap to rinse them. She heard Anna's stilettos clacking across the solid wood floor as she approached.

'You don't need to do that, Beth,' she said softly, standing beside her.

'It's fine. I don't mind. It's the least I can do after such a lovely meal.'

They stood without speaking, the sound of the running tap breaking the silence. Taking a plate from Beth, she crouched down to place it in the dishwasher.

'Charlie told me about your latest round of IVF,' Beth said. Anna smiled, but it failed to reach her eyes.

'Ah well. When it's meant to happen it will.'

The tone of Anna's voice suggested to Beth that she was not feeling hopeful.

'Anyway, are you okay?' She placed her hand on Beth's forearm.

'Me? Yeah, I'm fine. Why?'

'Charlie told Derek about the note you got.'

'Oh.'

Anna's face reddened slightly as her eyes darted away from Beth's. 'I'm sorry. Was I not supposed to say?'

'No, it's fine.' Beth picked up a tea towel, drying her hands, before folding it and placing it back on the worktop. She closed off the tap, turned around and leaned against the kitchen unit. 'I don't know what to say about it. It's... strange.'

'And you've no idea who it might be from?'

'No.'

Anna frowned.

Beth paused for a moment. 'Out of interest, what exactly *did* Charlie tell Derek?'

'That a letter came through the door on Friday night, and all it said was *found you*.'

'Right.' Charlie had chosen not to tell Derek about the second note. The one he received at work. Or about what had happened with Daisy. Beth was glad of that at least.

'You need to be careful, Beth. A friend of mine had a stalker. It all got out of hand. He started turning up outside her work, bumping into her in the supermarket, that sort of thing. She went to the police, but they weren't helpful.'

'I don't think we have a stalker, Anna. It's probably one of Peter's friends having a laugh. Besides, we don't even know who the note was intended for. It wasn't addressed to anyone.'

'Right. I'm just saying. You never know.'

'Thanks for your concern. I'm touched. Really. But don't worry. I'm sure it's nothing sinister.' Beth checked her watch, and was surprised to see it was almost ten. The plentiful supply of wine had fooled Beth into relaxing a little. Derek was an excellent host. But the conversation had reminded her that her children were at home.

And somebody was outside her house. Watching them.

She shivered, noticing Anna's eyes flick towards her.

'Are you cold? I can put the heating on if you like.'

'No, I'm daydreaming.'

Beth closed the dishwasher.

'I promised the babysitter we wouldn't be late, so I think we need to be getting home.'

Anna placed her hand on Beth's arm. 'Have I upset you?'

'No, not at all, I just... I need to go.'

Beth crossed the kitchen, heading down the vast hallway towards the front of the house where the men were sitting in the lounge.

'I don't know. She's being quite weird about it all...' she heard Charlie's voice explain as she neared the door. Derek and Charlie stopped talking at her arrival. As they looked up, Beth couldn't help thinking they were like naughty schoolboys, caught smoking behind the bike shed.

'Oh hi, love. You okay?' Charlie's face flushed. He wasn't good at hiding things.

'We need to go. I promised Margot we wouldn't be late.'

Charlie checked his watch, frowning, but thought better than to say anything.

'It's not even ten yet,' Derek whined. 'I'll open another bottle.'

Charlie glanced towards Beth for approval.

'No thanks. It's been a lovely night.'

Beth turned round. Anna was standing in the doorway looking sheepish, holding a tea towel. She'd kicked off her high heels and seemed much smaller now. Beth saw a look between Anna and Derek.

Charlie stood up from the red leather chesterfield he was slumped in, smoothing out his trousers.

'Right. Thanks for having us. It's been great. Sorry for shooting off so quickly.' Charlie approached Anna, giving her an awkward hug. 'Food really was delicious, Anna, thanks.'

The couple showed them to the door.

∼

As the door closed with a click behind them, Charlie hissed at Beth.

'What the hell was that? You were so rude.'

Beth turned to Charlie, swaying a little.

'Me? Why did you tell them about the note? I was mortified when Anna asked me about it. And I notice you conveniently omitted the bit about your office. They think it's all got something to do with me!' Beth's speech was slurred, angry.

'Don't be so ridiculous. Of course they don't think that.'

'Anna does. She started going on about stalkers, and a friend of hers, and telling me I need to be careful. *I* need to be careful? It was you that had someone creeping around your gym delivering you a note!'

'Yeah, about *you!*'

Beth turned away from Charlie and marched towards the car. 'You're an arsehole.'

'And you're drunk. Can you keep your voice down, please? They'll hear you. You've embarrassed me enough tonight already.'

'I don't understand why you had to tell Derek. Of all people.'

'He's my friend, that's why. We were chatting at lunch and I mentioned it. That's all. No big drama. A casual conversation. As you do.'

'And what were you talking about when I came in from the kitchen?'

'Oh... you know... bloke stuff.'

'You were talking about me. I heard you!'

'You're paranoid, Beth. We were talking about everything.

And you're my wife, so yes, obviously *you* came up. It would be odd if you didn't.'

Beth stumbled as she walked towards the car. But as she got closer, she stopped, eyes fixed on the vehicle. Charlie caught up with her and saw what she was staring at. The paintwork had a deep scratch across it, running its entire length.

An envelope was tucked under the wiper.

Beth didn't move. Charlie barged past her and lifted the envelope from the windscreen, tearing it open. He pulled out its contents. Charlie stared down at his hands, eyes wide.

'What the hell...'

'What is it?' Beth's voice trembled.

Trying to make sense of what he was looking at, Charlie's eyes darted about the page.

A smiling face. Somehow familiar.

It was too dark to read any of the smaller print, but thick black letters at the top stood out. This was all he needed to see.

And then it hit him. He knew that face. Those eyes.

Joining him at his side, Beth looked at the paper.

'Is this you?' Charlie asked slowly.

She didn't reply.

'Beth. Is this you?'

Beth looked down at the newspaper again. A pretty blonde girl, not much older than Daisy, beamed out from the page. Above the image in large capital letters, the stark headline.

SHE GOT AWAY WITH IT.

15

Kitty sat on a grown-up chair. Her feet didn't reach the ground. She swung her legs back and forth as she glanced around the stark room, catching her reflection in a large mirror spanning almost one whole wall. Her mother, who sat next to her, across from the policeman, wouldn't look at her.

She was upset. Kitty could tell. That was okay. She could cope with her mother being angry. But her father...

Another lady, who'd been introduced as Mrs Whitehouse, sat next to her on the other side. Kitty wasn't sure who she was. She'd already asked Kitty all sorts of questions about what happened to Billy. She'd told Kitty what to say, and more importantly, what not to say.

'Kitty, I need you to tell me the truth, okay? Do you understand how important this is?'

Kitty looked at her mother, but her mother stared straight ahead. Mrs Whitehouse nodded, and Kitty did the same.

The policeman spoke again.

'For the benefit of the tape, Kitty Briscoe is nodding. Kitty, you must speak up, okay. Do you understand?'

'Yes,' Kitty replied firmly.

'Kitty, do you know why you're here?'

'Yes.'

'Can you tell me why you think you are here?'

Mrs Whitehouse gave Kitty another nod.

'Because something bad happened to that little boy.'

'That's right. Now, do you know what happened to the little boy, Billy Noakes?'

Kitty shook her head. Tears welled up in her eyes. 'No.'

'Now you said you would tell the truth, didn't you, Kitty?'

'I am!'

'I don't think you are. You were at the summer fair in the park that night, weren't you?'

'Yes.'

'And can you tell me who you were there with please, Kitty?'

'Kieran. Kieran Taylor. He lives on the posh estate.'

'Okay. And what did you and Kieran do at the fair?'

There was a long pause. Kitty laced her fingers and fidgeted with them, staring down at the tabletop.

'Kitty?'

She bit her lip, but still refused to speak.

'Kitty, did you and Kieran take Billy away from the fair?'

Kitty nodded.

'Yes.'

'Right. And why did you do that?'

Kitty stared at her hands as she wrung one over the top of the other.

'Kieran wanted to play with him. He said it would be okay.'

Her mother let out a quiet sob and put her hand to her mouth. Kitty looked at her, but Mrs Briscoe wouldn't look at her daughter.

'Okay, Kitty, so how did you lure Billy away from his mother?'

'She was talking to another lady at the candyfloss stand. She had her back to him. Kieran made me do it. I didn't want to do it, but he said the boy would come to me. I waved until Billy saw me. I had this lollipop. Kieran stole it from one of the stalls, it was a big, bright colourful one with circles. I showed it to Billy... offered it to him from across the way.'

'And then what did you do?'

'I called him over. His mum wasn't paying any attention. He came over easy. I didn't have to try very hard.'

'Then what happened?'

'Kieran and me, we took him.'

'Where did you take him, Kitty?'

'Into the woods.'

'Why did you do that?'

'Kieran said he knew a cool place where we could play.'

'Can you remember where that was?'

'The old hotel. The one that had the fire.'

'And you took Billy there?'

'Yes.'

'Was Billy happy to go with you?'

Kitty looked down at the table again.

'Kitty?'

'At first, yes.'

'What do you mean at first?'

'He was okay cos he had the lollipop. But as we got further away, he started to get upset. He was crying for his mummy.'

'And then what happened?'

'Kieran was telling him to shut up. To stop crying, but he wouldn't.'

'You didn't think at that point that maybe you should take him back to his mother?'

Kitty shrugged.

'You thought it was okay that he was upset? A little boy? He was two. You thought that was okay?'

'No.'

'So why didn't you? Why didn't you take him back to his mum?'

Kitty looked at Mrs Whitehouse for reassurance. She nodded.

'I was scared.'

'Scared of what, Kitty.'

'Kieran. I was scared of Kieran. He's much bigger than me. And he's strong. He hurts me sometimes. I have to do what he tells me.'

Kitty's mother sobbed uncontrollably beside her. She held her hand over her mouth to stifle the noise.

'Do you want to take a break?' the policeman asked her mother. She shook her head.

'And then what happened, Kitty?' the policeman continued.

'Kieran walloped him. *Really* hard.'

16

Charlie stared at his wife. She was looking straight at him. He couldn't read her expression in the dim light. But he thought she looked hurt.

'Of course it's not me, Charlie.'

'It bloody well looks like you.' He waved the page of the newspaper at her.

'It's a little blonde girl. It could be anyone... but I'm telling you that is *not* me.'

Charlie stomped towards the driver's side door, unlocked it and climbed in.

'Can we get in the car, please? Before Derek and Anna hear us and come out.'

Beth opened her door and got into the passenger seat. She didn't look at Charlie.

'Beth, I need you to be honest with me.'

She snatched the newspaper from him, looking down at it. He watched her intently as she read the page.

'I remember this case. It was bloody awful what those kids did to that little boy.' Charlie sounded as if he was at breaking point.

Beth finished reading and tossed the paper back into Charlie's lap.

'You honestly think I could do that? What that is saying? To a two-year-old child? You think I'm capable of... *that*?'

Charlie swallowed hard before he spoke. His mouth was dry. He licked his lips. 'I don't know, Beth. It looks a lot like you. It's your eyes. I know your eyes.'

'It says here they tortured him. You think I could torture a child? *Kill* a child?'

'She didn't do it. I remember that. She was found not guilty. It was an older boy who tricked her into helping him snatch the kid. He went down for it. That newspaper got fined a fortune for printing her name and picture.'

'It doesn't matter. You're saying you think I could even be involved in this?'

'Beth, I don't know! You've been acting so weird lately. And then there's those fucking notes. And the incident with Daisy.'

'It's not me, Charlie! You know me. I'm your wife. You've known me for most of our adult lives. This...' she picked up the newspaper, screwing it up, she threw it back at him, 'is not me.'

'Well someone seems to think it is.'

They sat in silence. Charlie flattened out the paper and stared down at it. Random words and phrases jumped out of the page at him.

Tortured, over fifty separate injuries, painful, systematic beating, knife wounds.

Charlie screwed his eyes shut, shaking his head. This could not be Beth. But his mind kept seeing the note left at his work.

How well do you know your wife?

'Charlie, can we go home? Please.'

Charlie turned the key, and the engine roared to life. As he glanced up he noticed Anna holding the curtain back in one of the large bay windows.

Charlie put his foot on the accelerator and drove away from Derek's house.

'I can see why somebody might think it was you,' Charlie said eventually.

'There is a resemblance, I'll give you that.'

'It's spookily like you. When I first saw it something jarred in my head. I couldn't put my finger on it... then it clicked. I thought I was looking at Daisy.'

'Charlie, you *know* me. Please tell me you know I couldn't do anything like that.'

'Yes. I believe you. I do. It was a shock at first. That's all.'

'Honestly? I need to know that you're with me here. I don't want you thinking... wondering things. If you have any doubts, I need you to talk to me about it. Now.'

'I believe you.'

Beth nodded.

'I think we should tell the police.'

'Charlie, no. I'd rather not. It will cause problems. They'll want to talk to Daisy, and she'll be traumatised. I don't want that for her.'

Charlie flicked on the indicator and took the right turn into the long twisting lane that eventually led to their farmhouse.

'Beth, somebody has vandalised my car. This is not someone leaving us silly notes anymore, this is getting serious. If some crazy person believes that you are that girl, that you *hurt* a child... I don't want to think what might happen next.'

Beth remained silent.

'I knew we should have done something after what happened with Daisy. If some lunatic thinks you're wrapped up in *this*...' His voice trailed off.

'I'm begging you, Charlie. I'll sort the car. I'll pay for it so you don't even have to claim on your insurance. But please don't get the police involved. We'll have to explain why we think this is happening. And if it makes it into the papers, or gets leaked, then other people might think this girl is me... what would happen then? We would be...'

'Be what?'

'Finished here,' Beth said, sadly.

'But it's not you, so you don't have anything to worry about, do you?'

'Do you think that matters? Can't you remember the fuss surrounding this case? There was outrage when she was found not guilty. When the boy got out of jail he got a new identity. But there were all sorts of accusations. Random people got named as potentially being him, with absolutely *nothing* to back it up. Pure supposition. Their lives were ruined. Do you want that to happen to me... to us? If people thought for one second that I might be that little girl, that would be it for us. We would have to leave.'

'Do you really think so? People know us here.'

'*You* know me better than anyone. And it didn't stop you asking, did it?'

Charlie didn't reply. As he pulled up into their drive, he let out a long breath.

'Please don't say anything to Margot.'

'Of course I won't.'

Charlie turned off the engine, and they crunched their way over the gravel to the front door.

17

Beth and Charlie let themselves in quietly. No sooner had they set foot in the hallway, Cooper came scurrying out to greet them.

They made their way to the living room, poking their heads in the door. Margot sat reclined on the sofa, reading a trashy romance novel. She looked up and waved.

'Hello, darlings! How was it?'

Beth stepped into the room. 'Yeah, we had a nice time, thanks. And thanks again for looking after the kids.'

'No bother at all.'

'Was everything... okay?' Beth asked tentatively.

'Yes, of course. Hardly saw Peter. But Daisy was good as gold.'

The news made Beth relax a little. No danger at the door tonight.

'Zoe came over for a while. She's a lovely girl.'

'Yes. She is.'

There was an awkward silence. Margot glanced from Beth to Charlie, then hopped up off the couch.

'Right, well now you're back I'll be off.'

'Okay. Sure you don't want a coffee first?'

'No thanks, I'm fine. Can't drink caffeine this time of night. I'd never sleep and would be peeing non-stop.'

Beth walked with Margot to the front door.

'Is everything okay?' Margot mouthed to Beth as they stood in the hall.

'Yes, we're both tired,' Beth whispered back. Margot leaned in and gave her a tight hug.

'See you Monday,' she said casually as she crossed to her Audi at the end of the driveway.

As her car pulled away she gave Beth a wave through the window, and she was gone.

Beth shut the door, sliding the security chain on.

'I'm heading up to bed,' she called through the living room door as she passed.

'Night then,' Charlie replied. When he was sure she was upstairs, he pulled the newspaper from his pocket, unfolding it.

The story had been written the day after the trial verdict was reached.

The nation is outraged as seven-year-old Kitty Briscoe walked free from court yesterday. A jury found her not guilty of the abduction and murder of two-year-old Billy Noakes in July.

Billy was snatched from a fair in Perry Barr, Birmingham where he had been enjoying an evening out with his mother, Wendy (29). Briscoe, referred to throughout the trial simply as 'Girl A', along with eleven-year-old Kieran Taylor, referred to as 'Boy B', took Billy from his mother's side. They lured him away, then walked with him for over a mile to a disused hotel.

Once at the hotel the pair tortured and killed Billy, inflicting over fifty separate injuries. The toddler's parents had to leave the courtroom as pathologist Dr Michael Parkes spent over twenty-five minutes outlining the various injuries sustained. He concluded that the child had suffered a painful, systematic beating.

There were various knife wounds on the young boy's body. The police reports suggest that one or both of the accused had visited Billy's body several times after his death. The killer, or killers, had also cut some of Billy's hair off. Eventually the tiny body was set alight (the police believe in a juvenile attempt to dispose of it) but the fire failed to take hold.

The remains were discovered by the local fire crew, who were alerted to smoke by a passing member of the public.

Briscoe denies playing any part in the torture and subsequent murder. She places full responsibility at the hands of Taylor. Taylor also denied all charges through his legal aid but refused to speak during hours of police interviews.

Briscoe's lawyer, Beverly Whitehouse, claimed that Taylor had coerced Briscoe into helping him abduct Billy. She also claimed that Taylor had at times been violent to Briscoe if she did not do what he told her to. She was afraid, and claims that was why she helped Taylor abduct Billy. Whitehouse surmised that traces of Billy's blood found on Briscoe's clothing were transferred to her when she had comforted the child after Taylor struck him to stop him from crying. Whitehouse also argued that Briscoe was too young to understand the differences between right and wrong. She claimed that Briscoe would also not have completely understood the severity of her actions. Briscoe maintains that Billy was fine when she left the hotel.

The T-shirt Billy had been wearing when he disappeared, the lock of his hair, and the knife have never been recovered.

The jury cleared Briscoe, agreeing that at her age she was incapable of mischievous discretion, but found Taylor guilty of the abduction and murder. There was obvious shock from the public gallery as the jury delivered their verdicts. During the investigation, the Record spoke to chief investigating officer Detective Matt Simms who claimed that being in a room with 'Girl A' chilled him to his core.

The judge has ruled that Taylor's identity may be reported but has banned publication of Briscoe's identity. The Record is in contempt of court today by printing Briscoe's name and picture, but we believe the public has a right to know who this monster is. We believe she is a danger to all children, and we think her face should be made public. Her own father agrees and has provided us with her photograph.

We graciously await our punishment.

He placed the paper on his lap. Even now, over thirty years later, the story was shocking. He remembered it, of course, from when he was a kid. It was a huge case. The entire country lapped it all up, everyone feeling the pain of poor Wendy Noakes; a mother who took her eye off her child for a second and would have to live with the painful consequences for the rest of her life.

Charlie would only have been young; around the same age as Kitty Briscoe. His parents protected him from some grizzlier facts. Rumours had circulated the school, as they always did. But a lot of these details were new to him.

Feeling nauseous, Charlie tried to imagine what that poor boy must have been thinking as he was led away by two children.

As he was beaten, stabbed and tortured.

As he cried for his mother, but she never came.

Charlie stared at the grainy picture of the little blond boy, grinning out from underneath the larger photograph of Kitty Briscoe. At first glance it was two happy children. The sinister truth revealed by the shocking words below.

He thought of his own precious Daisy. Looking towards family photos on the shelf opposite him, he saw himself holding her in the park when she was roughly the same age as Billy Noakes.

So small.

So trusting.

So innocent.

He shook his head and folded the paper into quarters, placing it in his pocket, before switching out the lights and heading up the stairs to bed.

18

Zoe Granger sat at a bus stop. The early morning sun bounced off her freckled face. Her ginger curls tumbled loosely about her shoulders, her mother's emerald silk scarf knotted round her neck. She would have it folded neatly back where it belonged, long before her mother returned from work. Holding her phone in one hand, she unlocked it, scrolled for a few seconds with her thumb, then locked it again. A moment later she repeated the entire sequence.

She tapped *like* on a few of her friends' photos without paying much attention to what they were of.

She scrolled some more. Checking the time, she noted that the bus was late as usual. She glanced around and realised she was alone, so she checked her phone again to kill some time. In case she had missed something important in the last three seconds. Her mobile buzzed to life as a text came through. Seeing who it was from, she grinned.

Her heart always danced when she heard from Peter. She didn't know if she was in love. But she knew she hated being away from him. She had certainly never felt like this about anyone else so far in her fifteen years.

Where r you?

Zoe grinned again as she typed out a reply.

Bus stop. Going to school.

Peter's reply came quickly.

Come to my house.

Zoe frowned.

Now?

Yes. Parents at work. House to ourselves!!!!!

Her heart fluttered. She fidgeted with her blouse, as crimson blotches spread up her chest. Although there was nobody around, she fanned the ends of the scarf out over her skin.

Her fingers trembled as she hammered out her reply.

I'm going to school!

Three dots appeared under the message. Zoe held her breath without realising she was doing it.

Forget school. This will be much more fun. 😉

Zoe looked up and down the road. The bus was nowhere to be seen. She had never skipped school in her life. But she wanted to be wherever Peter was.

Ok. On my way!

She couldn't believe what she was doing. She felt excited and happy. She bit her lip as she thought about her parents. If they got wind of what she was doing, she would be in big trouble. She hadn't even dared to tell them she was dating Peter yet. They were quite particular, strict, in an old-fashioned sort of way. They wouldn't approve of her having a boyfriend. Her mother said she was too young for any of that nonsense. So her folks were blissfully unaware of Peter's existence. Life was simpler that way. Although it did mean a lot of lying about where she was going, and who with.

But it was worth it.

She rummaged around in her purse, finding a couple of screwed-up fivers. Should be enough for a cab, she thought. If not, Peter could help out.

She tucked her phone into the pocket of her tight stone-washed jeans, swung her bag over her shoulder and headed along the road towards the taxi rank.

19

Beth glanced up from her monitor as someone knocked on the door of her office. The mail guy stood in the doorway holding a bunch of letters.

'Come in,' Beth said, more cheerfully than she was feeling.

Her colleague strode across the office, placing a huge pile on Beth's desk.

'You've got a few today.'

'Thanks.'

He turned and scurried out, closing the door behind him.

Beth riffled through some of the submissions. Although most of her stuff came in by email these days, she still received a couple the old-fashioned way. A few of the more mature would-be authors hadn't quite mastered the digital age yet.

Skimming down the first page, she nodded to herself, placing it into her *to be read* pile. The next one she looked at was not so promising. She tossed it into her wastepaper bin. She used to feel guilty doing this, but she knew there was no point in wasting time with work that would never make it past Chloe Grey, the boss.

The third envelope was much lighter than she would have expected. It wasn't heavy enough to contain a manuscript.

She frowned as she slipped her letter opener between the folds of the stiff brown paper. The satisfying rip filled the otherwise quiet room.

She slid her hand inside. Puzzled, she pulled out a single sheet of crisp white paper.

Spidery black handwriting covered the page.

Beth felt sick.

One side of A4 paper, handwritten in marker.

Hello,

I have a story for you. Do you think it would make a good book?

Once upon a time there was a little girl called Kitty.

She was a naughty little girl. But everybody thought she was perfect, because she was blonde and pretty.

And she was a very good liar.

One day she and her friend Kieran did something bad.

They took a little boy from a funfair. And they hurt him. They hurt him very badly and he died.

Kitty put all the blame on Kieran, and Kieran went to jail for it. But Kitty wasn't so innocent. And she got away with it.

She fooled everyone.

Then when she was old enough she moved away.

She changed her name. She changed her accent. She got a new life.

Which was more than the little boy she killed could ever have.

But somebody found her.

And that person thinks Kitty should pay for her crime.

A knock at the door drew Beth's attention away from the note. Margot walked into the office as Beth quickly flipped the paper over on her desk.

'What's that you've got there? Love letter?' She winked.

'Oh, nothing. Submissions,' Beth replied.

Margot perched her bottom on the edge of Beth's desk.

'Are you okay? You look pale.' She placed the back of her hand against Beth's forehead.

'Yes, I'm fine. I skipped lunch and now I'm regretting it.'

'Want me to grab you a sandwich or something?'

'No, it's okay. I'll wait for dinner.'

Margot folded her arms in front of her chest.

'You've forgotten, haven't you?'

Beth stared into Margot's eyes, having absolutely no idea what she was talking about.

'Of course I haven't.' She paused. 'Forgotten what?'

Margot stood up indignantly.

'I knew it. You have! It's drinks in town tonight after work for Chloe's birthday. You *promised* you would come. I don't want to be the only fossil.' She pouted like a petulant child.

With everything that had been going on it had slipped Beth's mind.

Chloe Grey always organised a big night out for her birthday, with plenty of cash behind the bar. To miss it wasn't a good idea, particularly if you were hoping to work your way up the ladder.

It was usually quite messy.

Beth couldn't think of anything she'd rather do less.

'You know I'm not actually feeling all that well...' she began, but Margot cut her off.

'Don't you dare. You are coming. You appear to need a drink more than me. And that's saying something.'

'Margot, I–'

Before she could finish Margot had marched around to her side of the desk and was peeling her out of her black leather swivel chair.

'Come with me right now. We are going to the ladies. You are going to put on some lippy and we are going out.'

She dragged Beth out of the office.

'Hold on!' Beth shouted, pulling away. She darted back to her desk, picking up the note, folding it into quarters. She slipped it into her bag and threw the strap over her shoulder before rejoining Margot in the doorway.

As she stepped out of her office, her eyes flicked around the room.

And there she was.

Vicky.

Leaning on her desk and staring at Beth. That same old smile playing on her lips. She didn't wave this time. She watched as Margot dragged Beth into the lavatories.

'I'll have to text Charlie and get him to pick Daisy up from school.'

'I'm sure he can manage to be a father for *one* evening.'

'That's not fair. He does a lot. His job keeps him very busy.'

'And yours doesn't?'

'Of course it does, but it's easier for me to slip away. They're much more accommodating here.'

Margot applied a fresh coat of lip gloss, eyeing Beth in the mirror.

'All I'm saying is it won't hurt him to look after his children for a few hours while you come out and get shit-faced with me!'

Beth pulled her phone out of her bag, typing a quick message to Charlie.

Margot sprayed herself in a mist of floral-scented perfume, handing the bottle to Beth. She glanced at her reflection, then in Margot's direction.

'Do I look okay? I'm not prepared for a night out.'

Margot spun Beth around so she could assess her. She eyed Beth's black dress and matching patent stilettos.

'I'm loving the whole Morticia Addams vibe, darling. Very chic.' She winked.

Beth exhaled.

'I'm kidding, sweetie. You look amazing. Black is the new black, haven't you heard? Nobody would *ever* guess that you had completely forgotten your boss's birthday drinks.'

Margot cocked her head to one side. 'Hold on.'

She reached up, unclipping the comb holding Beth's hair in place, and it fell down around her shoulders. Margo ruffled Beth's locks energetically with both hands, then smiled.

'Beautiful.'

An hour later they were standing outside a noisy bar on the seafront. Beth stood alone, staring out at the coloured lights of Brighton Pier, as Margot mingled, laughing, working the crowd. She was good at this.

Beth, on the other hand, was hopeless.

She didn't go out much. She never had. She enjoyed a drink behind closed doors, in the comfort of her home, but in this setting she felt vulnerable.

'Beth, hey!'

Beth turned to see Vicky heading towards her with a brightly coloured cocktail. She had a good-looking guy in tow. Thirties. Messy short brown hair framed an angular jaw. His thick, bushy eyebrows almost met in the middle. Pale skin that was decorated with a dusting of designer stubble.

Beth imagined that people often warmed to him without him having to try very hard.

He reminded her a little of Charlie. When he was younger.

She tried to pretend she hadn't seen them, but she was too

late. Before she could escape, Vicky was in her face. Her companion stood looking shy in the background a few metres away.

Vicky leaned in and gave her a kiss on each cheek. Beth froze at the close contact with a virtual stranger.

'This is my friend, Mikey,' Vicky yelled, motioning behind her with her free hand. She placed her lips around a plastic straw protruding from her glass and slurped the fluorescent-green liquid noisily.

Mikey gave her a wave. Beth didn't return it.

'So I realised why I thought I know you.' The sickly-sweet smell of the drink wafted into Beth's face on Vicky's warm breath. Beth took a sip of her wine to dispel the aroma. She breathed in deeply, her nose inside the glass, as the cold liquid ran down her throat.

'Is that right?' Beth replied.

'Yeah. On my media studies course. We looked at *loads* of famous court cases and stuff, and how the press handled them. How they treated suspects and all that, you know.'

Beth didn't know. She didn't care. Why Vicky thought she would be interested was beyond her. She stared into Vicky's eyes. Waiting.

Mikey stood in the background looking at his phone. It rang, and he walked away onto the promenade as he answered the call.

'Anyway, you look *just* like that girl, Kitty Briscoe.'

Beth tried to keep any emotion from her face.

'Who?'

'You know... Her and her friend killed that little boy, Billy Noakes. But she was acquitted. That newspaper in Birmingham printed her name and picture. Got fined *shitloads* of money for it. It basically finished them.'

Beth raised herself up on her toes, looking over Vicky's shoulder. She saw Margot was facing the wrong direction. No chance of a rescue there.

'I'm sorry, I don't remember.'

Vicky frowned, cocking her head. 'Even I know about it and I wasn't born. It was like, a totally huge story. Still is. Most people think she should have gone down for it.'

Vicky raised her glass and drained the dregs of her drink.

'And you're telling me all this why?' Beth asked, her tone clipped.

'You look like her. That's why I thought I recognised you. You could *be her*. Like, she disappeared after the media leaked her name and picture, so you could *literally* be her.' Vicky laughed.

Beth reached up and grabbed Vicky's wrist.

'Ow-ch!' she cried overdramatically.

Beth leaned in close, so only Vicky could hear her.

'Let's get something straight, okay,' she hissed. 'We are not friends. We will never be friends. I don't care about your anecdotes. I don't care if you think I look like some kid from a case you studied at school. I don't care about any of that stuff.'

'Let go of my wrist, you're hurting me!'

'Keep away from me. Stop staring at me. Stop talking to me. Don't come anywhere near me. If you continue with whatever *this* is that you are doing, I will destroy you. I know what you've been doing. Do you understand?'

'What the hell is wrong with you, you psycho!'

'Do you understand?'

Vicky nodded frantically. She looked like she might cry.

Beth let go of Vicky's wrist.

Vicky raised her other hand and nursed it gently, looking at Beth with trepidation.

'I think we're done here,' Beth whispered.

Vicky looked indignantly at her.

'If Mikey comes back tell him I'm inside.' She spun around and disappeared into the noisy bar.

Beth glanced at her empty glass and was about to put it down on the floor and attempt to slip away unnoticed when Mikey reappeared next to her.

'Hey. Do you know where Vicky went?'

Beth felt embarrassed. She was glad he hadn't witnessed their altercation.

'She said she was going home.'

Mikey frowned, then glanced around the throng of people congregating outside the bar. He looked at the empty glass in Beth's hand.

'Can I get you another?' He nodded towards the glass.

Beth looked down. It took her a moment to realise what he was asking.

'Oh, no thanks. I think I've got to go, actually.'

'Go on. The only person I know here seems to have abandoned me. Let me buy you a drink?'

Beth looked around, trying to get Margot's attention, but she was deeply engrossed in a story. Huge hand gestures, lots of laughing. The life and soul of the party, eternally.

'Okay, just the one though.'

'White wine?'

Beth nodded, and Mikey smiled before heading into the bar.

He returned a few minutes later with two large glasses of wine in his hands, and two packets of crisps in his mouth. Beth took one of the glasses, and Mikey grabbed the crisps from his lips.

'Salt and vinegar or cheese and onion?'

'Either,' Beth replied. She took a sip.

'Sorry, I don't think I got your name.'

'I'm Beth.' She held out her hand and Mikey shook it.

'Hey, Beth. Nice to meet you. So you work with Vicky?'

'Kind of. I don't really know her.'

Mikey took a gulp of his drink.

'Right. So what do you do there?'

'I work in submissions. I basically vet all the manuscripts that get sent in. The good ones get passed on to Chloe for consideration, the others... don't!' She smiled guiltily.

Mikey sucked in air through his teeth.

'Cut-throat!'

'We kind of have to be. We're in this business to make money primarily. There's no point in wasting time on stuff we don't believe in.'

Mikey screwed up his face.

'Remind me not to get on your bad side.'

Beth laughed. 'Hey, I'm a nice person... at least I think I am. It's my job. I wouldn't last very long if I passed any old rubbish through to Chloe.'

'That's okay. I'm winding you up. You definitely seem like a nice person. And I'm an excellent judge of character.'

Beth wasn't sure if Mikey was flirting with her. It was such a long time since anyone had tried, she wasn't even sure how to tell anymore.

'How about you? How do you two know each other?'

'We were at school together.'

'Oh right.' Beth couldn't hide the surprise from her voice.

'What?' Mikey smiled.

And Beth actually blushed. His eyes bored deep into her. She couldn't remember the last time anybody looked at her that way.

'It's only... you seem older than her.'

'Thanks!' he replied with mock hurt in his voice, then laughed.

'No, I... I didn't mean you... she just looks quite young.' Beth smiled as she met his lingering gaze.

'Yeah, Vicky has always been blessed there. Apart from when we were teenagers. She couldn't get into any pubs.'

'I bet.'

Beth took a sip of her wine. Noticing that Mikey had emptied his glass, she nodded towards it.

'Fancy another?' she asked.

He checked his watch. 'I'd love to, but I've got to go.' He bent over, placing his empty glass on the floor beside him. 'Some other time?'

Beth looked down, then back up at Mikey, holding her hand up, wiggling her ring finger.

'I'm married,' she said.

'And?' Mikey held up his hand revealing a thick gold band. 'So am I! Doesn't mean we can't be friends, does it?'

Beth cringed. She had misread the situation.

'Sorry! No, of course not.' She felt a wave of heat rush up her neck and face.

Mikey pulled out his phone, looking at her. She took it from him and typed in her number. He gave her a drop call.

'There's mine.'

'Thanks.'

'Great to meet you, Beth,' he said with another deep smile.

'Likewise.'

He turned and disappeared down the promenade.

'Who the devil is *he*?' Margot slurred her words as she appeared in front of Beth.

'Friend of Vicky's.'

'Was he chatting you up?'

'I don't think so.'

'So I didn't see you give him your number then?' She raised an eyebrow.

Beth reddened again. 'Oh God. What the hell am I doing?'

'What do you mean?'

'You're right. Why am I giving a young guy I've only just *met*, my number?'

'It's okay, darling. You're allowed.'

'No. It's not okay. Nothing is okay.'

And at that, Beth burst into tears.

20

——————

Margot sat next to Beth on the sea wall with one arm draped loosely over her shoulder.

Beth dabbed at her eyes with the pile of tissues Margot had grabbed from her designer handbag.

After Margot had finally got Beth to stop crying, Beth had told her everything.

About the notes. About the texts. She told her about the newspaper cutting. And she showed her the latest addition that had arrived at work that day. After a seemingly endless pause, Margot clicked her tongue in the roof of her mouth, handing the paper back to Beth. 'And...?' she said questioningly.

'And what?'

'Are you her?'

Beth looked at Margot, slightly hurt that she had asked.

'No. Of course I'm not her.'

'I'm just checking. You never know! First thing in the morning, you must go to the police and tell them what has been happening–'

'No. That's exactly what Charlie said. But don't you see, if I do, this will all get out. It might end up in the papers. And if people think I'm that girl, my life here is over.'

Margot pursed her lips.

'Don't look at me like that, Margot. It's true. That bloody weirdo Vicky has already told me tonight that I look like Kitty Briscoe. That's why she's so obsessed with me. All it takes is a tiny seed to be planted in people's minds, and that will be it.'

'Hmmm...' Margot tapped her foot as she gently stroked Beth's back. 'You might have a point. I remember when this all happened. It was terrible. Very sad. And those kids were despised. Even her. She was acquitted, but the public weren't happy with that. She was seven, for Christ's sake. She couldn't have known what she was doing.'

'That's only a year older than Daisy. I look at her and I think it can't be possible, you know?'

'Okay. So we don't go to the police. What is the alternative? Do you have any idea who might be doing this?'

Beth thought for a moment, shaking her head.

'I'm not so sure about Vicky. This all started happening around the time she showed up. And she *clearly* has some sort of weird obsession with the story, and with me.'

'Right. Let's keep an eye on that one. And for now I think you should avoid being alone.'

'You can walk me to my car, then.'

'You're not driving.'

'I've had two glasses of wine. I'll be fine.'

'Two *big* glasses of wine.'

'I'm fine.'

'If you say so.' Margot held both hands up in surrender.

They walked together to the car park. They didn't speak, and Beth was fine with that. She felt like she had said too much. She couldn't remember the last time she had confided in someone like this. She had told Margot things she hadn't even told Charlie.

She thought of Charlie. She thought of Mikey, and she felt ashamed. If she found out that Charlie had given his number to a pretty girl at a work night out, she would be mortified.

As they arrived at her car, she turned to Margot.

'What do I do if he calls me?'

'Who? Your stalker?'

'No! Vicky's friend, Mikey.'

'Oh, Mr Sexy! I wouldn't worry. People of that generation don't call. They communicate solely by text message or Whatsup or whatever they call it.'

'Okay. So what if he texts?'

'Then you text him back. You haven't done anything wrong, Beth. You are allowed to have male friends.' She paused. 'Just don't sleep with him.'

Beth slapped Margot on the shoulder.

'It's not funny!'

'You have nothing to feel guilty about. You're married. He's married. He's clearly interested in your sparkling personality!' She winked.

Beth opened the car door, climbing into the driver's seat.

'Now you are sure you're okay?' Margot fixed Beth with a teacher-like stare.

'Positive. Can I give you a lift?'

'No, don't be silly. It's in the opposite direction.'

'I don't mind, really.'

'No, honestly, I'll get a cab. I'll see you tomorrow. Text me as soon as you're home.'

Beth was about to pull the door to, when Margot leaned into the car.

'Tell Charlie about what's been going on. About the letter

you got today and the text messages. He deserves to know. He's a good man. You need the support of a partner at times like these.'

She didn't wait for a reply. She simply closed the door and waved goodbye as Beth pulled away.

As Beth drove from town, she felt less embarrassed at having confided in Margot, and a feeling of relief washed over her instead. She had spent her entire life being independent. She had never needed anybody. She never even really needed Charlie. She *loved* him, but she didn't need him. She tended to keep her problems to herself and dealt with things on her own. And that's how it had always been.

Thinking of her mother briefly, her lip quivered as she blinked away tears, but pushed the memory from her head. Back to where it belonged.

As she recalled crying outside the bar, she hoped nobody from work had seen.

She headed out of town. The roads became less populated, and she relaxed. She knew she was likely to be over the limit, but she felt absolutely fine. She also knew that wouldn't stand up in court if there was an accident. She drove slowly, cautiously.

Glancing in the rear-view mirror, the headlights of a car behind dazzled her. She checked the clock. It was nine thirty. Probably someone else heading home from the bars. It was rare anyone would be on the road out towards her house at this time of night. She turned left onto the country road which would eventually bring her home and was surprised to see the car behind take the same turn.

Her heart beat a little faster.

She told herself it was nothing to worry about and concentrated on the road ahead.

The last thing she wanted was to strike a deer, or worse.

She continued along the winding road, pressing her foot

down slightly in an attempt to put some distance between her and the car behind.

But the other vehicle also increased its speed.

Beth felt uneasy. Her mouth was dry.

She pressed her foot down harder, watching the speedo climb up through the forties, fifties, and into the sixties.

The car behind did the same.

She tried to convince herself it was merely a coincidence.

Another driver heading home.

Her heart pounding, Beth suddenly turned right, off the road onto a narrow farm track, without indicating. It was the wrong direction, but she had to see what her *friend* would do.

Beth heard the squeal of tyres as the car behind made a sharp turn.

The driver flicked their headlights onto full beam. Beth was momentarily blinded and eased off the accelerator. The car behind drew closer. It was tailgating her, its bright lights dazzling her each time she glanced in her mirror.

She took the next available left turn, hoping it would bring her back in the correct direction. After a few minutes she felt relief as she approached a familiar junction. She turned right, back onto the road home, pressing her foot down to the floor. The relief faded fast as her pursuer came racing up behind her. Headlights dazzling once again.

Beth's heart raced.

She increased her speed.

Her pursuer accelerated too.

She pressed her foot on the brake, and the car gained on her.

Beth held on to the wheel with one hand as she reached down for her bag. She rummaged around for her phone, finally grasping it between her fingertips.

As she pulled it from the handbag it slipped out of her hand

and fell into the passenger-side footwell. She had no hope of getting it without stopping the car.

Something told her that would not be wise.

She kept driving, her speed creeping up.

The car behind sped up and bumped into the rear of her Range Rover.

Whoever was following her was not just trying to scare her.

Beth tried desperately to put some distance between them, but she couldn't get away.

The other vehicle veered sharply, clipping her rear end. As the cars impacted together, Beth swerved. Overcompensating, she crossed onto the wrong side of the road. She cursed as she corrected her steering.

Thank God there was nobody coming the other way.

Her knuckles turned pale as she gripped the wheel, trying to remain in control.

Once more, she was shunted aggressively.

She peered into her rear-view mirror, desperate to see who was behind her. Trying to make out a licence plate. Any detail at all about the car.

But all she saw was blinding white headlights.

The vehicle swerved out to Beth's right and back into the side of her car. She kept her eyes fixed firmly ahead, trying to keep to the road. Metal squealed and crunched.

The impact and speed were too much. Beth lost control.

She slammed on the brakes too late.

Her car collided with a barbed-wire fence and Beth's head bounced off the steering wheel as she came to a halt in a field.

Her pursuer screeched away. The tail lights disappeared into the night like two red eyes of a demon speedily retreating into the darkness.

And then there was silence.

21

R inging.

As Beth came round, that's what she heard. She felt dazed, momentarily unsure what had happened. Then the horror of the car chase flooded back to her. She didn't know how long she had been there, but she knew she had been knocked unconscious.

Her phone. It was buzzing. She grabbed her bag, sluggish from the knock on the head. And then she remembered she had dropped the handset. She scrambled about on the floor, finding it under the passenger seat. Her vision was still not right. She struggled to focus on the screen. The caller rang off.

The screen showed the time as 10.45.

'Damn, damn, damn,' Beth whispered. She scrolled her screen.

Two missed calls from Margot. Five from Charlie.

She slipped her phone back into her bag and tried the ignition. Surprisingly, the car started on the first try. She reversed out of the field, up onto the road and headed for home.

~

As she pulled in slowly to the gravel driveway, Charlie stood in the doorway of their house, a stern expression on his face.

He eyed the car as Beth parked up. She turned off the engine but remained sitting in the driver's seat.

Charlie strode over to her, wrenching the door open.

'Where the hell have you been? And what the fuck happened to the car? It's totally mangled!'

'I... had an accident.'

'My God! Are you okay?' He crouched down beside her.

'Yeah, I'm fine. I lost control and went into a field.'

Charlie embraced Beth before helping her up. He slipped an arm around her waist and walked her back to the house. As they stepped into the hallway, the warmth of her home hit her and she slumped, letting Charlie support her. He turned her towards him.

He sniffed, screwing up his face.

'You've been drinking.'

'I had two glasses of wine.'

Charlie looked at her, his disappointment apparent.

He sat her on the sofa and stood with his arms folded in front of his chest. His brown eyes fixed intently on her face.

'Charlie, I swear I'm not drunk.'

'So you drove your car into a field because you are totally sober, right?'

The sarcasm was thick in his voice, and it stung Beth like a slap.

'No. I went off the road because...' She stopped. She didn't want to tell him.

'Because what?'

She remembered Margot's final remarks before she had left her that evening.

'Because someone was trying to run me off the road.'

Charlie blinked a few times as the words sank in.

'Are you sure?'

'Yes. He slammed into the side of me at sixty-five miles an hour and I ended up in a field.'

'Right. That's it. This has gone far enough. I'm calling the police.'

Beth jumped up from the sofa.

'No, Charlie, please! Don't.'

Charlie pushed her with one hand and she fell back down onto the seat. He pulled his mobile from his jeans pocket. Beth stood up again, grabbing at the phone, desperately trying to stop him. He twisted away from her.

'Charlie, you can't! I've been drinking. If the police come, they will breathalyse me. And they'll arrest me. Think about this.'

Charlie stopped, staring blankly back at her. His lip quivered.

She reached up, clasping her hands around his. His face turned down to the floor. She slipped the phone out from between his fingers.

'I know you're scared. I am too. But this won't help. This will lose me my licence. And we can't afford for that to happen. We live in the middle of nowhere. Do you understand?'

Charlie nodded.

'Good.'

Beth sat down on the sofa, patting the cushion. Charlie resisted at first. Beth reached up and took his hand, gently tugging him downwards. He collapsed onto the seat beside her.

'We need to do something, Beth. We can't keep ignoring this. It's not going away. It won't stop. Someone will get hurt.'

'I know.'

They sat in silence for a while. Beth placed her hand on Charlie's leg, stroking lightly, her eyes closed.

Charlie finally broke the quiet in the room.

'So what do we do?'

Beth thought for a moment longer.

'I don't know. Somebody clearly thinks that I am Kitty Briscoe. Someone obviously wants me to pay for what *she* did. I think first, we need to establish who that someone is. We can't do anything until we know who's doing this to us.'

'It must be someone linked to the case. The boy's mother?'

'Maybe.'

'Or what about the lad? The kid who went to jail. He'd have as much reason as anyone to hate her.'

'Yes. True.'

'So Billy's family. The guy who did time. Anyone else you can think of?'

'I really don't know. There's a new girl at work. There's something... not right about her. And all this started happening pretty soon after she showed up. I don't like her.'

'Okay. You think she could be connected?'

'She wouldn't even have been born when Billy Noakes was murdered. I don't know what her connection is. Unless she's one of these weirdos who's obsessed with grisly murders. She was grilling me about it tonight. I got the impression she was digging. She wanted me to think she was joking, but I'm sure she meant it. I don't know how or why, but my gut tells me she's connected in some way.'

'Right. I'll see if I can find any info on Billy's family. The lad, he'll be harder to track down. He's protected. But someone will know where he is, I'm sure.'

Beth nodded.

Charlie placed his hand on top of Beth's.

'I love you. I won't let anyone hurt you. I'll protect our family. I promise.'

'Thank you.' She stood up. 'I need to get to bed.'

'You go. I'll be up soon,' Charlie replied.

Beth trudged up the stairs. Charlie heard running water from the en suite.

He pulled the folded newspaper from his pocket. Skimming it once more, he made a note of a few names. A quick internet search on his phone revealed that Detective Matt Simms had retired a few years earlier on medical grounds.

Hardly surprising, Charlie thought. He couldn't find any further information. So he changed tack. He scoured the page for the reporter.

Tom Cavanagh.

Bingo.

Charlie typed the name into the search engine, and within seconds he had all the details he needed.

He must have been a rookie at the time of the case; still looked relatively young now. He found a mobile number, tapping it into his phone.

After a couple of rings, Cavanagh picked up.

'Hello?' The voice was thick Brummie. Grouchy, probably from being called late at night by a stranger.

But when you're a journalist, that's par for the course. Charlie explained who he was.

'Okay, mate. So why are you calling me this late? You got a story for me?'

'No. Sorry, I don't.'

Silence. Charlie could hear the occasional long breath, maybe drawing on a cigarette.

'I'm trying to find Matt Simms.'

No reply.

'Matt Simms was–'

'I know who he is.'

'Okay. Do you know how I can get in touch with him?'

Another pause.

'Perhaps. What do you want him for?'

'It's complicated.'

'Mate, you've called me after midnight. I think the least you owe me is to tell me what this is about.'

'It's about Billy Noakes.'

'What about him?'

'It's actually more about Kitty Briscoe.'

More silence.

Not even the sound of breathing.

'Do you know where she is?' Cavanagh asked excitedly.

'No.'

'Are you sure? My paper would reward you handsomely for dirt on her.'

'Do you have a number for Simms or not?'

'Sorry, mate. No can do.'

The line went dead.

'Shit,' Charlie cursed under his breath.

He sat staring at his phone for a moment, then hammered a text message into it.

Someone thinks my wife is Kitty Briscoe.
That person is terrorising my family.
She's innocent. I need to find out what happened to Kieran Taylor.
He's our prime suspect.
Simms is the only one who can help me.

Charlie typed in Tom Cavanagh's mobile number and hit send.

A few minutes passed, and Charlie had almost given up hope, when three small dots appeared below his message. Cavanagh was replying. A few seconds later a reply buzzed onto his screen. An address in Birmingham, followed by a warning.

Simms was affected hugely by that case. He never really got over it.

Raking it up again now will open old wounds for him. Be sure you want to go there.

Charlie was sure.

He didn't want to cause upset to anyone else, but he had to do this. He had to protect his family.

Tomorrow he would drive to Birmingham.

22

As the setting sun fell on Kitty Briscoe's face she inhaled the sweet scents of honeysuckle and jasmine and smiled. She loved summer evenings. Smudge, her kitten, sidled up behind her, rubbing himself against her. His tail swayed above his head as he purred loudly.

Kitty turned and ran her hand across the soft fur of his back. Smudge dribbled as she stroked him.

Kitty's mother had brought the animal home a few weeks earlier. Her father had been furious, of course. Nothing new there.

She closed her eyes and reclined slowly onto the grass. Resting her fingers on Smudge she lay peacefully, watching the sun set.

She didn't like it when her mother was out. She tried hard to keep out of her father's way, but sometimes it didn't work.

A door slammed inside the house, and Kitty's eyes sprang open. She sat upright on the lawn.

'Kitty!' Her father's booming voice carried out into the garden and the cat scurried away.

It hadn't taken *him* long to learn.

'Kitty, get in here now!' her father roared.

He was getting closer.

Kitty jumped up. She didn't want to see him.

She ran to the fence, slipping through a gap. Crouching on the other side, she held her breath.

Didn't dare breathe. Didn't dare move.

'Kitty, where the hell are you?'

He was outside now.

A bead of sweat trickled down her forehead. She wiped it away carefully.

'I'm warning you, you little shit. You better get here right now or you'll bloody well regret it!'

Kitty backed away, the skirt of her pink gingham dress snagged on a rough edge, or a nail, she wasn't sure which. The fabric ripped.

She held her hand to her mouth, resisting the urge to cry.

Don't. Get. Caught.

She moved further from the fence, stepping on a twig.

The cracking sound may as well have been a gunshot. She ducked down again, peering through the gap. Her father span around, unsure which direction the noise had come from. Vodka had lessened his ability to think straight. Kitty had learned at a very young age that her father was stupid when he drank.

Stupid, but dangerous.

Kitty watched as his shirtless, fat body wobbled. He swayed back and forth. She hoped he might fall, but he held his balance, taking a step back.

'Where the hell are you?' He was furious now.

The kitten ran across the garden, past her father and in through the French doors. He glimpsed the flash of movement out of the corner of his eye and twisted towards the house. He lurched forwards, then half ran, half fell, over the lawn and into the living room.

Kitty took her chance. She stood up and scarpered.

She sprinted as fast as she could and didn't stop until she got to the tree house that she and Kieran had built in the woods the previous summer. She climbed up the ladder and pushed the hatch open, pulling herself into the safety of their den.

She sat huddled inside, hugging her knees to her chest. As the sun went down, the walls around her turned orange, then deep scarlet. The birds stopped chirping. Something scurried past beneath her in the bushes. She didn't care. Whatever it was couldn't be any worse than her pig of a father.

The warmth faded with the light, and as the red changed to black, Kitty shivered. It was a summer evening, but she'd left without a jacket. She didn't know how long she had been hiding, but she felt cold. She wanted to go home.

She slowly descended the ladder and made her way back.

Sliding through the gap in her fence, she tiptoed towards the house. The French doors were still wide open. There was a warm orange glow from one solitary lamp inside. The bright moon cast eerie shadows around the garden.

Kitty froze as she saw something lying on the grass midway between where she stood and the house.

She couldn't make out what it was. A small pile. A rag, perhaps.

As she approached, she saw a clearer shape. The rough outline of fur.

A shaft of moonlight illuminated the animal. Kitty smiled as she edged closer to Smudge.

But something wasn't right.

He would usually come running to her as soon as she was nearby.

But the kitten didn't move.

She took a few more tentative steps towards him until she was standing over him.

He looked all wrong. His eyes bulged. His tongue lolled outside his mouth.

Kitty knelt down beside her beloved cat, picking him up gently. She cradled his lifeless body in her arms. But of course, she was too young to understand.

'Smudge?' His head fell awkwardly to one side and Kitty gasped. She dropped the cat onto the lawn and screamed.

'Smudge, wake up!' she cried. But the kitten didn't move. He felt cold as she stroked his fur.

Kitty began to cry.

'Smudge!' she shouted, over and over again.

She didn't notice her father until he was almost on top of her.

'Daddy, something's wrong with Smudge. He won't wake up!' Kitty bellowed through her sobs.

Her father stood staring at her, a sneer on his face.

'He's dead.'

'What?'

'That's what you get. That'll teach you to hide from me. You remember that.'

He turned away from her and wobbled back inside the house, leaving a stench of sweat, cigarettes and alcohol in his wake.

Kitty sat stroking her pet for a few minutes. She knew now that he was dead, but she couldn't let go of him... not yet.

Eventually, after she had cried herself dry, she crawled to the edge of the garden and dug a hole in the flower bed with her hands. She returned to the cat, picking him up. She placed him into the hole and filled it in, patting it gently.

That was Kitty's first experience of death.

But not her last.

She stood and turned back towards the house.

Wiping at her eyes, smearing a streak of mud across her cheek, she edged closer to the French doors.

As she reached the entrance, she stood for a while, picking at the dirt beneath her fingernails.

'What are you waiting for?' Her father's voice came out in a growl. 'In you come.'

23
___

It was scrawled messily on a scrap of paper.

Written in a hurry, but definitely Charlie's handwriting.

He'd climbed into bed late the night before and had been up and away early. Beth assumed he was off to the gym before work. But when she got up, she found the note in the kitchen.

Beth turned it over in her hands, examining it carefully, searching for any sign that it was under duress. But she found none. It simply appeared to be a letter from her husband.

Nothing more, nothing less.

Nothing sinister.

Beth, I have to go away for a few days for work. Totally forgot to tell you yesterday. Sorry. Will be on the road a lot but will try to call when I can.

Love you.

C x

But something about it was odd.

Charlie hadn't mentioned a trip. It was unlikely he had forgotten. That was not in his nature. Why hadn't he spoken to her about it earlier when he bent over and kissed her as she lay in bed?

Beth screwed the note up, throwing it in the bin. She sipped her coffee, tapping her finger on the side of her mug.

The noise of a teenaged boy barrelling down the stairs filled the house and Peter appeared in the kitchen.

'Morning,' Beth shouted to him.

He grunted in her general direction, opened the fridge and removed a four-pinter of milk. He unscrewed the cap and gulped the contents down.

'Use a glass, please.'

He ignored her as usual. Replaced the lid, placing the plastic bottle back on the shelf.

'Where's Dad?' he asked.

'He's away with work, apparently.'

'Till when?'

'A few days.'

'He never said, yesterday.'

'No. He forgot.'

Peter raised an eyebrow. The lie wasn't fooling him either.

He skulked over to the island unit, threw himself down onto a stool and sat fidgeting, lacing his hands over one another, staring down at his grubby fingers.

'Have you seen my phone?' he asked finally.

'No. Where did you last have it?'

'Not sure. If I knew that I wouldn't be asking *you*, would I?'

'How long is it since you've had it?'

'Dunno. Couple of days?'

'Peter! How can you be so careless with that thing?'

'I swear I haven't lost it. I bet Daisy has got it.'

'We won't be buying you another one. So you had better hope it turns up.'

'Am I *asking* you to buy me another one?' he replied sarcastically.

He got up and crossed to a cupboard, grabbing a box of cereal.

Returning to his seat, he picked pieces from the carton, throwing them into his mouth.

'My God, Peter. What is wrong with you today? Can you use a bowl, please?'

Peter sighed loudly, slamming the box onto the counter, folding his arms across his chest. He eyed his mother from beneath his shaggy fringe.

'Zoe is away on a geography field trip. I've got no way of contacting her without my phone,' he said.

'Right. Don't you know her number?'

'Mum, do you *know* how a mobile phone works? It's not the dark ages. You don't *actually* have to dial a number anymore. You just press the person's name.'

'Okay. You'll have to wait until she's home then, won't you?'

'But she's away for *ages*!'

Peter unfolded his arms, shoving his hands into his trouser pockets.

'I'm sorry, Peter, I don't know what you want me to do. I'm not the one who lost your phone.'

He tutted overdramatically.

'I *didn't* lose it.'

Beth stood up. She wasn't in the mood to argue with a stroppy teenager.

'Okay, Peter. The fairies must have taken it. Maybe write a letter to Santa Claus and ask him to tell them to bring it back.'

As she turned and walked away, she heard Peter's stool scrape across the tiled kitchen floor.

'Whatever,' he shouted petulantly.

'Yes, whatever.' Beth held up her hands in surrender.

'Can I get a lift to school?'

'No.'

'Why?'

'Because I had an accident last night and I don't really want to drive the car until it's fixed. Daisy has already been picked up by Sarah's mum. I'm getting a lift in with Margot and the car is being collected by the garage tomorrow. It shouldn't take long for them to fix it, but until then you'll have to get the bus.'

'Great!' Peter shouted as he stormed past Beth, into the hallway. 'I hate my life!'

'Yes, Peter, your life is absolutely terrible. You're the first teenager in history who has had to get the bus to school, aren't you?'

'Most other teenagers don't live in a shitty old farmhouse out in the middle of nowhere.'

'Right. If you hate it so much you can move out, can't you.'

'I wish.'

The sound of a horn from outside halted their conversation. As Beth headed out the front door, she shouted to Peter to remember to lock up when he left.

Margot's silver TT was sitting in the drive. Beth jumped into the passenger seat. She caught Margot staring at her mangled Range Rover. She turned to Beth, her mouth hanging open.

'Don't,' Beth said firmly. Margot nodded and drove away from the house.

24

They sat staring at the animal for at least ten minutes. Kitty drew her hand across her eyes, wiping the tears onto her white lacy skirt.

'It'll be okay,' Kieran said softly.

'I didn't want to hurt it,' Kitty said through her sobs.

Kieran picked up the cat. Its body was still warm.

Kitty looked away. She didn't want to see it.

Intestines were hanging from its belly.

'Look at it,' Kieran said. 'It's so *weird*.'

'I don't want to!' Kitty shrieked.

'Kitty, look!'

'No.'

'Look at what we did!'

Kieran thrust the dead animal under Kitty's face. She screamed, turning away, but he grabbed her arm with one hand.

'Touch it,' he said, laughing.

Kitty screwed her eyes shut tightly and heard Kieran walking away from her, his feet trudging across gravel. She opened them in time to see him toss the cat like a piece of litter into the bushes at the side of the path. He came running back towards her, wiping blood from his hands down his muddy jeans.

'It was a stray. It wasn't wearing a collar,' Kieran said, placing his arm around Kitty's shoulder. A huge smile spread over his face.

Kitty didn't reply. She fiddled with the hem of her dress.

'It doesn't matter. It was just a stray.'

Kitty looked down at the floor.

'My Daddy hurt Smudge, you know. Last night.'

Kieran didn't reply. He glanced at the giant purple bruises on Kitty's arms.

'I buried him in the garden. He was my baby.'

Kieran still didn't reply. He looked confused.

Sometimes Kitty thought she understood more things than Kieran did. And he was much older than her.

Kitty kicked at the dry dirt on the path, covering over the patch of blood.

'Are you sure it was a stray?'

'Yeah. No collar. Would've had a collar on if it'd been someone's pet. Probably a wild cat.'

'There's no wild cats.'

'There are too. My mum told me. They're all over England.'

Kitty bit her bottom lip. She never knew if what Kieran was saying was true. She hadn't ever heard about wild cats.

Kieran turned and walked away down the path.

'Come on.'

Kitty ran after him. 'Where we goin'?' she asked.

'Have you ever been to the old hotel on the other side of the woods?' Kieran asked excitedly.

'No. What hotel?'

'It's closed now. All blocked up. But there's a few boards you can get through and go inside. It's *really* cool.'

Kitty didn't respond. She simply followed a few steps behind Kieran, like a little shadow.

They walked for a long time, the summer heat beating down on their heads. Kitty wished she had a drink with her, but she didn't complain.

She'd learned not to.

Eventually they arrived at a huge old building.

The structure loomed menacingly, way up into the sky. Chipboard covered the doors and windows. Parts of the roof were missing. They looked all black and burned. The bushes around the carcase were overgrown, but Kitty could tell this place had once been beautiful.

Now it felt sad.

And scary.

'There was a fire here years ago. Loads of people burned to death.'

Kitty wrapped her arms around her small body. Despite the heat from the sun, she shivered.

'No they didn't.'

'They did too. My mum says it's haunted and I shouldn't go in there,' Kieran continued, a menacing grin on his face.

'Give over!' Kitty shouted.

'It's true. If you're here at night, you'll see the ghost of Bloody Mary. She'll walk up behind you and tap you on the shoulder.'

'You're such a liar, Kieran!'

'It's true.'

'My mum says there's no such thing as ghosts.'

'Your mum is full of shit.'

Kitty stopped and stamped her foot.

'Take that back. It's not nice.'

Kieran smirks.

'No. It's true. My mum says your mum is a liar. Everyone around here knows it.'

Kitty stuck out her bottom lip.

'You're mean, Kieran Taylor. Sometimes I really hate you!'

Kieran swatted a dismissive hand in her direction, turning back towards the hotel. He pushed a few of the boards that sat in front of an old doorway and eventually one of them bowed inwards. He slipped inside through the gap.

Kitty looked around.

'Kieran?' she shouted after him.

There was no reply.

Kitty walked closer to the doorway, pushing her ear against the wall.

Silence.

'Kieran.' She trembled. She was whispering, but she didn't know why.

Kitty pushed a board where she had seen Kieran push it. She wasn't as strong as him, and she had to push with both hands, as hard as she could. The board gave way and Kitty tumbled in through the hole.

Into the darkness.

25

The rain had started about halfway into Charlie's journey and hadn't stopped. As he pulled up outside the terraced red-brick house, he yawned. Four hours on the road and an early start were taking their toll on him. But he couldn't afford to be tired. He stepped out onto the pavement and assessed his surroundings. A pleasant enough estate.

Large houses, bay windows, pretty, manicured front lawns. Marigolds growing in neat rows in a few of the flower beds. Nothing like a bit of gentrification, Charlie thought.

They would have been desirable, once. He looked over his shoulder. A group of teenagers who had been kicking a tennis ball around the road had stopped and were watching him. Or were they looking at his car? He glanced at the scratch along the length of his A5 and decided to take the risk.

Pulling out his phone, he checked he had the right address and descended the path before him.

He arrived at a white door, with small, coloured window panels in the top. Pressing the doorbell, he waited.

Eventually, he saw movement but couldn't make out anything other than dark, jumbled shapes, distorted by the glass. The door opened slowly. The smell of stale cigarettes wafted out, making Charlie grimace. He recoiled, then realised he was being assessed, trying to regain his composure.

A rotund woman of about seventy stood in the doorway, eyeing Charlie suspiciously. Her clothes were smart, but her white hair was wild.

'Can I help you?' she asked, her voice thick like treacle.

'I'm looking for Matt Simms.'

'And who are you?'

'Is he here?'

She stared at Charlie, waiting for an answer to her question.

'He doesn't know me, but I'd really like to talk to him.'

'What about?'

Charlie wished he had formulated more of a plan before he drove all the way to Birmingham.

He heard a series of knocks and rattles from inside the house.

'It's okay, Jude. You can let him in.' An old-sounding, raspy voice.

The woman stepped to one side, opening the door fully. Charlie saw a fat, elderly man in a wheelchair.

'Cavanagh told me to expect a visit. Didn't think you'd be here this quick though. You must be desperate.'

Charlie stood in the doorway, hands in his pockets.

'I suppose you'd better come in then. Jude, be a love and put the kettle on, would you?'

The woman's eyes flicked back and forth between her husband and Charlie, as she shut the door and scurried away down the hall.

The man manoeuvred himself into an adjacent room. Charlie followed. Simms was a different person from the pictures on the internet.

You wouldn't have called him handsome, but there was

something kind and intriguing about his face. He had been fit, healthy-looking.

A distant shadow of the creature before Charlie now, a cigarette tucked behind one ear of a pallid, grey-skinned face. Deep crevices and folds lined the surface. Thinning grey hair, stained yellow at the ends from nicotine, hung limply around his jowls.

'Sit down then,' he said as Charlie stepped into the living room. The house was tidy and soulless. There were no photos on the mantel. No art on the walls.

The furniture was clean and modern, but this didn't feel like a home. No ornaments. Nothing personal.

Charlie sat on a large floral settee, fidgeting with the buttons of his leather jacket.

'So what do you want, Mr...'

'Carter. Charlie Carter.'

Simms coughed. A repugnant, rasping noise. He sounded like he was choking on phlegm.

'Well?'

'I need some information about Kitty Briscoe.'

'I'm sure you're aware that her identity is unknown. She was relocated. Rebranded. She got the chance of a new life. To have her childhood. To grow up.' A sadness entered his eyes. Charlie felt there was more he wanted to say but didn't.

'Yes, I know. But I wondered if you perhaps had any idea where she might be. Or *who* she might be.'

'No, I don't. And I don't care.'

The wife shuffled into the room carrying a tray with three mugs and a teapot. She poured the tea and handed a cup to Charlie. No milk, no sugar.

'Jude, could you give us a minute please, love?' Simms said tenderly to her. She shot daggers at Charlie, then retreated, closing the door behind her.

'Why do you want to know, Mr Carter?' he continued.

Charlie watched him. He didn't look healthy. His eyes lingered on the wheelchair. Simms saw the direction of Charlie's gaze.

'There's not a lot right with me these days. Emphysema. Too many fags. My legs don't work too great either. Let's just say I've not treated my body well over the years. God knows why Jude stays with me. That's devotion for you.'

Charlie cleared his throat.

'Someone thinks my wife is Kitty Briscoe.'

Silence.

Charlie continued. 'She's not. But this person is making our lives hell. I'd like to find proof that she isn't, before somebody gets hurt. I'd also like to know who is doing this to us. We suspect it may be Kieran Taylor.'

'Taylor is long gone.'

'What do you mean?'

'When he got out of prison he disappeared. He was to report to a social worker regularly. After he'd been out a few months, he vanished.'

'Are you serious?'

'Yep. We weren't supposed to know who he was... but I had people keeping an eye for me. I called in favours and I found out. So one day, Taylor booked himself a flight out of the UK. Never returned. It's like he stopped existing.'

'So he could be anywhere?'

'I suppose. I've often wondered if he took his own life.'

Charlie stood up, slamming the hot tea down onto a side table.

'How the hell was this allowed to happen?' he said through gritted teeth.

'Served his time. Did his eight measly years. He was free. If somebody wants to disappear enough, then they will do it.'

'But he was dangerous!'

'Was he?'

'Excuse me?'

'What makes you think Kieran Taylor was dangerous?'

'He killed a little boy. *Tortured* him.'

'Mmm-hm.'

'What do you mean by that?'

'What I mean, Mr Carter, is that I was never convinced Kieran was the main protagonist in this story.'

He watched, smiling as Charlie let that sink in.

'The jury found him guilty,' he continued. 'They also found Kitty not guilty. I never agreed with *that* decision either.'

Simms coughed again, pulling a tissue out of his pocket. He filled it with something brown and lumpy from his mouth, tucking it away in his sleeve.

'They saw a pretty little blonde girl with big blue eyes who looked ever so sad. She had them all wrapped around her finger.'

'She was seven years old.'

'Yes, and she was wise beyond it. She knew exactly what she was doing. I spent *many, many* hours interviewing that girl, and I never once got the impression she was an innocent party. Her lies never washed with me. But I was in the minority. My superiors thought I had a vendetta against her.'

'Why were you so sure she was lying?'

'I watched her. I talked to her. I felt it was all an act. When she was alone and she didn't know we were looking, she didn't show an ounce of emotion. Her demeanour was totally passive. Like she was... bored. But the moment people entered the room, her face changed. She was as cold and calculating as any killer I have met. And I've met many.'

Charlie fidgeted nervously with the hem of his jacket as he

listened. Having a daughter of a similar age he struggled to see how it could be possible.

'But she was so young,' Charlie whispered.

'Yes, and that's how she got away with it. The jury couldn't entertain the idea that she had been a willing participant in the murder. Done those terrible things to another kid.'

'But you think she was?'

'Oh yes. Absolutely.'

'Why?'

'Gut feeling. That little girl... she wasn't right. I spent a lot of time with her. She was... well for want of a better word, terrifying.'

Simms sipped his tea and coughed again, spraying droplets of phlegm down his front.

'How can a seven-year-old girl be terrifying?' Charlie was incredulous.

Simms paused, considering the question. He looked Charlie straight in the face.

'Her eyes. There was nothing there. No compassion. No sorrow. No fear. A psychopath in the making. I've not come across anyone else quite like her. And I hope I never do.'

Charlie smirked, thinking Simms was being melodramatic.

'Do you know what actually killed Billy Noakes?'

Charlie stared at Simms, who didn't give him a chance to reply.

'Because I do. He was tortured and beaten, yes, but *that* didn't kill him. They took their time with that boy. They ignored his cries and his pleading screams for his mother. They *enjoyed* it. What they did to him was... well, it was evil. There's no other way to describe it. But what ultimately killed him... she took him up onto a balcony in that old hotel, about twenty feet high and she pushed him off. That boy had been traumatised beyond belief... what he must have gone through, nobody can imagine.

And then she tossed him to his death. Like a piece of trash. He was... broken. We couldn't let the parents identify the body. It would have been too harrowing for them. Had to rely on dental records.'

'Why are you so sure it was her?'

'We did some investigations at that hotel. It was dilapidated. The balcony was weak. We struggled to get any of our forensic team up onto that ledge. We had to use a cherry picker. The whole thing was so knackered, it wouldn't support much weight. Kieran Taylor wasn't a big lad by any stretch of the imagination, but he was much bigger than Kitty. We tried a sandbag the same weight as him on those floorboards and it went straight through. We tried a much lighter sandbag, around Kitty's weight, taking into account the extra mass from a toddler and it held firm. There is no way Kieran could have gone up onto that mezzanine alone, never mind carrying a small child with him. No way at all. But Kitty... she could. She could easily have gone up there.'

Charlie sat back down on the sofa.

'How come this wasn't used in court?'

'It was. But the defence solicitor, Beverly Whitehouse, piece of work she was... she put up a good argument. She knew her stuff. Convinced the jury that this theory was not rock solid, that it was simply hocus-pocus to convict an innocent child. They looked into those big baby blues and believed what you and every other person has *chosen* to believe. There's no way that sweet, pretty little girl could have done what they're accusing her of.'

They sat for a while, neither of them saying a word. Charlie couldn't bring himself to speak. Simms seemed exhausted.

'So you don't know where either of them are now?'

'I don't. And I don't care to know. That case has never escaped me. I haven't been able to forgive myself... I didn't do a good enough job to convict that girl. I will take that to my grave.

But I have no desire to find either of those children. I dread to think what sort of adults they became.'

Charlie stood up, smoothing down the front of his jeans.

'Right, well I guess we're done here. I'll let myself out.'

He turned and opened the door, stepping out into the hallway.

As he walked away, he heard the creak of the wheelchair behind him.

'Mr Carter...' The gravelly voice sickened him.

Charlie faced Simms.

'I've seen a lot of terrible things in my life, the job I did. But what they inflicted on that little boy... it will stay with me until the day I die. It haunts me. It ruined me. Destroyed my faith in humanity. That two children could do... *that*. Did you know one of them carved the letter K into Billy's torso? After he was dead.'

'I didn't know that.'

'No. Those grislier details were kept out of the papers. But that's what happened. Of course, with both their names beginning with *K,* we could never be entirely sure who did that to him. Though I have my suspicions.' His eyes lingered. 'Do you have a photo of your wife I could see?'

Charlie hesitated.

'If you're totally sure it's not her, then you can show me. What damage can it do?'

Nodding, he pulled his wallet from his pocket, slipping a wedding photo out from the folds. He crossed towards Simms, handing him the picture.

Simms stared at it, his eyes ominous. A grimace on his mouth.

He handed the photograph back to Charlie.

'Good luck, Mr Carter,' he said.

'Why do you say that?' Charlie took the picture and placed it back into his wallet.

'I've spent a lot of time looking into those eyes. I'd know them anywhere.'

'I'm sorry, but you're wrong.'

Simms cocked an eyebrow.

'If you say so.'

He stared at Charlie. Charlie couldn't read his expression.

'Do you have kids?'

'Yes. We have a teenaged son and a six-year-old daughter.'

Simms turned his chair and wheeled himself away without saying a word.

As Charlie opened the front door Simms shouted out from the living room, 'I hope you're right. For your family's sake.'

Charlie clicked the door shut, Simms' words ringing in his ears. As he walked down the garden path towards his Audi, he remembered the note he had received in the gym.

How well do you know your wife?

He unlocked the car and sat behind the wheel. The conversation played around his head.

He knew his wife. He trusted her. She was *not* Kitty Briscoe.

Simms was wrong. Charlie was sure of that.

He pulled his phone from his jeans pocket and typed in Beth's name. The only result was her work profile and email address at Greys.

Nothing else.

He typed in her maiden name, Morton.

Still no results.

Charlie knew Beth didn't engage in social media, she was a very private person.

But he had never met anybody who didn't throw back any Google results.

No photos, no news.

Absolutely nothing.

He added *St. Albans* to the search. This was where Beth had said she had been living with her parents when the accident happened. He also typed in *1996–1997*, an approximation of when he assumed the fire that killed her parents would have occurred, recalling she was around eighteen when it happened.

Zero.

No news stories. No headlines.

Charlie frowned.

He had never googled his wife before. He'd never felt the need.

But he found it odd that a fire that killed two people wouldn't have made it into at least the local press.

He added *house fire* to the search. Still nothing.

Charlie's brow furrowed as he typed in various phrases and words, each delivering the same result. Eventually, his frustration beat him, and he threw his phone into the passenger seat, cursing under his breath.

He considered embarking on the long drive back to Sussex, but the thought of another few hours on the motorway filled him with dread.

He decided to find a bed and breakfast instead.

He desperately wanted to talk to Beth, find out why the fire at her family's home when she was younger had not made it into the news. He wanted to believe she was not lying to him.

He needed this all to go away. But it would have to wait.

For now, he needed to rest.

26

The light broke through the cracks in the curtains as Beth woke from her slumber. It seemed dull, diffused, and for a moment she assumed she had awoken earlier than usual for a Saturday.

She glanced at the clock on her bedside table and it surprised her to note it was after eight.

'Shit,' she cursed as she dragged herself out of bed. Cooper would be desperate for the loo no doubt.

She crossed to the window and opened the curtains. A short while ago, this action would have been alien to her, but now, it had become part of her daily routine.

Thick fog enveloped the house, she couldn't see anything, only a cloud of white. Her Range Rover in the driveway was little more than a dark shape in the haze.

Beth threw on some jogging bottoms, a pale-pink T-shirt and her slippers. Pulling her hair into a ponytail, she tied it back off her face with an elastic band from the dresser.

She exited her bedroom, knocking on Peter's door, then Daisy's.

'Come on, kids. Time to get up!'

She heard a groan from Peter's room. On entering Daisy's room, she found her daughter sitting in the middle of her carpet, playing with a doll. Her curtains were already open. She had dressed herself in a pair of blue denim dungarees with nothing underneath, a pink, frilly tutu and wellies with frog faces on the toecaps.

'I've been awake for ages, Mummy. Look outside, it's all white! You can't see anything.'

'I know, love,' Beth said, scooping Daisy up from the floor into her arms. 'It's very foggy. I've not seen it like this for years.'

'I don't like it. It's scary.'

'It's just fog. Nothing to be afraid of.'

Beth carried Daisy out of the room. A blast of cool, damp air hit her as she descended the stairs, and she frowned. As she reached the bottom and stepped into the hallway, she hesitated. The house felt icy.

The front door was wide open.

'Peter!' she shouted.

No response. She hollered again.

She heard Peter's bedroom door creak open.

'What?' he yelled through a stifled yawn.

'You left the front door open last night when you got home!'

'No I didn't.'

'Well I certainly didn't, and you were the last one in.'

She heard weight on the stairs as Peter came to join her.

'I absolutely *did not* leave the door open.'

Beth popped Daisy down, and strode to the end of the hall, checking her car keys were still on the console table as she passed it. She stood on the threshold, looking out into a thick cloud of white in front of her face. She wrapped her arms around her body, shivering, then shut the door firmly.

'It's lucky we weren't all murdered in our beds, isn't it,' she said sarcastically to her son as she headed towards the kitchen.

'I didn't leave it open. I swear.'

Beth ignored him.

'Mum!' Daisy screamed suddenly, panic in her voice.

Beth ran the remaining few steps.

'What is it, Daisy? What's wrong?'

Daisy was standing by the French doors.

'It's Cooper. He's not here. He must have excaped.'

'It's *escaped,* you retard!' Peter muttered at his sister.

Beth joined Daisy. Cooper's bed was indeed empty.

She knelt down, placing one hand onto the cushion. It felt warm.

'It's okay, he can't have gone far. Peter, see if you can find him anywhere.'

Peter did a cursory patrol of the house but returned empty-handed, shaking his head solemnly.

Beth sprang into action. She hurried down the hallway, opened the front door, and out into the fog.

'Cooper!' she shouted.

Nothing. It was eerily silent, Beth's slippers crunching on gravel the only sound. She called out again. A muffled bark drifted from somewhere in the distance. He didn't sound nearby.

'Cooper!' she called again, taking a few steps out into the driveway. She turned around the side of the house, stepping cautiously through the fog, arms outstretched in front of her. She couldn't see more than a few inches ahead.

Now and then a muted bark would echo around the garden, but Beth's senses were out of kilter. She couldn't tell which direction it came from.

She didn't even know where she was anymore in relation to the house.

More barking. Frantic this time. Beth picked up the pace. She ran. The barking grew louder. Interspersed with the odd whimper.

'Cooper!' Beth was screaming now.

Desperate.

She could hear Peter and Daisy shouting somewhere behind her, disembodied voices floating through the damp clouds surrounding her.

'Peter, Daisy, go back to the house!'

They ignored her. They continued their search. Beth ran forwards. Something cold and wet hit her face and wrapped around her body.

The shock made Beth scream, as she battled with whatever was trying to suffocate her.

A familiar smell filled her nostrils. Fresh and pleasant.

She had run into the clean bed sheets hanging on the line at the side of the house. She flung the wet bed linen from her, and it slapped into a pile on the ground.

More barking, frenzied this time. Beth's heart pounded.

A high-pitched yelp. The sound of feet running on gravel. A car engine.

Beth ran faster, sprinting now. She tripped. Losing her balance, she plummeted to the gravel below, wincing as her hands scraped along the path.

She knelt for a moment. The ground was wet beneath her. She raised one hand slowly to her face.

Red.

Oh God, she thought, springing to her feet, examining herself.

She scoured her limbs, searching for a wound, but finding none.

And then she realised in horror.

Cooper was silent.

'Did you find him, Mummy?'

Daisy's voice was close behind Beth. She spun around.

'Keep back!' she shouted.

'Mum, what is it?' Peter sounded scared. Old enough to sense something was wrong.

'Peter, take Daisy. Go back to the house. I'll be right with you.'

'Mum?'

'Go!' Beth screamed.

Peter put a protective arm around his sister's shoulder and steered her away.

Beth glanced about. All she could see was white.

As her children's footsteps on the gravel got quieter, she stood and listened. Holding her breath, eyes wide. Not a sound. No playful chirping of birds. No car; it was long gone.

But still Beth listened.

A scream broke the silence. A terrified, blood-curdling scream.

Daisy.

Beth dashed back to the house. The front door still open. She darted into the hallway where she could see her kids in the kitchen at the end.

Daisy was crying, huddled into Peter, who enveloped her in his arms. He stroked her back gently, whilst staring straight into Beth's eyes, a look of horror on his face.

Beth hurried inside. Peter motioned to the worktop with his head. She followed the direction of his gesture. Her eyes widened in terror as she realised what she was looking at.

A pale blue-and-white polka-dot bandana. Cooper's collar.

Soaked in blood.

27

'Peter, take Daisy up to her room. Read her a story.'

Beth's voice was low, hard.

'Mum, what's going on? Who did that?'

Daisy's wailing stopped momentarily.

'Mummy, where is Cooper?' her tear-stained face threatening to explode into torrents again.

'Now.'

Her son didn't ask any further questions. He led his sister up the stairs, a worried glance over his shoulder, and then they were both gone.

Beth approached the counter, unable to take her eyes off the grotesque offering.

A small scrap of folded paper poked out from beneath the bandana. She tentatively took its corner and slid it out from under the pile, grimacing. It was spotted with blood, still wet.

She unfolded it carefully, taking in the black, scrawled words on the page.

She dropped it, running to the sink, and vomited. Her stomach was empty, she hadn't had breakfast yet. Stinking yellow bile tickled from her mouth, bubbling at the corners of her lips.

She spat, turning on the tap to rinse the rancid liquid away.

Bending down, she gulped down icy water, but she couldn't dispel the taste.

She returned to the note on the floor, crouching down beside it. She didn't want to touch it. But she forced herself to pick it up.

Forced herself to read the words again.

Next time it will be one of <u>YOUR</u> kids.

She stared at the scratchy black letters. She raised her trembling hands to her face and she sobbed.

She didn't hear Peter until he was beside her.

'Mum, are you okay?'

Beth shook her head.

'This is all such a mess.'

Peter sat on the floor next to his mother, placing an arm around her shoulder.

'Mum, what is going on? What's a mess?'

'Everything!' Beth spat through her sobs.

'What's that?'

Beth's head snapped up.

Peter reached for the note in her hand. She snatched it away.

'Nothing.'

'It's got blood on it.'

'It doesn't matter.'

Beth sprang to her feet. Peter eyed her suspiciously.

'What's happened to the dog, Mum?'

'I don't know.'

'You're lying.'

'Don't speak to me like that.'

Peter stood up. He was taller than Beth. He took a step towards her, leaning in, his face inches from her own.

'I'll speak to you however the fuck I like,' he growled.

Beth could feel his hot breath on her cheek.

'Something is going on here. You and Dad are both acting weird. Someone has done something terrible to our dog. Why?'

'I don't know, Peter. I heard a car. Maybe there was an accident.'

Peter slammed his fist down on the worktop. Beth flinched.

'That's bullshit!' he shouted, droplets of saliva splattering Beth's face.

'You actually expect me to believe somebody ran over the dog, and left his blood-soaked collar on the kitchen side, but didn't stick around to say anything? How stupid do you think I am?'

Beth didn't reply.

'What's on the paper?'

'It's nothing!' Beth held the note behind her back.

'Give it to me,' he demanded.

Beth shook her head. Peter reached round and grabbed her wrist, trying to force it round in front of her. She struggled, screwing the paper up tight in her hand.

Peter tightened his grip. For a skinny lad, he was strong.

'You're hurting me!' she whined.

He pushed forwards, the weight of his body forcing Beth down sideways onto the counter. Her arm was crushed painfully between her torso and the marble edge. He tried to force the note from her hand.

Beth wriggled free somehow, and Peter fell clumsily onto the floor. She ran, but he came after her, scrambling across the kitchen tiles, grabbing at her feet. She tumbled, banging her forehead on the ground.

Peter flipped her over onto her back, straddling her. He had both hands wrapped around her clenched fist, trying to prise it open. The paper screwed up into a tight ball in her sweaty hand.

She scratched at his arms.

'Give it to me!'

'No!'

Beth raised a knee into Peter's groin, and he rolled off her, doubled over in pain. She flipped onto all fours and tried to crawl away, reaching the edge of the island unit before she felt Peter's hands around her ankles. He yanked, and she collapsed down onto the tiles, screaming.

Peter dragged her towards him. She kicked. She flailed. But it was no use. He was stronger.

Once again, he tried to wrestle the note from her hand.

'What the hell is going on in here?'

Charlie's voice boomed through the kitchen.

And everything stopped.

28

C harlie's words echoed around the kitchen.

Beth rolled out from underneath Peter, who straightened up onto his knees, looking sheepish.

'Peter?' Charlie growled as Peter stood up.

He looked down at his feet, not saying a word.

Beth clambered up from the floor, brushing a loose strand of blonde hair from her face, tucking it up behind her ear.

'Beth?'

She didn't know what to say. How could she explain this? This wasn't a mother-and-son play-fight. This was aggressive. Nasty.

Charlie took a step forward into the kitchen, and his gaze drifted to the worktop. He looked confused, unsure at first, but as his brain made sense of what he was looking at, his eyes widened in disbelief.

'Is that... Cooper's collar?'

He strode to the counter, picking up the bandana. Realising the blood was still wet, he dropped it on the floor, wiping his hand on his jeans.

'What's going on?'

Beth picked up the collar.

'We think somebody hurt Cooper,' Peter replied. He still didn't dare look up at his father.

'What do you mean, *hurt* him?'

Beth took a few steps towards Charlie.

'I came down this morning... the front door was open. Cooper had escaped. It was so foggy, we couldn't find him... but we heard him. There was... a cry, and a car drove away. There was blood on the driveway and when we got back in the house...' Beth glanced at the collar.

Charlie stared at the red mess on the counter, trying to take it all in.

'So you haven't actually found the dog?'

'No, only *that*,' Peter chipped in.

'And what did I walk in on there? Why the hell were you two... *fighting*?'

Beth felt a crimson patch begin to spread up her chest and onto her neck, as the shame of the situation hit her.

'There was a note. With the collar. But she wouldn't let me see it.'

Charlie's eyes darted to Beth's. She shook her head almost imperceptibly. Charlie looked back at his son.

'She said it was nothing, but she was crying when I found her. She was trying to hide it from me. I wanted to know what was going on.'

Charlie stepped closer to Peter, towering over him. He leant in, his face right in front of his son's.

'And you think that gives you the right to attack your mother?'

Charlie's voice was low, rumbling. Peter turned away.

'Do you?' Charlie roared, shoving his son hard on both shoulders.

Peter stumbled backwards, steadying himself on the counter.

'Someone just killed our dog. I deserve to know. You two are hiding something. You've both been acting dodgy since that note came through the door.'

Charlie slammed his hand down on the worktop.

'We are your parents. We are the adults in this house, and while you are living under our roof, you abide by our rules. And if your mother doesn't want to tell you, you goddamn respect her decision! Do you understand?'

Peter didn't respond. Charlie grabbed the scruff of his son's T-shirt.

'Do you understand?' he bellowed.

'Yes!'

'Get out of my sight before I do something I regret!'

Peter scurried from the kitchen. Charlie didn't often reprimand the kids, so when he did lose his temper, it was terrifying.

Beth crossed to the island, pulling out a stool. She eased herself onto it, sore from the struggle.

Charlie stared at her, arms folded across his chest.

Beth looked back at him defiantly.

'The dog... is he...' Charlie whispered.

Beth shook her head, running both hands through her hair.

'I honestly don't know. There was a lot of blood. And the collar. He came *into* our house. Whoever it was walked in here and put that there.'

She nodded at the collar.

Charlie stepped towards his wife.

'And the note?'

Beth smoothed out the screwed-up ball of paper and handed it to Charlie. He grimaced as he saw the blood.

Beth watched as he read, his eyes widening in horror.

'My God. Are you okay?'

'No. No, I'm not. I'm scared.'

Charlie sat at the stool next to Beth, placing an arm around her shoulder. He pulled her into him.

'We have to tell the police now. This has gone far enough,' Charlie whispered. 'You know that, don't you?'

Beth shrugged his arm from her. She turned and stared into his face.

'Whoever this person is, they are threatening us. They have done... God knows what to our dog...' Charlie's voice wavered for a moment, but he cleared his throat, regaining his composure.

'I can't,' Beth replied in an almost inaudible whisper.

'You're being ridiculous. This is madness. Our family... our children are at risk. *We* are at risk. What's it going to take for you to listen to me?'

'I just can't,' she said again, louder this time.

'We have to!'

'You're not listening to me, Charlie. I can't!' she screamed.

'Why? For God's sake. Why are you so averse to talking to the police? They can protect us. We are an innocent party here.'

'Because I'm her.' Beth's voice was quiet again now, as if she didn't want anybody to overhear.

Charlie blinked. Once. Twice.

'What?'

'I am Kitty Briscoe.'

And Beth Carter's life as she knew it, it ceased to exist.

29

Charlie stared dumbfounded at his wife. His mouth hung open.

He stood from his stool.

'Charlie, please! Sit down. Let me explain.'

He walked away, but Beth grabbed at his shirt, pulling him backwards.

'Explain what? That you've been lying to me. Pretty much for our entire life together? Or how you were involved in the murder of a two-year-old boy when you were a child and kept that a secret from me too, perhaps?'

'Please.'

Charlie sat beside Beth. She touched his leg.

'Don't,' Charlie spat. Beth snatched her hand away.

'Charlie, look at me.'

He wouldn't. He stared ahead, jaw clenched, understandably upset. Angry, even.

'I don't... get it. How can that be you? And why have you never told me?'

'How would I? How do I begin to tell you that? It's not exactly *first date* material.'

'No. But now, with everything that's been going on. You've had every opportunity to tell me. And you chose not to. I even asked you straight out, and you lied. You lied to my face, Beth. You *swore* on your parents' graves.' Charlie paused, remembering his web searches the day before, the lack of results about a fire with two casualties, and something dawned on him.

'Was any of that even true? Your parents? The fire? I tried to find it online. I couldn't get anything. Now it makes sense. Because it was all bullshit, wasn't it?'

'No, Charlie. It wasn't. That part was true. My parents died in a fire when I was eighteen. I wasn't at home, and the house burned down with them asleep inside.'

'How am I supposed to believe *a single thing* you tell me anymore? You're clearly an *accomplished* liar.'

Beth stood, pacing across the kitchen, staring out into the garden, before turning to look at her husband.

'You have to understand. That girl... Kitty Briscoe. I *was* her. But that's not me now. I've spent my whole life trying to get away from her. I may not have gone to jail, but believe me when I say I have served a life sentence. I still am.'

She crossed back to the island, sitting down again beside Charlie.

'That newspaper printed my name, my photo. They ruined my life. My parents' lives. We had to move away. Every time we got settled, someone found out who we were, and we had to up sticks and move again. It was a nightmare.'

'How could you...' Charlie couldn't bring himself to finish the sentence, but Beth knew instinctively what he was asking.

'It wasn't me. I swear to you. I wasn't even there. *Yes*, I helped Kieran Taylor take him from the fair, but I had nothing to do with what happened to him. I ran away, I left him at that hotel with Kieran, and he was alive the last time I saw him.'

'Why didn't you tell anyone? You went home and kept quiet.

That boy was lying there for days. His parents anguished, not knowing if he was alive. And you carried on as normal.'

'Charlie, I was seven. Just think about that. I was only slightly older than Daisy. Kieran Taylor was eleven. He told me Billy was fine, and I believed him because I didn't know why he would lie.'

Charlie finally looked at her. His face red, angry.

'It doesn't matter now anyway, Beth. That's not even the issue. What hurts is that you have *lied* to me every day of our lives. Everything you have ever said about yourself. Your family. Your name! Where you come from. All lies. Do you understand how that makes me feel?'

'Yes.'

'No. You don't. I don't think you'd like it if the shoe was on the other foot. We've always said as long as we're honest with each other we can get through anything–'

'And we can!'

'No, Beth. No. We can't. Because... can't you see? We have *never* had honesty.' Charlie paused. 'At least, *you* haven't.'

'But everything else has been genuine. My feelings about you. The kids. None of that is lies.'

'Of course it is. It's all rubbish. I don't even *know* you. I don't know who you are.'

'I'm the woman you married. That little girl, Kitty Briscoe, she doesn't exist anymore. When you look at her, you're looking at a life through windows that were boarded up decades ago. She's... dead. I erased her.'

Charlie laughed humourlessly, standing. He strode across the room to a wall mounted cupboard, pulling the doors open. Suddenly, the man she loved seemed so distant from her.

She watched as Charlie took a bottle of whisky and a glass tumbler from the cabinet. He half-filled the glass, downed its contents, and refilled it. After emptying it a second time, he slammed it down on the counter. As he poured a third, Beth approached sheepishly as he drained the glass again. She placed her fingers on his arm.

'Charlie, please...'

He jerked away.

'Don't touch me,' he shouted.

He picked up the bottle and the glass, barging past Beth with such force that she almost fell. She steadied herself on the worktop, taking a deep breath.

He strode to the French doors, flinging them open. Stepping out onto the patio, he pulled a cast-iron chair from under the table, sliding down into it, and poured himself another drink. He sat sipping it while he stared out into the field at the back of the garden.

Beth followed him outside, standing beside him as he drank.

'This is all such a mess,' Charlie said sadly.

Beth dragged out a chair, sitting opposite him. Still, he refused to look her in the eye.

'I've been so scared, Charlie. Do you know how hard it is to carry a secret like this with you? Of course you don't. Not many people do. I always planned on telling you, in the early days. Until I realised I was falling in love with you, and I was so terrified that you would react... like this.'

Charlie slammed his glass down on the table. The sound, the level of aggression made Beth jump. She glanced up and saw Peter back away from his bedroom window.

'Don't you dare, Beth! Don't you try to turn this around on me. I'm angry because you have lied to me. About everything. If you had told me in the beginning, I wouldn't have reacted like this.'

'Yes, Charlie, you would have. I know you would. Because

people always do. I learned at a very young age that I could no longer be Kitty Briscoe. People despised her. They blamed her.'

'You took him!'

'Yes,' Beth replied quietly, nodding. She gazed into the distance, eyes glazing. 'And there is not a day that goes by that I don't regret it. Don't you think if I could go back and do things differently, I would? But we can't change the past. I was a child. But you have to believe me. I am innocent. I had nothing to do with Billy's death.'

Charlie looked up, locked his eyes on Beth's face. She couldn't read his expression. For a moment she thought he might embrace her, tell her he forgave her. That he believed her. Her heart fluttered as she imagined how good that would feel.

'This is all your fault,' he said coldly. 'I need you to go.'

It took a few seconds for the words to hit Beth.

'What?'

'Go. I need some time to process all this without you here. Can you do that for me?'

'I don't want to.'

'I don't care. I need space. You have put our family in danger. You knew exactly why all this was happening, and you acted like it was a mystery to you. You questioned *my* loyalty when I asked you about it.'

Beth reached her hand across the table, placing it on top of Charlie's.

He snatched it away.

'I can't even look at you. You disgust me.'

Charlie's words stung. Beth's lip quivered. But she held it back.

'Give me some space. I need to think and I'm so angry, I can't do that with you around. So please go.'

'Where?'

'I don't care. Anywhere but here.'

Beth knew Charlie well enough to know that he was being serious.

She crossed to the door, turning briefly back to her husband. He didn't look up. He sat staring into the bottom of his empty glass.

Beth entered the kitchen, looking once more at the bloodstained collar of their beloved spaniel. Picking up her car keys, she left the house. She didn't know where she was going, but she couldn't be here.

Charlie heard the front door slam shut, followed by Beth's Range Rover starting. He listened as she drove away across the gravel. The sound deteriorating until all that was left was the twittering of a solitary goldfinch.

The hot sun beat down on Charlie's face, but he shivered. He couldn't process what was going on in his head.

His wife, the woman he had loved for all of his adult life, was not who she said she was. She had a secret.

And it was horrifying.

Charlie tried to put himself in her position, asked himself if he would have acted differently. Part of him understood why she had lied. It must have been a terrible burden. But that didn't make him feel less angry. Less sad.

He thought of good times with Beth. He heard her laughter. He pictured the day they found out she was pregnant with Peter, and again with Daisy. He tried to reconcile that with what he had now learned, shaking his head.

He picked up his whisky tumbler, and before he realised what he was doing, he threw it as hard as he could.

It hit the back wall to the house beside the French doors, smashing into a thousand tiny shards. The splinters fell around the patio and Charlie thought how the shattered glass was an excellent metaphor for his life.

'Daddy?'

Charlie's eyes darted up quickly. Daisy was standing on the doorstep, looking at him with fear and confusion.

She'd been crying.

'Don't come out here, honey, Daddy has broken a glass.'

'Are you okay? Where's Mummy?'

Charlie stood.

'Go inside, Daisy. Go upstairs and pack some clothes. Tell Peter to do the same. We're leaving.'

'Where are we going?'

'For an adventure. You'd like that, wouldn't you?'

'What about Mummy?'

Charlie crossed to the door, crouching down so he was face to face with his daughter.

'Mummy will meet us there, okay, so go up to your room and pack a bag.'

Daisy scurried away and up the stairs, and Charlie thought, *funny, it is easy to lie to your family after all.*

He stepped into the kitchen, crossing to what was affectionately known as *the shit drawer* in the Carter household.

Opening it, he rummaged through charging cables for long-dead mobile phones, old wallets, and antiseptic wipes. He eventually found a notepad, creased and dog-eared, towards the bottom of the drawer. He placed the pad on the bench and fished around once again for something to write with. Finding one of Daisy's thick colouring pens in fuchsia pink, he poised, ready to pour his heart out.

Beth... he wrote.

Closing his eyes for a moment, he pictured the scene where they first met. Or at least where he had first seen her. It took him a few weeks to pluck up the courage to actually *speak* to her. But he had first spotted her in the university library, second week of term.

Her hair had been dark brown, almost black back then, cut into a short pixie. She wore thick-rimmed tortoiseshell glasses.

Charlie admired her for looking different to all the other girls on campus. Having her own sense of style.

In hindsight, he now realised this was an attempt to alter her appearance. She must have been terrified of being recognised. Her clothing was plain. She wore baggy blue denim dungarees over a dark sweatshirt. She had been sitting on her own reading a book, something lofty, but the title and subject escaped him now.

Charlie could see her clearly, as if it were yesterday.

Two small, translucent, plastic, cherry-shaped earrings dangled gracefully from her lobes. Charlie had been transfixed by them. The light from an adjacent window shone through them, causing green and red shapes to dance over her cheek. Over the years at uni they would become Charlie's favourite thing that she wore, as they always reminded him of the first time he had seen her. These, along with the small silver key which Beth always wore on a chain around her neck; a twenty-first birthday gift, were two constants.

Two things which were quintessentially Beth.

He hadn't been able to stop staring at her. She didn't notice. Didn't glance up from her book once.

Over the following days he saw her many times, always sitting at the same spot. He eventually realised he was returning to the library each day simply to glimpse her.

But she never looked up. Never knew he was watching her.

Which made her more attractive.

Charlie was used to girls noticing him. So Beth's failure to do so made her a challenge for him.

He pictured those cherry earrings. Did she still have them

somewhere upstairs? He wondered how long ago she'd stopped wearing them. Wondered sadly why he hadn't noticed.

In that moment, he wanted nothing more than to see his wife in those stupid plastic earrings.

And his heart broke a tiny little bit.

30

Sitting in a lay-by, Beth cradled her head in her hands. How had it come to this? She had driven the winding lanes around her home for an hour, before pulling over. When the grief had hit her. The sudden realisation that life would never be the same.

That the man she loved may never look at her in the same way ever again.

Of course, she had fantasised about that moment, many times. Offloading her terrible secret. The one thing she did her utmost to make sure Charlie would never find out. She didn't know what she had expected. She had always imagined that he would be angry for the deception, but then embrace her tightly, telling her he still loved her. She was still his Beth. Nothing would change that.

But the look in his eyes in reality... was far different.

Anger. Hatred. Suspicion?

When he had told her to go, she hadn't quite believed it at first. His lack of empathy for how hard it had been for her to confess to him felt like a betrayal. It hurt. Real, physical pain.

An aching in her heart that she had never known. Not even

when her father had refused to come to court to support her. Nor when he had shouted she was no daughter of his and spat at her.

But she hadn't loved him. He was a weak, pathetic excuse for a man, so she hadn't expected anything from him. Charlie was different.

Or so Beth had thought.

'Stupid, stupid, stupid!' Beth screamed, as she thumped the steering wheel hard with both hands.

When she had failed to reveal the truth to Charlie within their first year together, she had decided she should never tell him. To have kept a secret for so long was bound to upset him. So she knew in her gut that it had to remain just that. And she had done so well.

Even when she had wanted more than anything to pour her heart out, to scream it in his face. She'd held back. And after she became pregnant with Peter, that simply sealed the deal. She would take her identity to the grave.

But Charlie had backed her into a corner today. She had run out of excuses to not get the police involved. A note threatening their children, and their dog's blood spilled on their driveway.

No rational person would think attempting to tackle the situation alone was the sensible thing to do. And so she'd been left with no choice. The truth, as hard as it was, the only option.

She pulled her phone from her pocket, dialling Charlie's number. Straight to voicemail. She hammered out a text asking if she could come home. Demanding he call her.

The waiting drove her insane.

She longed to see her family; to hold her children. How dare Charlie tell her to leave? It was her house. He had no right. Anger replaced her grief.

For better or for worse appeared to be another broken promise.

She started the engine and headed for home. As she drove, she thought of Charlie. Tried to picture his eyes when he laughed. All she could see was his expression as her words sank in.

I am Kitty Briscoe.

Shock, followed by disappointment, then something darker. Far worse.

She wanted to make things right. She shouldn't have left. Should have demanded that they talk it out. That they hug. She should have insisted they go for ice cream as a family, and then a walk on the beach.

Anything but walking out the door.

A feeling she had not experienced since childhood overwhelmed her. This was the exact reason she had vowed as a teenager that she would never give her heart to a man. She thought of the first boy she had truly trusted. How he had thrown that back in her face without regard for her feelings.

Glenn Jones. She almost said the name out loud.

Her mother had warned her not to get too close.

Beth could hear her mother's thick Brummie accent ringing in her ears.

'It'll only end in tears. You mark my words...'

31

The summer passed in a blur. Kitty wished it could be the beginning of the holidays again, but alas, she was more aware than most her age that you can never go back. The last day of term as the kids were all getting ready to head home for the break; that's when Glenn Jones had first approached her.

He wasn't what you would call a good-looking boy. Not classically. But he was funny and popular. He had caught up with Kitty at her locker, slightly out of breath. But, of course, by that point she was no longer called Kitty.

This time she was Lucy. She had been through so many identities. Inevitably, someone would find out. And her family would run again. She knew it was all her fault.

Her father made sure she never forgot that fact.

She'd been working hard to hide her accent, but sometimes, when she was feeling relaxed, it slipped. Glenn had shouted her name a few times. She still wasn't used to it.

'So I was wondering if you'd like to... er... hang out over the summer at all?' Glenn looked down at the floor nervously.

Kitty blushed. She had always blushed so easily.

'My parents don't really... I mean, I'm not supposed to.' Kitty opened her locker, pretending not to notice how crushed Glenn had been by her reply.

'Do you have to tell them?' he asked, a cheeky glint in his eye.

Kitty shut the metal door, smiling.

'I suppose not.'

And that had been it. They had spent pretty much every day that summer together. Hiding in fields of wheat where nobody could see them. Climbing tall trees, then sitting in branches above the river, watching as folk passed by below, oblivious to Glenn and Kitty's existence high over their heads.

And kissing. There had been *lots* of kissing.

Kitty had never kissed a boy before. She was worried she wasn't doing it properly. But Glenn kept wanting to do it again, so she assumed she must have been doing something right. Kitty may only have been fifteen, but she had an older head on her shoulders. The hand she'd been dealt had deprived her of the luxury of a normal childhood.

Eventually, her mother grew suspicious of her sneaking out every day and not returning until it was dark, and Kitty told her.

'His name's Glenn, he's in my year at school... and I'm in love.'

Her mother had been furious; had forbidden Kitty to see him again. But Kitty was defiant, and you can't stop a teenager from going out in the summer holidays.

'It'll only end in tears. You mark my words!' her mother screamed at her.

'You're wrong! Glenn is different. He loves me too!' Kitty had assured her, slamming the door as she left. And on a warm August evening, when Glenn Jones had slid his fingers tentatively inside the elastic waistband of Kitty's knickers, whispering in her ear with hot breath that he loved her, she had known.

This was *exactly* what she wanted. And Glenn was the one.

A few days later Kitty had been woken early by a commotion downstairs. Lots of shouting. As she pulled on her dressing gown and stepped out onto the landing, her father had sneered at her from his bedroom door.

'Did you think they wouldn't find out this time?' he said, a grin on his lips.

Kitty's heart thumped. She took a few steps down the stairs, perching halfway, peering through the bannisters. She knew who it was before seeing the face. She recognised her voice.

Glenn's mother. Kitty craned her neck to hear better what was being said.

'And don't you even try to deny it. We all know exactly who you are. Who *she* is!'

Kitty had heard that venom many times in her life. That tone. Almost those exact words. Every time.

'I knew she looked familiar the first time Glenn brought her to the house, but I couldn't put my finger on it. I said to my John, I said, *she looks awful familiar, that girl.*'

Kitty leaned further down the stairs for a better view. Why wasn't her mother defending her?

She just stood on the doorstep, head hung low. She had come to expect this. The first time had been a shock. But not anymore.

Kitty fidgeted, making more noise than intended. Glenn's mother's eyes darted up, and she saw Kitty. She lurched forwards into the hallway, pointing a trembling finger at her.

'You keep away from my son! You hear me? I don't want you in my house again, you evil little bitch!'

'That's enough!' Kitty's mother had hissed. 'She didn't do it!'

'You're disgusting. We don't want your family here. We've all got children, and you're not welcome.'

She turned abruptly and stormed off down the path. Kitty's

mother closed the door, looking sadly at her daughter, but the pity changed quickly to anger. Her mother lost her temper often these days.

'I hope you're happy with yourself. Was he worth it?' her mother spat, before storming down the hall into the kitchen.

Kitty heard her father sniggering from upstairs.

The following day she had waited at their usual spot. But Glenn didn't arrive. When she finally saw him at school a week later, he blanked her.

Everyone had blanked her.

The truth was out. Nobody wanted to know her anymore. Even her teachers were looking at her warily in lessons.

She caught up with Glenn at lunchtime in the canteen. He didn't want to speak to her. He tried to walk away, but she grabbed his sleeve, tearing his cuff. She saw a flicker of something, then his eyes darted around the room, took in the surroundings.

Everyone was looking.

'Look what you've done, you stupid cow!' he shouted.

'I don't care. I need to talk to you. I need to explain.'

'There's nothing to explain. And there's nothing to say. You're a child killer. And your name isn't even Lucy!' He walked away from her.

'Glenn, I'm still the same girl I've been all summer. Please... can we go somewhere more... private, and talk about this?' Kitty glanced nervously around the canteen, painfully aware that people were staring at them. 'Nothing has changed,' she pleaded.

Glenn spun around to face her, and she saw that familiar hatred in his eyes.

'Yes it has,' he spat. 'Everything's changed. Leave me alone. Don't ever speak to me again, you hear me? Just fuck off.' And he walked away.

There were a few sniggers. Some people whispered. Some simply looked at her, waiting for her to react, to cry, or run away. But she didn't give them the satisfaction. She walked out of the canteen, her head held high. Over the years, she'd learned to put on a brave face.

With her rucksack slung over one shoulder, she headed home, away from yet another school.

A week later Kitty and her family moved, again.

32

The driveway was empty as Beth pulled up outside. She left her car door open, running towards the house. With a trembling hand, she slipped her key into the lock.

Stepping into the hallway, she half expected Cooper to come scurrying out from the kitchen.

And then she remembered.

'Charlie?' Beth shouted as she rushed through the corridor. 'Daisy? Peter?'

Her shouts were met with an unfamiliar silence. It wasn't often the house was quiet.

No dog barking. No kids arguing. No television.

Nothing.

She hurried up the stairs and along the landing, poking her head into each of the children's rooms on the way. Empty.

She checked the bathroom, the door wide open. The whole place, still and quiet. Deserted.

A wave of panic shot through her. She ran into her own bedroom, throwing open the wardrobe. Some of Charlie's suits and shirts were missing, the hangers dangling empty on the rail.

Down the stairs, Beth made her way into the kitchen. A crisp sheet of white paper lay on the island unit. A pen beside it. She picked it up. The writing was Charlie's.

Beth,

I appreciate it must have been difficult telling me the truth after all these years. I thank you for finally being honest with me.

While I am grateful, and also aware that this is a stressful time for you, I can't pretend I'm not hurt and angry. It's a lot to take in.

It's not the details that you have divulged, but the fact that you've been lying for so long that's so painful. I feel that you have put our family, my children, at risk, and continued to do so by not coming clean when this situation first arose.

It's clear that somebody is targeting you because of your past. It is also clear that our children are not safe around you. They may as well have targets on their backs while somebody is trying to hurt you.

I need time to think.

And I have to keep the kids out of harm's way. That's my primary concern now.

I implore you to talk to the police. It's obvious this has got to a point where you are in danger. I am in two minds to tell them myself, but I feel it's your decision. Please make the right one.

Stay safe.

Charlie

Beth stared at the note. The words swam around in her head, stinging like a paper cut in her brain. She screwed the sheet up into a ball, and dropped it on the floor, fishing her phone from her pocket. She hammered Charlie's number into the keypad. He answered after a few rings.

'Oh thank God, Charlie, I didn't think you would pick up for a second there.'

'I almost didn't.'

'Charlie, please, can we talk?'

'There's nothing to say. Everything I have to say for the time being is in the note.'

'But I love you. And I love the kids.'

'Then you'll understand why I have to do this. It's for the best. They're not safe with you.'

Beth flinched, as she wondered if there was a double meaning in Charlie's statement.

'Where are you?'

The sound of Charlie's heavy breathing was the only answer she received.

'They're my children too. I have a right to know where you have taken them!'

Eventually, a sigh.

'We're gonna stay at Derek's rental for a while. It's empty, and he said it's fine for as long as I need it.'

'Does he know?'

'About you? Of course he doesn't. You think I'd want to advertise... that?' Charlie's spiteful tone was painful.

Beth sat, her ear to the phone for a few moments.

'When can I see the kids?'

'Beth, I really don't think it's a good idea.'

'Charlie, please–'

'No. Not at the moment. If you go to the police, get them to sort out what's happening, then we can discuss it. But for now, it's not safe. Surely you understand that?'

Beth didn't answer. She knew he was right, but that didn't make it hurt any less. She had never spent a day away from her Daisy. Peter was older, he had slept over at friends' houses, stayed out at parties, but Daisy... she was Beth's baby.

She was Beth's world.

'Oh, and if you find Peter's phone in the house, can you let me know? He's doing my head in going on about it.'

'Okay.'

The line went dead before Beth could say any more.

She sank to the floor, her back against a kitchen cupboard. The phone clattered on the tiles as it slipped from her hand.

In all her years with Charlie, she'd never heard him sound like that. The fondness in his voice, his chirpy demeanour, absent.

Beth wondered if their relationship would recover. The worst part was that she couldn't blame him. Everything he had said was true. She had lied, repeatedly, and put her family in danger to protect her own dirty little secret.

A thought struck her as she glanced down at her phone. Picking it up, she scrolled through her messages. She found what she was looking for. The texts from her stalker. She typed out a message.

Who are you? What have you done to my dog?

She didn't expect a response, but it was worth a shot.

A picture message flashed up on her screen. She blinked, taking it in.

Matted fur.

Blood.

Entrails.

A tiny, broken, honey-coloured body, almost unrecognisable.

Another message appeared.

You'll find out who I am soon enough.

33

Having spent the best part of a day away from her family, Beth was starting to feel a little stir-crazy. Twice she had resisted the urge to drive around to Derek and Anna's flat. But she knew that wouldn't help. If Charlie said he needed time, then she would give it to him. Pushing him would only make things worse. She wasn't used to a world without having to entertain a six-year-old. Or walk the dog. Or find something Peter had misplaced.

This silence was crippling for Beth.

And she hated it. She thought about texting Margot, asking if she wanted to come over for a drink. But she realised other people had their own lives. It was selfish to impose herself on them because her world had suddenly stopped existing.

And so she sat in her big old farmhouse, alone, staring at the walls.

She sank a bottle of red. And she finally felt relaxed. She rarely drank during the afternoon, but she thought, *what the hell*.

At about four, her phone buzzed with a text. She eyed it suspiciously on the coffee table, wondering if it might be the stranger. She rose from her seat and picked up the phone.

It was Mikey. Beth felt a rush of excitement.

Hey you, was great to meet you in the week. Hope you've had a good one. Up to much this weekend?

It was familiar and friendly. Beth sat back down in her armchair, staring at the message, tapping her thumbnail on the screen for a moment. She typed her reply.

Was lovely to meet you too. Not up to much. You?

Mikey's reply came in seconds.

Going to see a band, got a spare ticket if you fancy it?

Maybe it was the wine, or fear of being alone, but Beth replied:

Sure. Can you pick me up? I've had a drink.

No probs. Where do you live?

Beth hammered in her address, fingers trembling like a schoolgirl. She held her breath as Mikey typed his reply.

See you at 7.

After a brief shower to wash away the shitty day, Beth almost felt human again.

The sorrow of the events still weighed on her mind. She smiled at herself in the mirror. It was convincing enough, although it didn't reach her eyes.

She pulled on some black wet-look leggings, and a loose-fitting silver T-shirt, with some black heels.

She didn't want to look like she'd made too much effort, so she put on a little mascara and lipstick, leaving it at that.

Glancing again in the mirror, a pang of guilt hit her.

'You're not doing anything wrong,' she told herself aloud. 'You're going for a drink. With a friend.' She paused.

'On the same evening your husband has walked out on you with the kids.'

She shook her head, her hair bouncing around her shoulders.

It had taken her such a long time to have the confidence to go back to her natural blonde. The fear that someone would recognise her. It never went away. But Charlie made her feel comfortable enough. She even stopped wearing the stupid thick-framed glasses. With Charlie, she didn't feel like she needed a disguise anymore.

She could still remember his face the day she got back from the hairdresser; they'd done a good job stripping out the brown.

'Wow,' Charlie had said, his chin almost hitting the floor as Beth walked into the kitchen.

Beth smiled to herself.

The buzz of a FaceTime call coming through to her phone jogged her back to reality. It was Charlie, as if he had read her mind. She cursed under her breath, rushing to her wardrobe. Riffling through, she grabbed a grey hoody from a hanger, pulling it over her head.

She hurried back to her phone, accepting the call.

'Charlie, hi!' she breathed, trying to sound relaxed. Trying not to slur her words.

There was a short delay before Charlie responded. The wifi signal at the farmhouse was shockingly bad. They couldn't expect anything better out in the middle of nowhere.

'Hey, I hope you don't mind me calling. Daisy wants to say hello before she goes to bed.'

Beth's heart fluttered.

'No, that's absolutely fine.'

'Right, I'll put her on.'

The delay was annoying, but in the years they had lived out in the sticks, they had all grown used to it. Peter hated it the most, especially when he was trying to play one of his daft games online.

Beth sat down on the edge of the bed.

'Mummy!' Daisy screeched

'Hello, love.'

Her daughter's excited face beamed through the screen of her phone. She wore pink pyjamas, and her hair was damp, pulled back in a loose plait after her evening bath.

Beth hated it when Charlie didn't dry Daisy's hair properly before bed.

'I miss you, Mummy.' The words were juddery, broken, and Beth despised her shitty wifi connection more than ever.

'Me too.' Beth tried to keep a smile on her face.

'You look pretty.' The line crackled a little, the video froze, Daisy's face caught in a grotesque expression halfway between a grin and a scream. Beth shook her head as her phone caught up.

'Thank you. So do you. What have you been up to today?'

Another delay.

The reply came through the phone, but the line was so bad it was indecipherable.

Beth shifted to the other side of the bed, closer to the window, to see if the line improved.

It didn't.

She turned her body towards the window, her back to the bedroom door. She extended her right arm out as far as she could, angling the phone towards her face, trying to avoid getting her bottom half into the shot.

Daisy said something else; again, Beth couldn't make it out.

White noise, and disjointed syllables.

'What was that, love?' Beth shouted towards the phone.

Another pause, Daisy's face jerked around on the screen. Jumping from one freeze frame to another, intermittent fragments of words breaking the silence.

'Sorry, Daisy, the line is really bad.'

'I said who's that behind you?'

34

B eth spun around on the bed, towards the door.
　　Nobody there. But the delay could have given someone time to duck out of view. She turned back to the phone.

'Daisy, I have to go. Nighty-night, sweetie pie.'

Beth blew a kiss into the phone and ended the call, dropping the phone onto the bed. She turned, looking out through the doorway. The landing was empty. She stood up slowly.

'Hello?' she called out into the empty house, telling herself she was being ridiculous.

Daisy must have been seeing shapes in the dark, through the jerky video call.

But Beth felt afraid. She had always relied on her instincts. It had served her well in life to do so. Slipping off her shoes, she stepped out onto the landing carpet. The soft pile felt good on her bare feet. She tiptoed across the landing to the top of the stairs, and stood, holding her breath. Listening.

There was no sound from the ground floor of the house. So she began her descent. Halfway down the stairs, she paused again. Silence.

Her heart was thumping so hard, she was sure she could

hear it. Letting out her breath, she continued down to the hallway below. Everything seemed okay as she glanced towards the kitchen. A quick look into the living room revealed it to be empty. She carried on. There was nobody there.

Turning, she froze.

The front door, wide open, swayed gently, the security chain rocked back and forth, as if someone had brushed against it on their way out. She darted to the doorway, gripping the edge of the frame with both hands, looking out into the driveway, searching.

No movement.

No people.

Nothing.

Slamming the door shut, she slid the chain into place and retreated inside the house. A quick scout reassured her that whoever had been in the house was gone. She was alone again.

Terrified.

She would have to get a locksmith in.

Returning to her bedroom, she removed the hoody.

As she began to fix her hair, the doorbell echoed through the house, and she wondered how much more of this her nerves could take. She crept down the stairs, holding her breath. She was sure a stalker wouldn't bother ringing the doorbell, but the back of her neck tingled, regardless.

A little caution never hurt anyone.

She approached the door. Opening it a crack, she peered through. Mikey loitered on the doorstep, his back to the house. Relieved, Beth pushed the door shut, sliding off the security chain.

Grabbing a short black leather jacket from the hall cupboard, she opened the door. Mikey turned towards her, and a smile crept onto his face.

'Hi,' he said. 'You ready to go?'

'Yep.'

Beth stepped out onto the gravel, closing the front door behind her. She looked Mikey up and down, trying to avoid making it obvious. He wore a tight black T-shirt, and a pair of black skinny jeans. He was toned, but not bulky. Beth didn't think any man should ever wear skinny jeans, but at least he had the thighs and calves to pull it off. He smiled again as they walked towards a sporty-looking red Citroen. His wedding ring glinted in the setting sunlight.

'Your wife couldn't make it tonight?' Beth asked, attempting to sound nonchalant.

'Our babysitter fell through at the last minute, so Suzie had to stay home with the little 'un.'

Beth relaxed at the mention of his child. She hadn't pegged him as a father, but now she did, she liked it.

'Your husband doesn't mind you heading out on a Saturday night with me?' Mikey's eyes flicked sideways. He was testing the water.

Beth hesitated. She didn't want to think about Charlie. It hurt too much.

'He trusts me. Who are we going to see?' she asked, changing the subject.

'The Hypnotronic Hamsters. It's kind of... electro, dancey, pop-type stuff.'

Beth raised an eyebrow, as she imagined it was the sort of thing Peter might listen to.

'They're awesome, I swear!'

'I'll be the judge of that.' Beth swung her legs into the car as Mikey closed the door for her, like a true gentleman.

They made small talk on the journey. Beth told Mikey about Daisy and Peter. Mikey gushed over his daughter, Bella, who was two.

Beth told Mikey how Charlie had been her university crush, and how they had been together ever since.

Mikey explained that he had met Suzie on a dating app, five years and still going strong. He seemed embarrassed at first, but Beth assured him it was the modern way. Loads of her colleagues had met their spouses online. It was just how things were done now. Too busy to meet in real life.

The venue was small but trendy. It had originally been a Victorian tea room, and at one point was a notorious biker café, but these days it was a live music spot, popular with the youngsters. Beth and Charlie used to go there a lot, but they hadn't been for years. She couldn't even recall the last time.

Standing in the queue surrounded by twenty-somethings, and the odd thirty-something, Beth suddenly worried she had made a mistake. The effects of the bottle of wine were beginning to wear off, and she felt like mutton dressed as lamb.

She thought about her children in a strange flat, wondering what reason Charlie had given them for the upheaval. She hoped Peter had not heard any of their conversation earlier in the day. It was bad enough that Charlie knew the truth about her past. She couldn't bear her children finding out.

Charlie would never tell them. She was confident of that.

But Peter knew something was going on. Beth prayed he would not try to do any investigating of his own.

'Here.' Mikey handed Beth a small silver hip flask.

She unscrewed the cap and sniffed the contents. The warming smell of bourbon burned her nostrils.

'We can get a taxi home,' he added, winking.

Beth took a swig. The liquid felt hot as it flowed down her gullet. She winced, downing another couple of swigs, then handed the flask back to Mikey, who did the same. He tucked it into the waist band of his jeans.

The queue moved fast, and before too long they were inside the venue.

It was dark and loud. As they made their way to the bar, the whisky began to go to Beth's head. The pounding bass coursed through her, moving her body with the beat.

'What are you drinking?' she bellowed over the music, leaning in close to Mikey's ear.

'Surprise me!' he shouted back, moving his face closer to her skin. His lips brushed against her ear and she stifled a grin.

Beth ordered two beers, handing one to Mikey. They pushed through the heaving crowd towards the stage. She removed her jacket and saw Mikey staring at her.

'You look great!'

She smiled again, and as the whisky took effect, the catastrophic events of the last twenty-four hours started to ebb away.

The image of Cooper's mutilated carcase flashed into her mind, and she screwed her eyes shut.

A warm hand on her arm drew her back to the room. She found Mikey staring at her.

'You okay?' he asked.

She nodded, starting to dance again. As more people filled the space, Mikey was shoved closer to her. He danced beside her, his body bumping against her now and then.

And she liked it.

She drained her beer, dropping the empty bottle onto the dance floor. It clattered against her feet and spun off across the concrete. Mikey handed Beth the flask again. She took a large gulp of the liquid. It burned, the way whisky always did, but she didn't care anymore. Reaching one hand up, she weaved her fingers into her hair, swaying back and forth to the music.

The band arrived on stage, and the crowd exploded into a cacophony of screams and whistles.

Beth turned towards the action as a drumbeat filled the room, accompanied by synthesisers and guitars, and a soothing, melodic vocal. Her body pulsated, as she lost herself in the rhythm.

A couple of songs in, she became aware of Mikey's crotch pressing up against her. She continued to dance. His hands played briefly on her hips, then he pulled away. Beth danced backwards, pushing her bottom into his groin. His hands appeared on her hips once more, firmer this time. More confident. His fingers slid up her skin, under her T-shirt and brushed against her bare stomach. Beth's whole body tingled. Electricity sparked in her brain.

She pivoted, they were face to face, and Mikey looked into her eyes. He cocked his head, and then he was on her. His lips locked on hers, his tongue in her mouth. He tasted of beer and whisky. Beth's head swam in the excitement. She felt as though she could swallow him whole as he probed her with his tongue.

In that moment, Beth felt more alive, more turned on than she had in years.

And then she pushed him away. He looked confused, a little hurt.

'I'm sorry!' Beth shouted. 'I can't.' And she weaved through the throng of hedonistic revellers, leaving Mikey on the dance floor. The music filled her ears, and she realised she really didn't want to be there.

As she reached the door of the venue, she felt a hand on her shoulder.

'Beth, wait!'

She spun around. Mikey was behind her.

'Let me go, Mikey, please.'

'I'm sorry, I thought you wanted to. I didn't mean to offend you.'

Beth stepped out into the evening air and shivered. She pulled her jacket from around her waist and slipped it onto her goosebump-covered arms. Mikey followed.

'You didn't offend me. It's not your fault.'

'Then what's wrong? I don't understand.'

'You're married. *I'm* married.'

He shrugged. 'We're both adults.'

'No. I don't do... this!' Beth gestured with both hands towards Mikey. 'I should never have come here with you tonight. I had a shitty day, and I didn't want to be alone. I apologise for leading you on. It was unfair of me.'

Mikey reached his hand out, placing it on Beth's shoulder.

'It's cool. Don't worry.' He squeezed gently. 'I get it.'

'Listen, you go back inside. No point you missing the gig because of me. I'll walk into town and grab a taxi.'

He frowned. 'Are you sure? I don't like you being on your own. You seem upset.'

'I'm a big girl, Mikey, but thanks.'

As Beth walked away, he called after her.

'Text me and let me know you get home okay?'

She held up her hand to acknowledge she had heard but didn't turn around.

35

Walking along the promenade towards the pier, Beth hugged her arms around her body. The sea breeze hit her face, her hair blowing behind her.

She looked out to the black mass of sea, a couple of tiny white dots of light; some fishing boats, the only thing visible for miles.

She regretted her jacket choice, as she picked up the pace, and hoped she wouldn't have to walk all the way to the train station to find a taxi.

She stumbled a little, drunker than she had realised.

The sound of her high heels on the pavement rang in her ears, as laughter and distant shouts echoed all around.

Youngsters out on a Saturday night as the summer drifted away.

She cursed under her breath as she remembered the kiss; screwing her eyes shut, she shook her head.

She'd *never* cheated on Charlie.

It was only a kiss, but it was enough.

A betrayal.

She pictured Charlie in a small flat in the town centre, with their children.

For a split second she thought about walking there and ringing the buzzer. Demanding that he speak to her.

Then she realised she was drunk, probably reeking of whisky, and dressed up to the nines.

Not a good idea. Especially if Peter and Daisy saw her. It wasn't late, they would still be up.

Beth couldn't believe she had allowed herself to be so stupid. A lifetime of being cool, calm and considered was now escaping her.

She had been reckless. That hadn't happened for a *long* time.

As Beth marched past the arches, she noticed a dark figure leaning against a wall in the shadows, smoking a cigarette. The orange glow illuminating a wisp of white as it rose into the evening air.

She smelled the smoke, and screwed her face up, picking up the pace a little.

She heard footsteps.

Turning her head, she saw the figure walking behind her.

Glancing around, she noticed some teenagers kicking a glass bottle. They saw Beth watching them and scurried away up the steps towards the clifftops, giggling, leaving her alone.

The steady sound of the man's shoes was getting louder.

He was gaining on her.

She turned; he was closer.

She sped up.

He did the same.

Beth panicked as visions of her recent car chase flashed through her mind.

Feeling sick, she fished around in her bag for a weapon. Her hand came to rest on a can of deodorant.

Better than nothing, she thought.

She slipped it out, holding it by her side.

The lights of the pier twinkled in her peripheral vision, the noises of people having fun drifted across the water.

But it all seemed so far away.

She spun around, the cannister in her outstretched arm, finger on the top, poised and ready.

The man looked confused, swerving to avoid her. He carried on walking straight past. He glanced briefly back over his shoulder, before pulling his mobile phone out of his pocket, pressing it up to his ear.

'Hello? Yeah, weirdest thing just happened...' Beth heard him say as he hurried away. She dropped back, embarrassed by her paranoia. She cringed as she imagined the conversation he was now having. Relaying how a strange woman had threatened him with an aerosol for no reason.

'Get a grip!' Beth whispered in the dark, shaking her head again.

She saw headlights coming towards her down the road, dazzling her. She held a hand up, fingers splayed over her eyes.

As the car drew nearer, she clocked a taxi sign on its roof. She waved and it pulled over.

'Can you take me to Falmer, please? Cranbrooke Farmhouse, if you know it?'

'Sure, hop in,' the cabbie replied cheerfully. Beth felt instantly safer.

As she climbed into the back seat, she noticed the cabbie's eyes on her in the rear-view mirror. They lingered a second too long, and she drew her jacket across her chest.

'Been out on the razz?'

'Just a gig.'

'Oh right, anyone good?'

'Not really.'

'My daughter was at a gig tonight up this way.'

Beth felt embarrassed, as she tried to guess how young the cabbie's daughter would be.

'Surely it ain't finished yet?' the driver asked. 'I'm supposed to pick her up. She said midnight.'

'Wasn't my cup of tea. Decided to go home early.'

The conversation trailed off, and they drove the rest of the way in silence.

Beth paid the cabbie. He thanked her and retreated down the drive to the main road. As his lights faded, so did Beth's sense of safety.

She looked at her house, large, dark, and looming. The trees behind it swaying in the wind.

As she stepped forwards, the security light clicked on, flooding the driveway with a harsh white synthetic beam.

She cursed herself for not leaving a lamp on inside. She wasn't used to returning to an empty home. Pulling her key from her handbag, she pushed it into the lock, but the door swung inwards before she turned it.

Beth stood frozen on the doorstep, a chasm of black stretching out ahead of her. A shaft of moonlight fell through from the kitchen, casting swirling shadows from the towering firs outside, across the floor. She waited for her eyes to become accustomed to the darkness, then stepped into the hallway, holding her breath. She crept silently along the corridor to the bottom of the stairs.

She stood, afraid to breathe, and waited.

A loud creak, then the sound of footsteps above her head from the bedroom.

Beth's survival instincts kicked in. She turned, kicking off her heels into the hallway, running out of the front door onto the gravel. Her bare feet crunched on jagged edges, but she felt no pain, adrenaline coursing through her.

The security light sprung to life once more, as Beth sprinted across the driveway.

She afforded herself a glance over her shoulder and saw in horror a dark figure illuminated by the moonlight in an upstairs window.

She turned down the side of the house and headed towards the old barn. She heard the front door clatter against the inside wall, and the loud crunch of boots on gravel. He was coming.

Running fast.

Beth reached the stable doors and quickly lifted the latch as quietly as she could. She slipped through the gap, closing the heavy wooden door behind her. She knew she didn't have long. Whoever was chasing was close. She dropped to her knees, running her hands over the floorboards, searching for the trapdoor down to the crawlspace below.

If you didn't know it was there, you would never see it.

She slipped her fingers into a gap at the edge, lifting up the hatch. She eased herself below the stable building, lowering the panel down above her head.

A crunch of stones outside the door.

There wasn't much room to move. A roll of thick plastic filled most of the area. Charlie had used it to repair the shed roof last summer. Holding her breath, she peered up through cracks in the floorboards, her face almost pressed against the underside of the planks.

She watched and waited.

The metal latch clicked, and the door creaked open. There was a series of thuds on the wooden floor as someone stepped into the barn.

Footsteps above her, as the person moved slowly around.

Beth heard a click.

Slithers of light fell through the cracks as a torch was shone around the building. She winced., sucking in a little air. Too afraid to breathe properly.

He was directly above her now.

Dust fell down from the boards into Beth's eyes as the figure shifted weight from one foot to the other. She blinked through the pain.

She heard slow and steady breathing. The torch beam swooped over the ground again.

Beth remained as still as she could.

Silent.

The light shone directly downwards now, through the cracks, as the stranger stood with the torch down to one side. Thin splinters of light caught the edges of the plastic to Beth's side. She turned her head to avoid more dust.

As her vision adjusted, she gasped silently in horror.

Two bulging, dead eyes peered at her, frozen in a look of pure terror. A tongue protruded from pale lips.

Tangled red curls tumbled from behind the plastic.

Beth stifled a scream, placing her fist over her open mouth. The person above her strode to the barn door, opening it, and stepped outside.

Beth remained hidden.

After a few minutes she heard the distant roar of a motorcycle engine starting and then grow quieter as it rode away. She turned on the light from her phone, shining it through the plastic, illuminating the body. An emerald-green scarf knotted tightly around the neck.

Beth pushed the hatch up above her, escaping her hiding place. She ran. As fast as she could. She sprinted to the house, grabbing her car key from the hall table. With the front door wide open behind her, she rushed to her Range Rover, climbing into the driver's seat, phone still in hand. She tossed it into the passenger side. She didn't care that she was drunk. She needed to get away.

Away from the house. Away from the stables, and the body wrapped in plastic.

Starting the engine, she screeched away from the house, tyres spinning on gravel as she escaped. She drove until she reached the safety of warm amber street lights, far away from her home. Grabbing her phone, she punched a number into it and held it to her ear. It took a few rings, but eventually he answered.

'Charlie!' Beth screamed through sobs. 'Please, you've got to come now. It's Zoe. She... she's dead!'

36

Charlie stood scratching his head, while Beth lingered in the doorway, afraid to step inside the stable building.

'Whereabouts?' Charlie shouted over his shoulder, making little effort to hide the scepticism in his voice.

'Under the hatch in the crawl space. Wrapped in plastic.'

Charlie stepped forward, lifting the panel. He shone his phone down below him. He crouched, and Beth heard him rummaging.

'Careful, fingerprints!' Beth hissed.

He stood up.

'I think I'll be all right.' A grim expression on his face, somewhere between sorrow and anger.

'Come on in.'

'I don't want to, Charlie, I've seen enough.'

'Beth, come here.' His voice was firm, commanding.

Beth crossed the dusty floor, joining Charlie by his side. She looked down.

'I... I don't understand. She was there, I swear...'

'I'm honestly shocked that you stooped this low to get me over here. Meanwhile, the kids are alone in the flat, so you'd better hope that nothing bad happens to them while I'm here with you.'

Beth crouched, lifting the plastic. But that's all that was there.

The body was gone.

'I'm not making this up! I promise you, it was Zoe, wrapped up in that sheeting, right there!' Beth pointed down towards the ground. 'I think she'd been strangled. It was... horrible!'

'So where is she now?'

Beth stood, scanning the barn.

'I don't know. He must have... moved her.'

Charlie exhaled loudly.

'Beth, stop, please. This is... pathetic, quite frankly. I don't recognise you.'

'Charlie... I–'

Charlie grabbed her by the shoulders, his fingers dug into her flesh painfully.

'ENOUGH!' he shouted, shaking her violently. 'Do you hear me? I've had enough.'

He let go, his shoulders slumped.

'Charlie, please...'

'You're drunk. I could smell it off you a mile away. And you're slurring your speech. I'm going to give you the benefit of the doubt, and assume you're not totally crazy, and that you didn't make this all up just to get me over here. You've had too much to drink and thought you saw something... clearly, you were mistaken.'

'I'm not mad, Charlie, I know what I saw. It was a body. Zoe's body! I swear it, I swear on–'

Charlie didn't let her finish.

'Like you swore to me that you're not Kitty Briscoe?'

Silence.

'Beth, don't you see what you've done? I'll never be able to believe *anything* you say anymore. There will always be a niggling doubt. Everything you've ever told me is bullshit.'

Beth looked down at the floor. The truth in Charlie's words stung.

'Where were you tonight?'

The question caught Beth off guard.

'What?'

'You're pissed as a fart. Dressed up like you've been to a club. Where have you been?'

Beth hesitated.

'I... I went for a drink in town... with Margot.'

'So you weren't at a gig down on the seafront?'

Beth's eyes widened.

'No. I was with Margot at the Hilton.'

'More lies, Beth. You see? You seem incapable of telling me the truth. James from work saw you. He was there with his girlfriend, and he texted me to say he'd seen you in the queue and was I there.'

Beth's face flushed as pictures of Mikey with his hands on her hips, his tongue in her mouth, flashed into her mind.

'I–'

'Don't even bother, Beth. You need help... I'm not sure who you are anymore. You're not the woman I fell in love with.'

Charlie turned and walked towards the barn door. Beth rushed after him, grabbing his arm.

'Wait, I'm not making this up and I'm not mistaken. Ask Peter. Ask him if Zoe's parents have heard from her. She's supposed to be on a school trip.'

Charlie spun around to face Beth.

'No, Beth, I won't. I'm not going to mention this to Peter, and you won't either. He's stressed out enough as it is, without putting ideas into his head about his girlfriend.'

'Why? What's wrong with him?'

'He thinks we're getting divorced. He's totally freaking out.'

'And are we?'

Charlie looked at Beth, the sadness in his eyes broke her heart. He didn't reply. As he walked away, he glanced over his shoulder.

'Talk to someone, Beth. You need help. I don't think you're well. I think your secrets have finally caught up with you.'

Beth watched him go. She heard him walk across the gravel and slam his car door as he climbed in. The engine started, and he drove away. Leaving her alone, afraid.

She collapsed to her knees. The rush of anger and sorrow that filled her was unbearable. For the first time in years, she let go. She screamed. Cried until her throat was hoarse.

For Zoe, who despite what Charlie said, was definitely dead. Beth knew what she had seen.

She mourned the loss of her perfect family, her perfect life.

But most of all, she cried for herself. For choices she made when she was seven. And the consequences of that upon her life. No matter how hard she tried to escape from that night. No matter how far she ran, or how much she buried those events deep inside her, she would never, *ever* be free.

It would follow her until the day she died. Hanging over her, throwing shade on any joy she might allow herself to feel, reminding her that she didn't deserve it. She didn't have the right.

When her energy waned, she curled up into a tight little ball on the stable floor and sobbed until she had nothing else inside.

She knew she had to find out who was doing this to her. Whatever the cost.

After all, what did she have left to lose?

37

The warm sunlight streamed through the office window but brought Charlie no joy. He stared at his monitor; he had done no work today. His mind had been drifting.

He kept thinking about Beth's face on Saturday night. The fear in her eyes.

He hoped he was doing the right thing.

She was understandably scared being in the house alone, but she was an adult, and at least she could look after herself.

Daisy, on the other hand, needed protecting.

Charlie felt guilty. He loved Beth, of course he did. She was his world.

But he couldn't help feeling betrayed.

He was also trying to get his head around the fact of who his wife actually was.

Kitty Briscoe. The girl who got away with murder.

Allegedly.

He had no doubt that he'd go back to her, but not until the current situation was sorted.

They had received a clear threat to their children. He couldn't allow anything to happen to them.

Beth had been drunk. Charlie was sure she had not really seen what she claimed. The more he thought about the events of Saturday night, the more he convinced himself it was a desperate attempt to get him back. He had tentatively checked with Peter, and Zoe was away on a field trip. Her friends at school had been giving regular updates.

But why claim to have found Zoe's body? Why not just say someone was in the house? That would have been enough to convince Charlie to go over. Something niggled at the back of his mind. Despite what he may have said to Beth in anger on Saturday, he didn't believe she was crazy.

He knew that she was a calm and measured person. She rarely freaked out. She'd been spooked, but he wasn't sure what by. She'd seen something. But it can't have been Zoe.

Some mail landed with a loud thud on top of an already large pile on Charlie's desk. He had about a week's worth to open. The admin guy smirked and walked away.

Charlie began flicking through the letters.

Nothing of any interest. Until he found a bulky brown padded envelope towards the bottom. It had been there a few days, he couldn't remember when it arrived.

It was hand-addressed, his name at the top. He eyed the scrawl nervously; it was similar to the notes. How had he not noticed the writing before?

He tore it open. Slipping his hand inside, he felt something cold and hard. He pulled it out to reveal a small glass bottle. Turning it over, he saw the label, raising both his eyebrows.

Chanel No.5.

People sent him corporate gifts all the time. Trying to curry his favour. But there was no note. No compliments slip. No indication who it was from. He would usually take stuff like this home for Beth, but at the moment he didn't see the point.

'Oooh, Chanel! Someone is trying to impress you,' a high-pitched, whiney voice came from the bank of desks behind him.

Charlie looked over his shoulder to see one of the team beside him, craning her neck to see the bottle. A tall redhead, Charlie couldn't remember her name.

'Yeah,' Charlie replied indifferently.

She stood up and crossed to his side.

'Has your wife got a birthday coming up? She'd be dead chuffed with that.'

Charlie placed the package down on his desk, pushing it aside.

'No. She doesn't really wear this sort of stuff anyway.'

The girl's expression changed. She smiled, twiddling her hair. She loitered next to Charlie's desk, not saying anything. Smiling.

'Would you like it?' Charlie finally asked.

'Me? Oh well, if it's going begging I'll take it off your hands, yeah,' she said as if she wasn't bothered. But Charlie could tell she was itching to grab the bottle and run. 'If you're sure you don't want it?'

'Nah, it's yours.' Charlie picked it up and handed it to her.

'Thanks. Rob is going to be so jealous. He'll be like, *an older man giving you expensive perfume at work, hey?*' She gripped the glass as if she never intended to let it go. Her eyes wide, like an excited child.

'I hope you're not flirting with me, Charlie.' She winked, her grin widening.

'No,' Charlie replied firmly. 'Definitely not.'

The smile fell from her face, and she returned to her desk. Charlie shivered at the idea.

He heard the group behind him giggling, no doubt as the girl told them how Charlie must fancy her.

Older man? he thought, smiling to himself. He wondered

when did girls start to think of him like that. He supposed he was now. He was the wrong side of forty.

But he still felt the same as he did at twenty. Apart from his neck clicking every time he turned his head. Or groaning whenever he stood up. At some point in the last ten years, without realising it, he had been slowly metamorphosing into his dad.

Derek bounded down the steps from the kitchen, pulling up a chair. He punched Charlie playfully on the shoulder.

'How you holding up, big guy?' he asked nervously.

'Yeah, I'm fine, mate.'

'If you need a few days, you know... we can cope without you this week.'

'No. I'm okay. Thanks though.'

Derek nodded. Charlie could tell there was more coming. Derek was choosing his words.

'You know, you're welcome at the flat as long as you want it. But I really think you should sort things out with Beth and go home. Anna and I could tell things were tense the other weekend when you were round, but... Beth is a catch. Whatever has gone on between you two, I'm sure you can fix it. No point throwing it away over a silly row, is there.'

'Thanks, mate. I have to get my head around things.'

'I've never seen you like this. We can go into my office for a chat. If you want to... talk, or whatever.'

Derek was clearly uncomfortable. He wasn't a touchy-feely type of guy. He hated talking about emotions, or anything other than sport... maybe sex sometimes, but definitely *not* feelings. Anna had obviously ordered him to find out what was happening.

'No thanks, Derek. Honestly, I'm fine.'

Derek looked relieved.

'Look, mate, whatever it is you've done, just say you're sorry and send her a big bunch of flowers. Usually works for me.' Derek winked.

'Why do you automatically assume it's me who's guilty of something?' Charlie's voice was flat.

Derek picked up a pen lying on Charlie's desk, twirling it in the fingers of his right hand.

'Come on. She's perfect. What's she gonna have done?'

'You'd be surprised. Are we finished here?' Charlie turned to face the computer screen and began typing on his keyboard.

Derek frowned, dropping the pen.

'Yep. Yes we are.'

He stood, rolling the chair back under the neighbouring desk and skulked away like a sad schoolboy.

Charlie sighed. He'd never argued with Derek. And although what had just occurred couldn't really be described as an argument, their relationship was usually one of light-hearted banter.

Charlie was sure Derek would get over it though.

Until recently he would have agreed with his friend. He had always thought of Beth as perfect. But he was no longer so sure. The woman he had devoted his entire adult life to, seemed like a complete stranger to him.

If she could lie so easily, so convincingly... what else had she been lying about?

38

I t was the first Monday Beth could remember in a long time when she had not wanted to go to work. Sunday had dragged. She hadn't left the house; had no desire to. She could have easily stayed in bed today too.

But she couldn't afford to lose her job, as well as everything else in her life.

As she stepped out of the lift, she scanned the office. It was early and most people hadn't arrived yet. But Vicky was at her desk, talking to someone from IT. She glanced up. When she saw Beth, she held her gaze. Didn't look away, didn't smile, didn't wave.

Just stared at her, sizing her up.

Beth looked straight back as she crossed the room to her office. Feeling uncomfortable, she eventually looked away. But as she closed her door behind her, she looked through the window.

Vicky was still staring.

Beth powered on her computer, taking off her jacket and hanging it on her coat stand. There was a knock at the door. She craned her neck but couldn't see who it was.

'Come in!' she shouted as she got herself ready to start work.

Margot breezed in, all teeth and perfume. A vision in a cerulean playsuit and a pair of bright orange stilettos. She had a knack of looking fabulous in outfits that would make anybody else look ridiculous. Beth often envied her clothes, generally purchasing most of hers from the bargain section of the supermarkets these days.

'Darling, how are you? Good weekend? Mine was dire. We've got a lot going on today. Have you started yet?'

Beth sat down behind her desk, nodding.

Margot frowned.

'Are you okay?'

'Yes, I'm fine. What's up?'

Margot paused for a moment, cocking her head to one side, but carried on regardless.

'There's a problem with a new title. We released it yesterday, and we've had an email this morning from an author in New Zealand claiming we've plagiarised her work.'

'Oh.'

Margot held up the paperback in her hand.

'I'm looking into the claims. In my professional opinion she hasn't got a leg to stand on, but would you mind contacting the writer and giving him a heads-up? Warn him not to discuss the matter if he's contacted about it.'

Beth sighed.

'Fine.'

Margot closed the door, crossing the room to Beth's desk, perching her bottom on the corner. She crossed one of her Amazonian legs over the other.

'Right. What's going on with you?'

'It's nothing. I'm tired.' Beth couldn't tell Margot about Charlie and the kids, because she'd want to know why. And Beth had no intention of telling her the truth about who she was.

She didn't want to lose another person from her life over this. Given Margot's feelings about children, she couldn't be sure how she would react to Beth's past.

'Honey, I'm not an idiot. I'll ask one more time, and if you choose not to tell me, on your head be it. I will not be responsible for my actions.'

Beth smiled. Margot always had an ability to cheer her up. Everything was high drama with her.

'Honestly, I'm okay. I promise. Now get out of here so I can do some bloody work!'

Beth made a shooing motion with her hand, and Margot hopped up from the desk, scurrying out of the room, perfectly balanced on her impossibly high heels.

Beth glanced at her monitor. There was another knock, Beth didn't look up.

'What did you forget?' she said through a laugh.

The door clicked shut, and Beth's eyes shot up.

Vicky was standing in Beth's office, her arms folded in front of her chest.

'What do you want?' Beth didn't afford her any pleasantries.

'Did you have a pleasant Saturday, Beth?' Vicky asked sarcastically, raising an eyebrow.

'Was it... eventful?' She winked.

'Excuse me?'

'I wondered if you had an... exciting weekend. You know? Did anything interesting happen?'

Vicky wasn't smiling. She was deadly serious. Her eyes fixed on Beth's.

'Get out of my office.'

Instead, Vicky took a few steps towards Beth's desk, and sat on the edge, in the exact spot where Margot had perched only moments earlier.

She glanced around conspiratorially.

'I know who you are,' she whispered.

'You don't know anything.'

'Oh I do. *A lot* more than you realise. And let me tell you, I was a little drunk the other night at Chloe's birthday drinks, and I wasn't thinking straight. But if you *ever* threaten me again, I'll make sure you regret it.'

Beth swallowed hard but didn't look away from Vicky's face.

'Vicky, I really don't think you want to be threatening a senior member of staff. Not when you're still on probation.'

'I'm not scared of you.'

'You should be.'

'Why? What exactly are you going to do?'

Beth said nothing. Vicky waited, pursing her lips.

'No, didn't think so.' She stood up, pushing Beth's stationery caddy off the edge of the desk. It clattered to the floor, and an array of paper clips and pens spilled across the carpet.

'Oops,' Vicky breathed, as she casually strolled out, leaving the door open.

Beth's heart pounded. She crouched and began clearing up the mess. She glanced up to find Vicky watching her, smiling.

Beth wondered what Vicky had meant when she said she knew more than Beth realised.

She was now convinced that Vicky was involved. Had she been watching her on Saturday night with Mikey? Whatever her part, it was clear Beth's warning hadn't worked.

It seemed to have made things worse.

39

Kitty heard the front door slam, indicating that her father was home from the pub. The TV clicked on and the sound of muffled laughter came through the ceiling into her room. She knew it was only a matter of time until he would start on her. He always did when he'd been drinking.

She decided to get out.

She quietly opened her bedroom door and stood listening, holding her breath. She heard no movement from downstairs. Her mother was out gallivanting. Probably with some new man. Things were worse when her mother wasn't around to stick up for her.

Kitty stepped cautiously out to the landing, faded denim jacket under one arm. Still afraid to breathe, she placed a foot onto the stairs.

As she descended, the neon-blue glow from the telly hit the wall in the hallway below. Through the living room doorway, she saw the back of her father's head poking over the top of his chair, facing the television in front of him.

Now and then he would cough or belch. A smouldering cigarette lay in a glass ashtray on a small table beside him.

She tiptoed down the stairs, but as she reached the bottom, a loud creak escaped from beneath her.

She froze. Too late.

Her father spun around in his chair; his face contorted into a sneer.

'Where the hell do you think you're going?' he slurred.

Kitty ignored him, faster now down the hallway towards the front door.

'Oi! Don't you dare walk away from me when I'm talking to you, you little whore!'

Kitty stopped, closed her eyes and breathed deeply.

You need to calm down, she told herself. *Don't rise to it*. She began to count slowly in her head.

She heard the springs squeak as her father heaved his gargantuan mass up from his chair. She turned around, afraid to have her back to him. He lumbered towards her unsteadily.

'Just like your mother... drop your knickers for anyone!'

He lurched forwards, grabbing at her denim jacket. She held on tightly as he tried to wrestle it from her hands. Her father pulled harder, tearing a lapel from the collar.

He laughed, tossing it down onto the floor.

The familiar anger that Kitty had felt towards him for many years welled up inside her like a monsoon.

'I hate you,' she said through gritted teeth.

'The feeling is mutual, *Kitty*.' He always had an edge to his voice when he used her real name. Like he was enjoying it.

'Don't call me that,' she hissed back.

'Oh yeah, who are you this week?' He sniggered.

She ignored him.

'You can pretend all you want, but you will always be Kitty Briscoe. That's never going away. What you did. You nasty little cow.'

'I didn't do anything!' she shouted.

'Bullshit.' The smell of alcohol, cigarettes and sweat hit Kitty's nostrils all at once. She detested him with all her being.

'Why have you always hated me?' Kitty asked.

'Do you really need to ask that? You ruined our lives. You and your little queer friend Kieran Taylor.'

'You're a liar. It was before that. You *never* loved me!'

'No, you're spot on.'

'Why?'

He laughed again.

'Because I never wanted you,' he spat.

She supposed she had always known, but to have it confirmed was still a blow.

'Get me a beer!' her father shouted as he returned to his chair.

'No,' Kitty said defiantly.

Her father turned slowly to face her.

'What did you say?'

'I said no. Get your own fucking beer.'

Kitty's father took a step towards her.

'Now you listen to me, you little bitch, while you're in my house–'

'I'm eighteen. I'm leaving for uni soon, so I won't be in your house anymore. And I'm never coming back. You're a pig. You disgust me. I pity you. But I pity Mum more.'

Her father's face reddened. He reached forwards, grabbing a handful of Kitty's short black hair, screwing it up in his clenched fist, he pulled her head towards him. She could smell his rancid breath.

'I disgust you?' His fat cheeks wobbled. 'Let me tell you–' But her father didn't finish his sentence.

Kitty had stretched out her flailing arm, grappling for something, anything she could grasp. Her hand came to rest on a bronze bust of a horse that her mother kept on the hall console table. In that split second, Kitty's hand, complete with horse, connected with her father's temple. He stood, mouth wide open like a fish, staring at Kitty as blood trickled down his face.

She didn't give him a chance to react. She turned and lurched towards the front door. Yanking it open, she fell out into the street. She turned briefly, looking back at her father from the floor, but he wasn't following her. He reached his hand up to the side of his head, dabbing at the blood. He looked at his wet fingers, confusion, then anger on his face. As he bellowed, Kitty sprang to her feet and ran. She ran as fast as she could and didn't stop until she was sure her father wasn't behind her.

That was the first and last time she stood up to him.

40

Heavy drops of rain bounced off the ground. Charlie inhaled the smell of wet concrete as he soldiered through the car park, holding his rucksack above him. He might not have a full head of hair, but he didn't like looking a state. A leggy blonde in front of him held the door open, and he ran the last few steps into the building. She smiled at him, her eyes lingering a second too long. His cheeks felt hot, and he looked away. Rick, the security guard, winked, raising his newspaper to Charlie as he walked through the lobby. Charlie nodded back, swiping his pass to get into the lift.

He usually took the stairs, but this morning he couldn't face them. He'd had a rough time with Daisy when he dropped her off. She'd been asking all sorts of questions about Beth. Where was she? When would she see her? Why were they not at home? Charlie didn't know what to tell her. The truth wasn't an option, that was for sure.

She'd ended up in tears, and he had to carry her into school kicking and screaming. Her teacher had looked perplexed. And so early into the new term as well. Mind you, at least she was talking to him. Which was more than could be said for Peter.

Peter was ignoring Charlie entirely. He'd decided whatever was going on must all be Charlie's fault. Because it was *always* the man. Everybody thought Beth was so perfect. He couldn't blame them, he had always felt the same. He smirked grimly as he imagined what they would say if they knew the truth.

As he stepped out of the lift, there was a strange atmosphere in the office. Something felt off. People stood in small groups, chatting. Worried expressions on their faces. What's more, they were staring.

At Charlie.

He walked past the annoying twenty-somethings at the desks behind his. They stopped gossiping as he approached.

'Morning,' he said, trying to sound cheerful.

A chubby girl with black hair shot daggers at him. Charlie frowned, placing his rucksack on the floor beside his desk. He switched on his computer, turning briefly as he heard Derek's door open.

'Charlie! My office, now.'

The youngsters glared at him as he walked past. It seemed that everyone was staring at him.

'Close the door,' Derek commanded tersely as Charlie entered the room.

Again Charlie frowned, but he followed the instruction. Derek was sitting at his desk. He didn't offer Charlie a seat.

'What's going on?' Charlie asked.

'What can you tell me about a bottle of perfume?'

'Eh?'

'Perfume, Charlie. Expensive stuff, birds wear it to smell nice. *Chanel* to be precise.'

Charlie didn't understand. Gifts came into the office all the time. Derek had given Anna loads of stuff, he always called dibs on the best items. He'd once taken her an entire lingerie set from Victoria's Secret and passed it off as a birthday gift.

'Is there a problem?'

'Yes, mate, you could say that. A bloody huge one!'

'Derek, what the hell is going on?'

'Ellie Beeson, from accounts. Sits behind you. Apparently, you gave her a bottle yesterday?'

'I didn't exactly give it to her, it got sent in, and she asked if she could have it. What about it?'

Derek stood up, pulling off his jacket. Huge dark patches pooled beneath his armpits.

'When she went home and sprayed it on herself it burned half her fucking face off.'

The blood flowed out of Charlie's head, fast, as if it was all falling straight out through his ankles. He felt dizzy. He blinked a few times, as the world seemed to go quiet and the room span. Everything appeared to be happening in slow motion.

'Wh... what?'

'Acid, they think. The police are running tests.'

A bead of sweat formed above Charlie's eyebrow and ran down to his chin. It dripped, and he watched as it fell to the carpet below. He felt hot, thought he might pass out. He stepped towards Derek's desk, steadying himself on the corner.

'So?'

'So what? You don't think I had anything to do with it?'

'No, mate, of course not. But this is bad. Very bad. I've got a duty of care here.'

Derek sat down in his chair, running his hands over his head.

'Where did it come from?'

'It was sent in. I found it with all the mail yesterday.'

'Addressed to you?'

Charlie paused. If he admitted that the envelope had his name on it, it would make him involved. And he didn't want to be involved.

'No,' he lied. 'Nothing on it.'

'Do you still have it?'

'I threw it in the recycling. It will have been emptied by now.'

'Damn. Right. The police are gonna want to talk to you.'

'I'm not sure I can tell them anything of any use, to be honest.'

'Doesn't matter. You're the person her husband has said gave her the perfume, so they will need to ask you some questions.'

'Right, of course. How... how is she?'

'She's in hospital. Pretty shaken. The burns are nasty. She's going to have... extensive scarring.'

If things had been different, Charlie would have taken the bottle home. Beth, maybe even Daisy, would have sprayed it on themselves. It didn't bear thinking about. But Beth was clearly the intended target. Charlie was absolutely sure of that.

'I'll have to get security to start vetting the mail. This is a PR nightmare.'

'Mate, I don't know what to say... it's horrendous.'

'Imagine if I'd found it before you, taken it home for Anna.'

'We've both been very lucky.'

'Okay, Charlie, you get to work, buddy. I've given the police your details, so you can expect a visit at some point today, I reckon.'

Charlie walked out of the office, back to his desk. Again the chatter stopped as he approached. He sat, aware that all the attention was on him. He turned around.

'I'm really sorry about your friend. I... I had no idea about the perfume. It was sent in. I had nothing to do with it.'

They glared at him, suspicion in their eyes. But nobody spoke. *At least it had shut them up for a minute*, Charlie thought, instantly regretting it. He sat in front of his computer and scrolled through his emails. He had a backlog to work through. He didn't know where the time had gone this week.

One email caught his eye. It had been sent a few days earlier.

The subject line said *Perfume* and the sender's name appeared as *unknown*.

Charlie's head swam. A tiny vein in his temple pulsed and bulged, and more perspiration ran down the back of his neck, soaking into his collar. He glanced around nervously, as if people knew what he was looking at.

He clicked the email.

```
Hope Kitty liked the perfume.
```

Charlie looked about the office again. Then clicked delete on the message.

He was aware that what he was doing was wrong, but he was scared.

He emptied his deleted messages folder. He was sure this wouldn't be enough if the police felt inclined to go through his computer, but he'd have to make sure it didn't come to that.

He would try to charm them. He was usually able to get people on side. It was a skill he'd possessed since his teens. If it was a female detective, perhaps he could even flirt a little.

He stood and walked through the office to the toilets. Past the room full of eyes on him. He pushed the door, and it banged against the wall. He was burning up. Standing at a sink, he ran water into his hands, splashing it on his hot face. It trickled down, soothing his skin. Feeling suddenly dizzy and nauseous, he lowered himself to the ground, with the tap still running. He lay on his side, the cold tiles felt good against his body. He pressed his cheek into the surface, sighing as he did so. He didn't care that it was a communal toilet floor. He needed it. Let them see. Let them laugh.

Charlie wasn't sure how long he lay there, but eventually his phone beeped. He sat up and pulled it out of his trouser pocket.

A text. From an unknown number.

He opened it.

Kitty had a lucky escape. She still has her pretty face...

A second message appeared immediately on the screen.

For now.

41

As Kitty's eyes adjusted to the dark, she stood up and looked around the vast space she now found herself in. She couldn't see Kieran, didn't know where he had gone.

'Kieran?' she called out feebly.

No reply. Something dripped, echoing in a far corner. A noise to her right. Scurrying.

The interior of the old hotel was huge. Shafts of pale sunlight shone down through splits and gaps in the roof, illuminating areas, making others look darker.

The smell. Kitty didn't know what it was. But it was unpleasant. She screwed up her face.

A lot of the internal walls had collapsed, reduced to piles of bricks, rubble, scattered around the floor. An old chandelier sat shattered a few feet from where she stood. She took a few steps into the darkness.

'Kieran. I don't like this. I'm going home.'

Still no reply. Out of the corner of her eye she saw something move quickly through a shaft of light. She turned, terrified.

'Kieran?'

'Kitty! Help me!' A strange, scratchy voice, then a low gurgling noise.

She followed the sound through a dilapidated doorway. The next room was darker. She could hardly see anything. But in the middle, a dark shape lay on the floor.

The noise had ceased. Everything was quiet.

Kitty heard birds twittering outside in the sunshine and desperately wished she was out there with them. But rather than turn and run, she walked towards the mass. As she drew nearer and her eyes grew accustomed to the dim light, she realised it was Kieran. His eyes closed, hands by his side.

'Kieran, this isn't funny. What are you doing?'

He didn't react. He lay deathly still. Kitty crouched, holding her breath, leaning over his body. She reached out her hand, touching his shoulder.

His arms shot up and grabbed her. She screamed.

Kieran sat up in fits of laughter.

'You should have seen your face!' he shouted in between hysterical cackles.

'I hate you, Kieran! That wasn't funny. I thought Bloody Mary had got you. You're a pig!'

'There is no Bloody Mary. I made that up. This place isn't haunted. It's cool. Don't you think?'

Kieran stood up, dusting himself off, brushing gravel from the seat of his jeans.

Kitty did a slow three-hundred-and-sixty-degree rotation, taking in the space they were standing in.

'I don't like it,' she said finally.

'How come? It's a fab place to play. We can make it our hideout. It can be our secret.'

'But it smells funny.'

'It's only damp. You'll get used to it. It's the rats you should be more worried about.'

'Rats?' Kitty shivered, wrapping her arms around her bare shoulders.

Kieran slapped her back.

'I'm kidding. It's fine here. Relax, won't you? Come on, come see this other room.'

Kieran grabbed Kitty's hand and rushed to the other side of the space, dragging her behind him. There was a large archway, derelict like the rest of the structure. Three shallow steps led up into a huge cavernous space with a high ceiling. Huge domed skylights in the roof were covered in leaves and dirt. Dappled light filtered through in between.

'I think this was the ballroom or something,' Kieran said. Kitty looked around the space. To her left was an old staircase, leading up to a balcony. Kitty had never seen anything like it in her life. She ran to the steps, placing one foot onto the bottom. She climbed a couple, gripping what remained of the bannister.

Her leg went straight through the mouldy board, like it was made of paper. She screamed, managing to catch herself on the handrail, which came away from the wall. Fortunately, she had regained her balance already. She gulped, eyes shooting to Kieran.

'Careful. Don't wanna be taking you home to your mum in bits.' He giggled.

Kitty continue to climb the stairs, sticking to the perimeter. When she reached the top, she crawled carefully along the floor. From this new position she could see the area was even larger than she had initially thought. She made her way to the outer edge, glancing down from time to time through holes in rotting floorboards. It looked much higher from where she was now situated than it had from the ground.

Peering down at Kieran on the other side of the ballroom, it amazed her how small, how insignificant he seemed in the space. Like a tiny insect.

'Woah, it is *so* cool up here!' she shouted.

'Oh wait up!' he replied, running over to the steps.

He ascended the staircase, taking his time, having already seen Kitty nearly go through.

'Stick close to the wall, it's safer!' she warned.

Once he reached the top, he stood, rather than crawled, probably to prove to Kitty that he wasn't scared. He edged along towards her. As he took a step into the centre, the whole structure wobbled. Kitty screamed, clutching frantically at the edge of the balcony. Kieran took another step forward; his foot went straight through the plasterboard. He fell to all fours, and again the floor trembled. Rubble and dust tumbled to the ground.

'Kieran, don't! Get down. You're too heavy!' Kitty screeched fearfully.

'But I want to see!' he shouted. 'I'll crawl, like you did.'

'No! You're too big! Please!'

Kieran's face crumpled, but he obeyed, descending the stairs tentatively.

'How high do you think this is?' Kitty wondered aloud.

'Dunno. Pretty high.'

'Do you think I would die if I jumped from up here?'

'Yeah. Probably. Depends how you landed. Give it a go.'

Kitty dangled her legs over the ledge, swinging them playfully. She shuffled her buttocks forward until she was perched on the outermost edge. For a moment, Kieran looked like he believed she might actually do it.

'I'd like to push my dad from up here,' she said, brushing some dirt from her dress, absent-mindedly.

'Your dad would *never* get up there. He's definitely too fat.'

Kitty crawled back to the stairs and joined Kieran on the
Th nd, where he was drawing lines in the dirt with a stick he'd
nd.

'He's a bad man,' Kieran said quietly, without looking at Kitty.

Kitty remained silent, nodding slowly.

'We should kill him,' Kieran continued. He shot her a sideways glance.

'Yeah. I wish. I hate him.'

'Let's do it!' Kieran had a wicked grin on his face. 'We could leave him for the foxes to eat.'

'Do foxes eat people?'

'Course they do. They eat anything. They're wild!'

'I wish somebody *would* kill my dad.'

They both stood, staring at the ground. Kieran took Kitty's hand in his.

'I would do it, if he wasn't so big,' Kieran said, sticking out his chest like Superman.

'But we're too small. If he was little we could do it. Like that cat,' Kitty replied. They looked at each other, bursting into laughter.

'Come on,' Kieran said eventually. 'This is boring. Let's go.'

He dropped her hand, running away into the darkness.

42

BRIGHTON, EAST SUSSEX, ENGLAND.

The detective sat staring at Charlie, notebook in hand, pen poised, ready to write.

'So in your own time, Mr Carter. If you could tell us about the perfume?'

Charlie cleared his throat.

'It's like I told Derek at the office. It was sent in. We get stuff sent in from clients frequently, so it wasn't out of the ordinary.'

'I see,' said the detective, who had identified herself as DI Burns. 'Was there anything distinguishing about the envelope?'

'No. Nothing. It was just a brown jiffy bag. Nothing suspicious.'

'Printed?'

Charlie hesitated. 'No, handwritten.'

'Okay. What was the writing like?'

'It was... handwriting. Black pen. I don't know what else to say.'

'And you told your boss you threw it away, is that right?'

'Yep. Straight in the recycling bin with all the other rubbish. at gets emptied every day a few times. We get through a lot.'

The detective scribbled some notes down on her pad.

'And how did the perfume come to be in the possession of Ellie Beeson?'

'I gave it to her.'

'Right. Why?' Burns' dark-brown eyes surveyed Charlie coldly. Watching. Waiting for him to slip up. As he returned her gaze, taking in her muscular physique, and rather masculine looking attire, he suspected his charms were not going to have any effect on her. Beth would probably have more luck.

'Because she asked for it,' he replied, regretting his choice of words immediately.

The detective glanced at Charlie's wedding ring.

'You didn't think your wife would want it?'

'My wife?'

'You are married?' She nodded towards Charlie's hand.

'Yes, I am. But we're... I suppose we're separated... at the moment.'

'You suppose?'

'We are. We're separated.'

'Since when?'

'Is that relevant?'

'I'm trying to get the bigger picture here, Mr Carter.'

'Yeah, sorry. Since... the weekend.'

'Right. So this is a new thing?'

'Yes. So that's why I didn't take the perfume. Not much use to me. The girl... Ellie, she *asked* if she could have it, so I gave it to her.'

'I see.'

More note-scribbling. Charlie wished he could see what she was writing.

'How is she?'

The detective looked up.

'She's stable. She's obviously distraught. The substance

caused considerable damage to her skin. It's not particularly pleasant for her.'

Charlie swallowed. Why did he feel like he was being interrogated? He hadn't done anything.

'Do you know what it was yet?'

'Sulphuric acid. Probably common DIY-store drain cleaner. You can pick it up anywhere for a few quid. Nasty stuff in the wrong hands.'

She looked up from her pad, making eye contact with Charlie. Her face deadpan. Her cocoa-brown skin smooth, reflecting the sunlight that streamed in through the window.

'Is there anything else you'd like to tell me, Mr Carter? Anything that might help us?'

Charlie shook his head.

'Nothing?'

'No.'

'Right. We will have the bottle sent to forensics. Hopefully, we'll be able to lift a print from it, or some other DNA. Should shed a little more light on this situation, don't you think?'

She paused, looking at Charlie again for a reaction.

She didn't get one, so she continued.

'Do you have any idea why anyone would be sending a bottle of sulphuric acid disguised as perfume, into you at your place of work?'

'They didn't. Not to me directly anyway... it was sent to the office.'

'Really?'

'Yeah.'

'Because we spoke to the bloke who deals with the mail, and he told us categorically that he would never put random stuff on somebody's desk. Only personally-addressed letters would end up on their desk. Anything else goes to a different pile.'

Charlie swallowed hard. His mouth and throat were parched.

'Then he must have made a mistake. He's human. It happens. Can I get a drink, please?'

'Sure, it's your apartment.'

Charlie stood and walked to the open-plan kitchen at the opposite side of the room. He turned on the tap, grabbing a glass from the draining board. He filled the glass, knocked it back, filling it again. He returned to his seat slowly.

'I'd like to remind you, Mr Carter, that lying to a police officer investigating a crime is an offence punishable by law. A very serious incident has occurred here. May I also remind you that an innocent girl has been permanently disfigured. If you know anything, you need to tell me.'

Charlie took another sip of water, stalling. Her eyes didn't leave his face.

'It's my wife,' he said finally.

'Your wife?'

'Yep. I think maybe... the perfume might have been meant for her.'

'Why would you think that?'

'Because of something that happened in her past. We suspect someone is targeting her.'

'Okay, and your wife's name is?'

The detective lifted her hand and tucked a lock of curly black hair behind her ear.

'Beth. Her maiden name was Morton. But back then she was Kitty. Kitty Briscoe.'

43

Hot water spilled into the bathtub, mixing with scented oils, and the soothing fragrance of eucalyptus and rosemary filled Beth's nostrils. She couldn't stop thinking about her confrontation with Vicky in the office. Something had changed. She was being more threatening. More aggressive.

Beth left the bath to run, tying her robe around her, she made her way downstairs to refill her wine. She topped up her glass, placing the bottle back on the worktop. Turning to head back upstairs, she spun around at the last minute, grabbing it. She sipped, and the cool amber liquid flowed down her throat. As she drank, she tried to picture her life as it had been only a few weeks earlier.

How different everything was now. She would never have believed her life, which she had so meticulously crafted, could fall apart so quickly. It had all begun around about the same time that Vicky started at Greys. Those two things could not be coincidence.

She was dangerous. Beth was sure of it.

But why? What did any of this have to do with a girl who

wouldn't even have been born when Billy Noakes was murdered?

Beth took another sip, ambling into Peter's room to retrieve his speakers. She searched under dirty laundry, old plates and general teenager junk. She found them beside the bed on the floor, hidden beneath some boxers which she hoped to God were clean. Returning to the bathroom, she opened the door as wide as it would go, propping it with a heavy ornament from the sideboard.

Flicking the speakers on, she paired her phone with them and turned the volume up as loud as it would go, placing them on the windowsill.

She scrolled through her music, searching for something appropriate, settling for a *chilled moods* playlist.

The first song was Debussy's 'Clare De Lune', and Beth smiled to herself. It had always been one of her mother's favourites.

Placing her glass on the floor beside her, she untied her robe, slipping it off her shoulders, letting it fall down. She tested the water with her hand, then placed one foot into the tub, then the other. She slowly lowered herself down with her back to the door, wincing as the hot, scented water stung her skin.

But it felt good.

The aromas swirled around her head with the steam, and she closed her eyes, allowing herself to relax for the first time in weeks. She clutched her glass, taking a large sip, then lay back into the tub.

The haunting melody blasted out, slightly tinny, but endlessly beautiful.

Vicky's face flashed into her mind. Her frumpy clothes, her irritating smile.

Beth clenched her fist around the stem of the glass as the feelings consumed her.

She blinked it away, taking another gulp of wine.

A creak from the landing drew her attention. She peered awkwardly over her shoulder, through the vapour rising from the surface. She'd left Peter's bedroom door open. It had caught in the breeze from an open window, blowing open further.

She slid back down into the water.

She wanted to wash the day away, the hotter the better.

Her phone buzzed from the floor beside the bath. She reached down, grabbing it, wiping her hand on a towel to read the message.

It was from Mikey.

Hey. Are you ghosting me?

Beth sat staring at the phone for a moment, considering her response.

No. Been busy.

Mikey's reply came straight away.

Can I see you?

Beth didn't want to lead him on. She'd behaved inappropriately. She hadn't been in her right mind at the weekend, reeling from the shock of the dog, and Charlie walking out. She was drunk, and upset, and she had wanted to live someone else's life for a moment.

She'd regretted it instantly.

I don't think that's a good idea.

Why?

You know why.

I need to see you.

No.

Beth tossed her phone on top of her robe and sunk back down, closing her eyes. As she dipped her head right under the water, the muted sound of the music rippled in her ears, distorted and ghostly. She opened her eyes and they stung a little from the oils. She stared straight up to the skylight above her. It was dark outside, so all she could see was her own reflection staring back at her, naked and reclining. Her hair splayed out around her in the water like weeds in a lake. She exhaled, screwing her eyes tightly shut once more, wishing she could sink down further, beyond the base of the tub, away from this place. Away from this life. She exhaled the air from her lungs steadily, bubbles rising up above her head.

And then she remembered Daisy. Her pure, perfect little Daisy. And that was enough to will her to stay and fight.

She raised her head above the surface, pushing her hands up over her face and through her hair, pressing the excess water from it.

She drained the last of the wine, toying with the idea of opening another bottle but deciding against it. She had to work in the morning.

Her phone buzzed again.

'Mikey. Please leave me alone,' she whispered to the empty house.

The next song boomed from the speakers. A nineties trip-hop tune, which she remembered, but the name of which eluded her.

She and Charlie had danced to it in a club when they had

first started dating. She smiled at the memory, wondering if she would ever dance with him again.

She sighed, reaching down to the floor to retrieve her phone. The message wasn't from Mikey.

Her heart thumped as she opened it.

A picture filled her screen.

Despite the temperature of the bath, she shivered.

It was the front of her house, snapped from right outside.

She sat up, turning around to see behind her.

No movement through the steam. Nothing untoward. No dark figure lurking outside the door in the clouds of white.

The phone buzzed again in her hand. She glanced down, holding her breath.

A series of images filled her message inbox.

As she began to scroll through them, Beth felt panic spread over her.

She saw herself, a few minutes earlier, slipping the robe from her shoulders. Then in another, standing naked in the bathroom. She felt sick as she stared at a photo of herself testing the water with her hand.

All shot from inside the house. From the landing. She spun round again, staring out into the darkness. Trying to figure out the vantage point from which images had been snapped.

Someone had been near the top of the stairs, watching her.

The phone buzzed once more.

Another picture.

Beth naked, her head under the water, eyes screwed shut. Her hair splayed out around her, bubbles rising to the surface. Taken from above her. The bastard had been standing next to the bath.

It would have been beautiful if it hadn't been so damn terrifying.

She sprang up, grabbing her robe, covering herself. She slipped it on quickly as she tiptoed out of the bathroom.

The hypnotic beat faded out, and another song began.

Beethoven's 'Moonlight Sonata' echoed around the house. Beth stopped the music from her phone.

It buzzed again.

Another picture. Beth sitting up in the bath, looking at her screen.

'I'm calling the police!' Beth screamed out into the darkness.

Her phone vibrated in her hand.

No you won't.

'I will!' she screeched. 'I'm dialling right now, so you better get out of my house! You hear me?'

She heard the front door clatter against the hall wall. She ran down the stairs. A blast of icy air against her hot flesh made her feel dizzy.

She rushed into the kitchen, grabbing a carving knife from the block on the counter. Holding it out in front of her, arm trembling, she edged forwards.

'Hello?' Beth shouted.

Silence.

She moved slowly towards the front of the house, standing at the perimeter, looking out into the drive. The security light was on. No movement. She shivered.

Her breath swirled in patterns, mixing with the steam rising from her hot, wet flesh. She stepped out, wincing, as the gravel dug into her bare feet. She hopped backwards onto the carpet.

Shutting herself in, she slid the chain in place.

But what if he's still inside? she thought, turning her back to the wall, knife held out ahead. She did a quick scout of the ground floor. Satisfied all the rooms were empty, she made her way up the stairs. Daisy's room first. All as it should be. Peter's room was still empty. She stuck her head in. Just to be sure. She pushed her own bedroom door, and it creaked open.

An emerald-green scarf sat neatly folded in the middle of her bed. She recognised it immediately.

The last time she saw it, it had been bound in a knot around Zoe's neck, under the floorboards in the barn.

44

Beth didn't go to work the following day. She'd hardly slept. She sat in bed all night, clutching a knife to her chest. In the morning, she phoned her boss, claiming to have a migraine. Chloe wished her a speedy recovery, and the deed was done. Beth had called in sick when she wasn't, for the first time in her life. But she felt this warranted it.

She hadn't even showered today. Another first.

As she paced the kitchen, drinking an especially strong coffee, she heard tyres on gravel outside, and she held her breath.

Footsteps crunched across the drive.

She glanced towards the knife beside her on the counter. Picking it up, she tiptoed into the hall, edging her way towards the door.

A dark figure approached the glass. The sound of a key in the lock.

Beth stood silently, raising her weapon aloft, ready to swipe at her attacker. The door swung open and Beth took a step forward.

Charlie stood in the doorway. The blade clattered to the floor.

'Charlie! What are you doing here?'

'Jesus Christ, Beth! What's going on? Are you okay?'

'Not really. Why are you here?'

Charlie picked up the knife, pushing the door closed behind him. He placed a hand on Beth's shoulder and guided her back down the hall into the kitchen.

'Is there any more of that?' Charlie nodded towards the coffee.

Beth poured him a cup, sliding it across the worktop.

'I went to your office, they told me you were sick.'

'Right.'

'So what's going on?'

Beth fished her mobile out of her dressing-gown pocket and unlocked it, presenting Charlie with the messages from the previous evening.

'My God...' Charlie whispered. He swiped the screen.

'He was in here. With me. And I didn't know. I've not slept at all. I'm so scared, Charlie.'

She looked at her husband. Her eyes were red-ringed, dark circles beneath them.

'I know. I am too. Something happened at work.'

'To you?'

'Sort of... not really.'

Beth frowned. Charlie relayed the incident with the perfume. Her face contorted in an expression of horror as he reached the ending.

'Charlie, that's awful.'

'It was meant for you.'

He handed Beth his phone, showing her the message he received. She passed it back without saying a word.

'There's more,' Charlie mumbled.

Beth waited.

'You're not going to like it. At all.'

'What?'

'I had a visit from the police because I was the one who had given the girl the bottle. They asked me all sorts of questions. I tried to lie to them, Beth, I did, I swear. But she knew I wasn't telling the truth... the way she looked at me. You should have seen it.'

Beth reached her hand out, gently stroking Charlie's fingers on the counter.

'They said they would probably find fingerprints. They thought I had something to do with it. I'm so sorry.'

Beth's eyes narrowed.

'Charlie, what did you do?'

The room was quiet.

'I told them.'

'Told them what?'

'They were pressing me, threatening me. They said I could be arrested if I was lying. She knew, Beth.'

'Charlie, please tell me you didn't.'

There was a lengthy pause.

'I told them who you are.'

Beth pulled her hand away. The sound of the morning news on the radio drifted away from her ears, and for a moment, all she could hear was the twittering of some sparrows from the garden, without a care in the world. She wished she could be a bird, and fly away into the distance. Her face felt hot, her heart pounded.

'How could you do that to me?'

'It was the police, Beth. You can't expect me to lie to the police.'

'Do you realise what you've done? My life is over. Everything I have fought so hard to build here, from scratch, it's all ruined.

Do you understand that? Our lives are over. Mine, yours, Peter's and Daisy's. There's no coming back from this.'

She stood up and paced.

'Beth, this is a good thing. The secret's out now. You won't have to pretend anymore.'

'It wasn't your secret to tell!' Beth screamed at Charlie across the kitchen. 'It was mine; you hear me. My secret!'

'No more lying. No more pretending.'

'And you think that's a good thing, do you?'

'Well–'

'No, Charlie, its most definitely *not*. I've been through this many times. I've lived so many lives, I can't even begin to tell you. It always ends the same way when people find out. Trust me.'

Charlie lowered his head.

'I can't believe you've done this to me ... to *us*. Do you realise you've ruined everything, you stupid, stupid man!'

Charlie stood up, walking round the island to stand beside her. He reached his hand out towards her arm, but she slapped it away.

'Why don't we wait and see what happens. Maybe it won't get out.'

Beth laughed.

'Of course it will. People hate *her*. They despise Kitty Briscoe. They blame her for what happened to Billy Noakes as much as they blame Kieran Taylor. And they're right. I *am* responsible. It was my fault. I took him. If I hadn't... maybe Billy would be alive now, with a family of his own.'

Charlie grabbed Beth, she tried to force him away, but he pulled her close to him, hugging her head into his chest.

'No, Beth. It wasn't your fault. You were a little girl. You can't have known.'

'Can't I? Really? Because I look at Daisy, I watch her, how she behaves, and I think she is definitely capable of making decisions. She knows right from wrong. So I must have done too. I was a year older than her! I would have known it was wrong to lure that poor little boy away from his mother.'

Beth sobbed uncontrollably. Charlie stroked her head.

'He was two years old for Christ's sake. A baby! I go over this every single day of my life. I think about it. It's all such a blur. I barely remember it. Of course, I've read the stories so often that I feel like they are my truth, but I was seven. Can you really recall specific things that occurred when you were that young?'

Beth stopped rambling. She stood, hugging Charlie, letting him hug her. Crying into his shirt.

'What if I'm a bad person, Charlie. What if there's something evil in me? And I've passed it on to our kids somehow.'

'You're not a bad person, Beth. You're... amazing. And look at those kids. They don't have a bad bone in their bodies. So you can stop worrying about that. They are perfect, both of them.'

'But–'

'But nothing, Beth. You know it.'

They stood in the kitchen together. No words between them. Only love and support in an endless void of nothing. Charlie held his wife, and she let him.

With the sound of Beth's sobs filling the house, as if years of sorrow were pouring out of her, seeping from every inch of her, they stood like that for a long while, until Beth pulled away. She wiped her eyes, and suddenly she was calm, collected, the familiar Beth again. The emotion gone.

'So what do we do now?' she finally asked.

'We need to find out who is doing this to us.'

'And then what?'

'And then we get the bastard.'

45

Charlie had stayed with her until lunchtime, but eventually made his excuses and left. He told Beth not to worry, they'd get through this.

She wasn't so sure.

He seemed optimistic. But Beth had been here many times; experienced the hatred once people discovered who she was.

This was Charlie's first time, she couldn't blame him for not understanding. But she couldn't shake the overwhelming sense of foreboding that consumed her. It always ended the same way. With her leaving. Starting again somewhere new. It was easier in the past. She had no ties, no family. Packing a bag and moving was simple. But now, with Charlie, Peter and Daisy, things were different.

She had allowed herself to believe she could live this life. She had foolishly thought she was safe. But deep down she'd always known that it could all come crashing around her. She had learned from her mistakes.

Don't confide. Trust no one. Never allow yourself to get too close.

And the last time, when she ran away to university here in

Brighton, she had fully intended to live by those rules. But then she met Charlie. Big, handsome Charlie, with his kind face and goofy smile.

Of course she was attracted to him, *everybody* was. But she had convinced herself that happiness wasn't written into her storyline. So she told him no.

Over and over she declined his advances. And sometimes she even meant it. But he wouldn't give up.

He followed her. He hounded her. She'd look up and there he'd be, grinning at her. She would pretend not to notice. She didn't want to lead him on.

But he wore her down. Chipped away.

These days, snowflakes would probably call it stalking.

It's hard being a loner. Being nineteen and watching everyone around you make new pals, form relationships. Meet their *one*. While the whole time, you isolate, you go home to an empty flat, you eat microwave meals alone.

So when one day in the library, Charlie asked her again to go for a drink, she thought, *what the hell, why not?*

They could be friends, she supposed, perhaps naively. And the rest, as they say, is history.

Peter had been unplanned. They weren't even married at that point. A quick trip to the registry office soon fixed that. No fuss. No guests. Charlie's parents had been furious.

Peter may not have been planned, but he *was* loved. Beth was overjoyed. She hadn't ever factored children into her future. Didn't dare. She had never known it was possible to love something as much. And then a few years later, when Daisy came along, Beth felt complete. She would sit and watch her family, her beautiful, perfect family, and she couldn't believe how things had turned out. If you had told her seven-year-old self that she would have all this one day, she would never have believed it. There were times when self-doubt took over, and she convinced herself she didn't deserve this life. But as time went on, she grew to accept that she just might.

Her mother warned her. 'Don't you *ever* have children, Kitty. You're not the mothering kind.'

But her mother was wrong. Beth loved her kids. There was nothing that she wouldn't do to protect them. She thought of Daisy, then glanced at the clock. 3pm.

If she left now, she might get to the school in time to see her before Charlie arrived.

Be able to talk to her. To touch her.

She grabbed her keys from the hall table, rushing out to the car.

When she pulled up outside the school gates, the usual array of mothers, and the odd father, were milling around. Some with dogs. Some in posh cars.

She parked up and sat, waiting.

Julia, Daisy's friend's mother was standing by the gate, chatting to another mum who Beth didn't recognise.

Julia glanced up in Beth's direction. Beth waved, smiling.

Julia didn't wave back. She frowned, then turned away, whispering something to her companion. The woman turned, looking at Beth over her shoulder.

And so it begins, Beth thought.

She saw the kids starting to pile out into the playground, so she climbed out of her car, approaching the gate.

Daisy's friend Isla came skipping up to Julia, who crouched down, enveloping her daughter in a huge hug.

'Hi, Isla, hi, Julia!' Beth shouted as she strolled towards them, beaming.

Julia straightened up. Taking Isla's hand, she hurried off in the opposite direction without saying a word. The woman Julia had been talking to shuffled away from Beth.

'Mummy!'

The sound of Daisy's excited voice made Beth forget about the shun. She turned, smiling towards the playground. Daisy was hurtling at her, carrying a piece of paper. Her rucksack, almost as big as she was, bouncing around on her back.

'I've missed you so much! Look! I did a picture of you. I put Cooper in it too, because I miss him as well.'

Beth crouched down and Daisy handed the masterpiece to her. Splodges of multicoloured paint adorned the crumpled sheet. The odd bit of glitter.

An artist, Daisy was *not*.

'Are we going home, Mummy? I don't like staying at Uncle Derek's.'

'No, love, I've come to say hello. Your dad will be here soon to pick you up.'

Daisy stuck out her bottom lip, folding her arms across her chest.

Beth glanced up. Groups of nervous parents, some who she knew, others she didn't, were watching her warily. Holding their children close.

What did they think? That Beth would snatch one of their kids and run off with them? Maybe butcher them somewhere?

She straightened up, returning their stares. She would not be bullied. Not this time.

'Hi, Mandy. How's things?' she shouted towards one group.

No response. An icy glare.

She noticed a father shoot her a look, before rushing across the playground into the school building.

Ignore them, Beth thought. It's funny. That was the advice her mother had always given her as a kid. As if it was that easy.

Beth held her head high.

'Daisy, I want you to promise me something.'

'Yes, Mummy?'

'Whatever you might hear, if people say things about me, bad things, promise me you will always remember that Mummy loves you, very, very much. And nothing will ever change that. Okay?'

'Are you all right, Mummy? You look sad.'

Beth lowered herself beside her daughter again, and Daisy placed a hand on her shoulder gently, melting her heart.

'I'm fine, darling. Just promise me.'

'I promise. I love you too.'

Daisy hugged Beth and her heart felt as if it were splitting in two.

'Excuse me, Mrs Carter, may I have a word please?'

Beth straightened to see Mrs Everson, the headmistress, rushing in her direction across the playground. The father who had no doubt reported her, skulked away back to his family, not daring to look at Beth.

'Daisy, why don't you go and play? Daddy will be here soon to pick you up,' Beth said softly to her daughter. Daisy obediently skipped off towards a group of girls, a plethora of plaits and pigtails.

'Mrs Carter, it has come to my attention... that is, a parent has voiced concerns... I mean...'

Mrs Everson was becoming increasingly flustered. Beth tried not to smile.

'Are you okay, Mrs Everson?'

'Yes. I'm fine. But I think, you know, under the circumstances... that it might not be appropriate for you to be on school grounds anymore.'

Beth fixed her with an unfaltering stare.

'And which circumstances would those be?' She wanted to hear her say it out loud.

To her face.

The teacher's cheeks flushed as she averted Beth's gaze.

'Do you really need me to spell it out?'

'Yes. I think I do.'

She leaned closer, conspiratorially.

'We know who you are,' she whispered. As if she were afraid that even saying the name would bring some curse or plague on her.

Beth cleared her throat.

'May I remind you I was unanimously acquitted by a jury. I was seven. I made a mistake, and I did something wrong. But I am by no means responsible for the actions of Kieran Taylor. I was not a party to it, and I do not condone it. I have spent my entire life feeling guilty about what happened to that little boy, but let's put things into perspective, shall we?'

Beth's voice grew louder. Mrs Everson looked uncomfortable, glancing around at the gathering crowds of parents.

'I have successfully raised two children, without killing either of them. I have been a model citizen since that day. Haven't even picked up a parking fine. I have gone out of my way to make sure I live a good, honest life. I know this won't change what I did, or bring Billy Noakes back. But I have done nothing to you people. I don't deserve to be treated like this.'

'Mrs Carter, can you please keep your voice down? You're upsetting the children.'

Kids of varying ages stood with their parents, looking worried. Daisy and her group of friends had stopped chatting.

Beth considered screaming at them all. Telling them all to get lost. But she knew that would do no good. It would only make things more difficult for Daisy.

'Please can you leave? I think it would be best for everyone if you refrain from coming here from now on.'

Beth's head snapped towards the teacher, who visibly shrunk away, terrified.

'Fine, I'll go. But let me tell you this; I will not be alienated from my daughter because *you* feel uncomfortable around me.'

She marched to her car and climbed in, driving away from the school. As she glanced in her mirror, she saw Daisy standing at the gate staring after her.

46

Peter was sitting on the doorstep when Beth arrived home, his chin resting on his balled-up fists, looking extremely sorry for himself.

It was nice to see him without his phone.

Beth pulled on the handbrake as Peter stood up, dusting himself off. Guessing the news of her identity had reached him, she prepared herself for what was about to come her way.

She climbed out of the car.

'I forgot my key,' Peter said glumly as Beth approached the house.

'Does your dad know you're here?'

'No.'

Beth unlocked the door, standing to one side. Peter loitered for a moment, as if he was nervous to step inside, then crossed the threshold. He trudged down the hallway into the kitchen, throwing his school bag onto the floor.

He slumped down onto a stool at the breakfast bar.

'Is it true?'

'Peter, look–'

'Is it true, Mum? Did you kill a kid?'

Beth wasn't ready for that.

'No, Peter! Of course I didn't. Do you honestly have to ask me that?'

'That's what people are saying. Alex says his dad told him you killed this boy years ago and got away with it.'

Beth slid onto a stool beside her son.

'Peter, that's not what happened. When I was seven, I made a mistake–'

'Yeah, I've googled it, Mum. I know the official story. I'm asking you, did you do it?'

Beth stared at her son. His frankness impressed her.

'No. I didn't.'

'Does Dad know?'

'Yes.'

'Is that why we're not living here?'

'Yes. Sort of.'

'And is that why Cooper got... hurt?'

'I think so.'

'That note, the one that came through the door the other weekend. That was meant for you, wasn't it?'

'Looks like it.'

Peter sat fidgeting with his hands for a while, peeling bits of flaky dry skin from the ends of his fingertips, exposing pink flesh underneath.

Beth didn't know what to say. The look on his face, he was disappointed. He was clearly struggling with the version of his mother that he knew and loved, versus the version of his mother people were gossiping about.

The child killer.

'Do you want me to explain it from my side? In my own words?'

'No. I don't want to think about it. About you... doing *that*.'

'Okay. I understand.'

Beth reached her hand out to stroke Peter's hair. He flinched, moving his head away.

Beth stood, filling the kettle and flicking it on. She turned her back to hide the hurt on her face. Her son was afraid of her.

'Who's doing this to us?' Peter asked finally.

'I don't know.'

'Do you think it's that Kieran guy?'

'It could be. He got a new identity after he was released from prison. I don't know where he is.'

'Seems like you really shafted him. He didn't say anything under caution. You told them everything. He would have plenty of reasons to want revenge. Eight years' worth of reasons.'

'I didn't shaft anyone. I told the police what happened. Kieran Taylor killed a child. He deserved to go to jail for that. He didn't speak during the interview because he's a psychopath. He didn't feel the need to defend his horrendous actions.'

'I'm just saying. If you're trying to narrow down a list of suspects, you could do worse than looking at him. Or maybe Billy Noakes' mother. Although she'd be too old by now, so that's unlikely.'

'She's in her fifties. That's not old.'

'Yeah, I guess, but I doubt it's her. I think it's a man.'

'What makes you say that?'

Peter paused for a moment, considering the question.

'The dog. Pretty nasty. It has to be a man.'

'You don't think a woman is capable of that?'

'Yeah, but statistically it's more likely to be a man.'

Something about Peter's matter-of-fact tone made Beth uncomfortable.

'Do you want some lunch?' she asked.

'No thanks. Not hungry. So what's Dad saying about it?'

'Obviously he's upset.'

'You think?'

'But I'm sure we will sort it out. He's keeping away more to protect you and Daisy than because of anything I've done.'

'Are we in danger?'

Beth considered lying but thought better of it. Peter wasn't stupid.

'I don't know, Peter. But given what's been happening, we feel it's better to be safe than sorry.'

Peter nodded. As he looked towards his mother, then past her out into the hall. He blinked, his eyes widened. He stood up and marched out of the kitchen. Beth followed the direction of his gaze. He stopped next to the coat hook in the hall. Staring at the emerald-green scarf. Beth pretended not to notice.

'Where did you get this?'

'What, love?'

'This scarf. It looks exactly like one that Zoe wears... it's her mum's... but she... borrows it sometimes. She likes it cos it matches her eyes.'

Beth was about to make up some lie about it being Margot's when Peter leaned forward, pulling the scarf to his nose.

He inhaled deeply, eyes closed tight.

'My God. It *is* Zoe's. It smells of her. Why do you have this?'

Peter plucked the scarf from the hook, storming back to Beth's side.

'Mum? Why do you have Zoe's scarf?'

'I found it when I was tidying up. It was getting crumpled, and it felt expensive. It's silk! I brought it down to hang it up.'

Peter looked at his mother with narrowed eyes. Beth hoped her face wouldn't give her away.

'Are you sure it belongs to Zoe?' Beth asked nonchalantly.

'Yep. One hundred per cent.'

'Could you do me a favour? Can you take this scarf with you and show it to your dad? Tell him where you found it and tell him it's Zoe's.'

'Why?'

'Because I'm asking you to. He'll know why.'

Beth looked away, as red blotches began to spread up her neck. She wanted to tell Peter about Zoe, but how could she? She hadn't told the police. A decision she was beginning to regret. Charlie had maintained she had imagined it, convinced her they would want proof. And there was none. Just the word of a hysterical drunk lady. Who was on trial for murder when she was a child.

So she kept quiet, knowing that when her son found out the truth, it may destroy her relationship with him forever.

And it *was* a matter of when, not if.

Beth stroked Peter's shoulder.

'Come on, I'll give you a lift back.'

She watched sadly as he headed out towards the front door, then she followed him to the car.

He would have to find out about Zoe.

But not yet.

47

B eth's office was situated above an antiques shop among a labyrinth of narrow lanes in Brighton. From outside, you'd be forgiven for thinking it was a small, bohemian type of business. But once you crossed the boundary of the old wooden front door, you were greeted with glass, stainless steel and a gleaming interior. Although the building was narrow, it went back across a few shops, and occupied three floors upwards.

This was precisely the look Chloe Grey had wanted to create when she paid her architect husband a small fortune to remodel the office.

Greys was one of the city's hidden gems. Beth often felt immensely lucky when she was at work.

She swiped her pass at the front door, and the entry system beeped.

The door didn't open.

She frowned, swiping it again. Nothing.

She pressed the buzzer.

'Hello?' The receptionist's nasal voice crackled through the intercom.

'Hi, it's Beth Carter from submissions. My pass doesn't seem to be working.'

A long pause, an ominous crackling as Beth waited, unsure what was going on.

'One moment, please.'

Beth stood fiddling with her hair. She checked her watch and tutted.

'I'll buzz you in, if you could come to reception.'

Beth frowned again. The door clicked and she pushed it inwards. She stepped inside the narrow entrance hallway and climbed the spiral staircase to the first floor.

Lola, the young receptionist, sat behind her desk, looking daggers at Beth as she approached. Without saying a word, she picked up her phone and jabbed at the keypad.

'Yes, she's here now. Okay, I'll let her know.'

She placed the receiver back down.

'Ms Grey will be with you in a moment. Take a seat.'

She nodded towards a sleek, white leather sofa against the far wall. Beth raised her eyebrow, but the receptionist simply looked away, and tapped at her keyboard.

Beth perched on the edge of a cushion, her unease filling her mind like a storm cloud, growing with every second she was forced to wait.

The sound of stilettos clicking on the polished wooden floor drew Beth's attention down the corridor. Chloe was marching towards her, wearing a bright-red trouser suit, with a white blouse underneath. She didn't smile. No warm greeting.

'Beth, come down to my office.'

Beth stood, following Chloe. As she passed the floor-to-ceiling glass panels that separated the main office, she noticed people watching her. She saw Vicky, leaning on the edge of her desk, twiddling with her greasy hair. She smiled, but didn't wave.

It was definitely *not* a friendly smile. It was smug. Victorious.

Beth looked away, entering Chloe's office.

'Close the door.' Chloe's tone was off, terse.

Beth did as she was told. Chloe sat behind her computer. Beth approached the chair on the other side.

'No, don't sit. This won't take long,' Chloe barked.

'What's going on, Chloe? Is everything okay?' Beth suspected she already knew, but she had to play the game.

'No, Beth. Or should I call you Kitty? Which would you prefer?'

Beth's face flushed, but she didn't look away.

'You heard then,' Beth said. A statement rather than a question.

'Of course I heard. The whole bloody company has heard. Christ, it's been all over the socials. I'd be surprised if there's anyone in the country who doesn't know.'

'Chloe let me explain–'

'No. You let me explain. I won't waste either of our time here. Your services with us are no longer required, with immediate effect. You can collect your belongings if you want, or I can have them mailed to you if you would prefer.'

Beth clenched her jaw.

'Excuse me?'

'You heard. You're fired. I want you off the premises. Leave your pass with Lola on the way out.'

'But... you can't do that! You have no grounds.'

'I think you'll find I can.' She picked a pile of papers up from her desk.

'I have here your application form, along with the details you submitted to Human Resources on your first day.'

Chloe slid the documents towards Beth.

'That *is* your signature, is it not?'

Beth nodded.

'And there, in the top left-hand corner of your contract, what does that say?' Chloe pointed an immaculately-manicured, glossy scarlet nail at Beth's name, tapping it twice. The sound seemed to echo around the room.

'It says Beth Carter.'

'Yes. And is your name not in fact *Kitty* Carter?'

'No, I–'

'There is no record of you *legally* changing it. I had Margot check.'

'No, I... I didn't.'

'So you lied. When you applied for this job, you lied about who you are.'

'No–'

'You lied, Beth. And therefore the contract is null and void. You fraudulently gained employment at my company using a false identity.'

Chloe picked the papers up, tossing them across the desk at Beth. They scattered to the carpet around her feet.

'This isn't fair!' Beth shouted. 'I've given you everything. I have gone above and beyond time and again, cancelled holidays, put you first over my family. I have bent over backwards to be a model employee and help you make money! And this is how you repay me? Look at me, Chloe. I'm your friend. It's me!'

Beth placed her hands on Chloe's desk, staring straight into her eyes.

Chloe cleared her throat.

'We are a family company. We have a reputation to uphold. I can't risk it getting out that... *you* work for us. Now I suggest you get out of my office, before I have you thrown out.'

Beth turned, storming out of the room. She marched down the corridor. As she reached the top of the stairs, Lola bounced up from behind her desk.

'Er, your pass!' she yelled irritably, with the assumed authority that only a receptionist can believe herself to hold.

Beth ignored her, carried on walking, blocking out the shouts of protest.

She ran down the spiral staircase and exited the building, slamming the door hard behind her. She turned, kicking it, much to the bewilderment of the passing tourists.

'Fuck you!' she screamed at the building.

She turned and hurried down the lane, her eyes stinging.

'Beth!'

A voice called after her. She ignored it, carried on walking. A hand suddenly gripped her shoulder, spinning her around. Margot stood in front of her. Beth couldn't read her expression.

She stared, ready for the insults.

Instead, Margot grabbed her, pulling her into a hug. The familiar scent of Margot's perfume filled Beth's nostrils, and she relaxed into the embrace.

'Are you okay?' Margot asked.

Beth shrugged.

'I can't quite... I mean, I don't really know what to say.' It was rare for Margot to be lost for words.

'I'm sorry, Margot, I really am.'

Margot pursed her lips.

'You've nothing to apologise to me for. I'll be honest, I did wonder after you told me what was going on the other night, but it was a shock. But, darling, come on, it was a long time ago. I am here for you, no matter what.'

Beth nodded.

'Chloe fired me.'

'I know. I'm sorry. She made me look into your contract, I had no choice. My hands were tied. I've got to get back, but don't worry. You'll get through this. If you need any legal advice, you can call me, any time. Okay?'

Margot hugged her again, then turned and tottered off back down the alley towards the office.

Beth sighed. She'd half expected this. It had been such a long time since it had happened that she'd almost forgotten how much it hurt.

The rejection. The vitriol. Friends turning their backs on you. Disowning you. These things had made Beth the woman she was today. Whether or not that was a good thing, she wasn't sure.

As the smell of Margot's perfume dissipated, Beth made a decision. She had to pay someone a visit. Someone she hadn't seen for a long time. She pulled her phone from her bag and typed the name into a search engine.

She was easy enough to find.

48

She still resided in Birmingham. Surprisingly, the same area. Perhaps she cherished the memories? She lived in a bigger house now, a nicer street. But she hadn't moved far in over thirty years, compared to how much Beth's life had changed in that time; the distance she had come.

Finding her general location had been the straightforward part. Getting an address had proven trickier. It had taken a few phone calls, and a fair bit of cash, but Beth had eventually found what she was looking for. She'd been so bloody-minded when she decided to do this. But now, sitting outside the house, Beth wasn't feeling quite so brave.

She deliberated for well over an hour, and on more than one occasion she nearly started the engine and drove away. But the time had come. Beth finally had to face her demons, whether she liked it or not.

She locked her car, and slowly forced herself through the gate, and along the path. As she approached the door, a mixture of feelings swam around her head.

Trepidation.

Sorrow.

Feeling a knot in the pit of her stomach as she got closer, she was unsure when she last felt so nervous.

The garden was immaculate. The lawn mowed neatly in wide stripes. An abundance of rose bushes lined the perimeter, the blooms now past their best, but still pretty. Their perfume filled the air, reminding Beth of her mother. Smiling sadly, she reached the front door, resisting the urge to run away. Suddenly feeling seven years old again. She wanted to vomit but held it back. She had known this would be difficult, but she hadn't prepared herself fully for it.

Now or never.

She pressed the doorbell and a loud chime rang out from within the house. Beth swallowed hard. After some time, the door slowly opened.

Wendy Noakes had hardly changed at all.

She looked older, yes. But Beth recognised her straight away. She saw a flash in the woman's eyes and wondered if Wendy knew her too. Beth had picked up a cheap pair of thick-framed reading glasses and scraped her hair up into a tight bun. She hoped this was enough of a disguise. She was about to find out.

'Mrs Noakes?'

The woman stared at Beth blankly without replying.

'Wendy Noakes?'

'Yes.'

Beth flashed her staff lanyard, not giving her time to see it properly.

'My name is Celia Walsh. I'm from the council. May I come in, please?'

The Birmingham accent she had tried so hard to get rid of over the years, came easily back to her.

Wendy Noakes frowned.

'What's this about?'

Beth had found several social media posts from Wendy,

voicing pejorative opinions about bin collections, or lack of. Beth was clutching at straws, but she needed something to convince Wendy she was there in an official capacity, just long enough to get inside.

'I understand you've been having some issues with your bins not being emptied?'

Wendy paused, narrowing her eyes.

'Yes, but–'

'We take these complaints extremely seriously, Mrs Noakes. I'd like to get some information for my investigation.'

'The bloke I spoke to on the phone didn't seem to give a toss.'

'He passed your complaint on to me, and I have decided to investigate further. The last thing we want is vermin infesting the streets. Wouldn't you agree?'

'No, quite. You'd better come in.'

She stood to one side, allowing Beth to step in.

Tastefully decorated. Neutral, but clean and bright. An overpowering floral air freshener assaulted Beth's nostrils as she entered the house. A stark contrast to the scent of the roses from the garden.

Wendy Noakes traversed the hallway into a large open-plan kitchen.

'Would you like a cuppa?'

'Yes please, that would be wonderful.'

She busied herself opening cupboards, pulling out mugs and a jar of coffee.

Beth glanced around the room. To her left, beside the door she had entered through, was an old-fashioned Welsh dresser overcrowded with photographs.

Centre stage, in an opulent white frame, adorned with flowers, was a picture of Billy. Beth blinked, wanting to shut the image out.

It can't have been taken long before his... *death*. She couldn't bear to look at it.

Wendy handed Beth a cup of coffee, then sat in a wicker rocking chair in the corner. A small ginger cat hopped up onto her lap and began to purr loudly as it arched its back, rubbing itself against Wendy's hand. She stroked it softly, looking at Beth.

'Would you like to sit?' Wendy motioned towards a small sofa a few feet away. Beth nodded, lowering herself onto the plush cushions, pulling a notepad from her handbag for authenticity.

She wasn't ready to come clean. Not yet.

'So I take it this problem has been ongoing for a while now?' Beth asked nervously, feeling ridiculous as the words came out of her mouth.

Wendy stared at her coolly. The cat continued to purr, and for a while it was the only sound in the room. Other than Beth's heart pounding.

'You can cut the charade,' Wendy finally said.

Beth looked up from her pad.

'I know who you are. I knew it the moment I opened the door. I wanted to see how far you'd take it.'

Beth sat silently, looking at the woman. Her face full of sadness. Beth hadn't noticed it at first, too nervous about being recognised. But now, as she *really* took time to see her, it was obvious.

She had lived a life of pain.

'What name do you go by these days?' Wendy asked.

'Beth.'

'A nice name. And why are you here, Beth?'

'I... I felt that it was time.'

Wendy let out a slight laugh. 'Why now?'

'It's not that I haven't wanted to before. I think of you often. Every day, in fact.'

No reply.

'I guess I want to say I'm sorry. For what happened. For... everything.'

'Is that for your benefit or mine?'

Beth looked away.

'I think I owe it to you.'

'And what would you like from me in return? Forgiveness?'

Beth didn't answer.

'Is that why you've come here? To clear your conscience? I know you were very young. You've had an entire lifetime to reflect on what you did. You might not have understood then, that's debatable, but you certainly understand now, I'm sure.'

Beth tried to avert her eyes from the photo of Billy, but kept flicking back to it.

'Beautiful, wasn't he?' Wendy stood from the chair, the cat scurrying out into the hall, and up the stairs. She crossed the room, picking up the frame. She walked to Beth and turned it around to face her. Beth looked away.

'*Look* at him!' Wendy said firmly.

Beth reluctantly obeyed. The face beamed out at her, eyes full of life and happiness. It broke her heart.

'It wasn't only Billy who lost his life that day. What you did, you and Kieran Taylor, you destroyed so many lives. You might not have put a hand to him, but you were as complicit in my mind. My husband and I tried to make things work. To raise our new child together, as best we could, but it wasn't to be. It's hard to recover from... something like that.'

Beth looked up into Wendy's wide, red-ringed eyes.

'You had another baby?'

'Oh yes. I was already pregnant the night you took him. It

was only very early days, so we hadn't told anyone. But Billy knew he was going to have a little sibling. He was so excited.'

Wendy's voice was laced with melancholy, so thick, so strong; it was heartbreaking. She returned the photograph to the dresser, and stood staring at it for a while, her face hidden from Beth.

'But thanks to you my son had to grow up without his big brother.'

Wendy sat back down in the wicker chair, placing her hands on her lap.

'Doug, my husband, he suffered a great deal. Blamed himself. He stayed at home that night watching sport. Convinced himself if he'd been at the fair with us Billy would never have been snatched. I suppose he's probably right. The chances we would have both taken our eyes off him...' She trailed off, looking out into the garden towards a solitary yellow rose bush in the middle of an immaculate lawn.

'That's Billy's. I planted it for him not long after I moved in here. I talk to him all the time, you know. Every day. I tell him how sorry I am. Doug, we lost him to suicide about ten years ago. But we lost him to drink long before that. He was never the same. I couldn't blame him though. How could I? I spent so long thinking it was *me*. My fault. Because I took my eye off him. I let go of his little hand. So many what ifs. What if I'd held on to him? What if that stupid cow from school hadn't distracted me?'

She stopped herself. As if she wanted to say more but wouldn't allow herself. Beth stood up, taking a step towards Wendy's chair.

'Have you got children?' Wendy asked from nowhere.

Beth thought of her beautiful family, averting Wendy's stare.

'Yes. I have a son and a daughter.'

All the colour drained from Wendy's face. Her eyes glazed

over. She seemed to be looking at Beth, but... not. She started to talk again, but Beth felt that she wasn't really talking to *her*.

'They are precious. You know that of course. You never actually understand how much until... until they're gone. You look away for a second. You make a stupid mistake... I made a mistake. There is *evil* lurking everywhere. Sometimes the most nefarious forces can hide beneath a pretty exterior.' She looked directly at Beth, straight into her eyes.

'You assume that other people are good, that they are all kind, like you were raised to be. But they're *not*. And that is the fatal misjudgement that people make.'

'Wendy, please. You mustn't blame yourself. It wasn't your fault.'

Wendy rose suddenly from her chair.

'No, of course it wasn't. It was yours!' she scolded, her voice growing louder.

'How dare you come into my house after all this time and tell me it wasn't my fault. Who do you think you are?' She was getting agitated. Angry.

Wendy stepped towards Beth, jabbing a bony finger painfully into Beth's sternum.

'Did you assume I would absolve you? Is that what you hoped for?'

'No, I thought–'

'Shut up! You've said enough. Now it's my turn. I don't. I know I'm probably supposed to, but I don't forgive you. I will *never*...' She began to sob uncontrollably, her chest, her whole body convulsing.

'Perhaps I should leave.' Beth pivoted, and Wendy shoved her from behind.

'I think you're right. Go on, get out of my house!'

As Wendy jostled Beth towards the door, her gaze drifted one last time to Billy. But something else caught her attention.

She'd been so distracted by the image of Billy that she hadn't noticed it before. She stopped, planted herself firmly to the spot. Reached her hand out, plucking up the small silver-framed photo from the back of the dresser.

'What are you doing? Put that down right now!' Wendy shouted.

Beth stared in horror at the object in her hands.

'Mrs Noakes... who is this?'

She pointed her finger at the man in the photo.

'That's my son. That's Michael.'

Beth swallowed hard.

Michael Noakes.

Or *Mikey*, as Beth knew him.

49

B eth sat in her car. Not ready to drive. Her head spinning. She felt numb.

She didn't know exactly what she had expected from Wendy Noakes. Beth tried to imagine how she would feel if it had been Daisy. If someone had... taken her.

Hurt her.

Worse.

She closed her eyes, trying to shake the thought away. Wendy's hatred was nothing compared to the revelation about Mikey. Beth had avoided looking into the Noakes family. She hadn't wanted to know how those events had damaged them. Ruined them. She suffered enough guilt without reading about their pain. So she simply didn't look.

Ignorance is bliss.

Her phone vibrated in her handbag. She pulled it out.

'Peter, hi, now's not a good time, I–'

'Why did you have Zoe's scarf?'

Beth was taken aback by the venom in her son's voice.

'She must have left it at the house.'

'Bullshit.'

'Peter, what's wrong?'

'Zoe is missing. I thought she was away on a field trip. But she's not. Her parents don't know where she is. She messaged her mum and told her she was staying at a mate's house the night before because it was an early start. She also texted her friends saying she had glandular fever and couldn't make it. Someone has been in contact with her parents the whole time she was supposed to be away. Her mum didn't even realise until today that anything was wrong. Someone's been using her phone so nobody knew.'

Beth felt bile rise up in her throat. She knew he would find out eventually, but she wasn't prepared.

'Peter, I'm sorry, that's... awful. Why don't we meet to talk? I'm driving back from... a work thing. I'll be a few hours, but I can pick you up later.'

'No. You were acting really weird when I told you that scarf was hers. You had this look on your face. I knew something was off at the time.'

'Peter, I can't do this now.'

'Do what? Mum! What the hell is going on? I swear to you, if anything has happened to her, I will never forgive you.'

The line went dead. Beth stared at her phone. A few weeks earlier, she would have told anyone she had the perfect life. She hoped she had finally left the past behind her. It had taken a long time, and yes, perhaps she might not ever be completely free from what happened, but she had settled somewhere. She had a husband. A family.

She was content.

Her father had told her many years ago that she would never be happy; she didn't deserve it. As much as it hurt her to admit, she believed he was right. But she didn't have time to think about her father now. How would she explain this? What would she say?

As soon as she confessed that she had seen Zoe's body in the stable that night, her relationship with her son would be over. She thought of Peter, four years old, learning to swim. Smiling at her from the pool as he splashed about, bright orange armbands flailing.

She pictured the red BMX he had asked for one Christmas when he was small. The sheer joy on his face as he tore the wrapping paper away.

He had been such a beautiful child. She had spent many years worrying something would happen to him. That somebody would find out who she was and hurt him to get at her.

It was crazy, she realised eventually. And as time went by, she relaxed. She never completely let her guard down. She was always vigilant. But she softened. She learned to enjoy her children.

Yes, Peter could be a surly, antisocial teenager at times. But he was *her* surly, antisocial teenager.

She had worked so hard to make sure she didn't lose him.

Now she feared their relationship would be irreparably damaged, and there was nothing she could do about it.

Michael Noakes had found her. He had tricked her. And he had targeted her family.

She shuddered as she remembered kissing him. How could she have been so stupid? All her usual barriers were down. She got drunk, and she allowed herself to be taken in by his good looks and charm. His compliments. Beth had been foolish. It wouldn't happen again. As she sat pondering Michael Noakes, she tried to look at things from his perspective.

A heinous act had torn his family apart. An event that he clearly blamed Beth for, or held her jointly responsible for at least.

She imagined how Peter would react if somebody hurt Daisy.

Would he hunt them down? Spend his entire life searching? Would she condone it?

Beth suddenly thought of the person who had facilitated all this. The person who had recognised her. The individual who all of these events had started with. She felt a terrible anger boiling up inside her. A rage like she had not experienced in decades surged through her. Clenching her fists, she hadn't felt this way since... her father.

She knew what she had to do. She had to find Vicky.

50

The rain ran down the outside of the office window, although rain was an overstatement. It was that drizzly spatter that was colder, more irritating than a heavy downpour. Vicky Kershaw checked her watch.

Five minutes until she clocked off for the day. Great.

She had come into work without a jacket. The September sun had been pleasant enough that morning. She shut down her computer and pulled her phone out, tapping out a text message to Mikey.

Any developments with KB?

Smiling to herself, she slipped it back into her pocket. She'd been after Mikey for a long time, since she saw him give a talk at her uni. She hoped that this would seal the deal. He owed her for this. She had gone above and beyond. She almost felt sorry for Beth, or Kitty, or whatever she was supposed to call her. But then she remembered what she'd done.

The pain she had caused. The evil crime she had committed. And got away with.

Vicky waited a few minutes to see if the rain abated, but when it became apparent that it was here to stay, she decided to take her chances.

She grabbed her bag and walked the length of the building to the exit, waving at various people on her way, saying goodnight.

As she glanced at Beth's empty office, she saw the tall woman with dyed auburn hair, from legal, slipping out of the door. Vicky waved, receiving a death stare in return.

She was odd, that one. Vicky shrugged, continuing her exit. She stood in the alley, the drizzle splashing into her face. She blinked, holding her bag above her, making a dash for it.

Footsteps behind her caused her to turn abruptly. Nobody there.

She shook her head and half ran, half walked towards the multi-storey. She climbed the stairs to the top level, and once again found herself battling the elements. As she reached her car, she fumbled for her keys in her bag, dropping them as she pulled them out.

'Shit,' she muttered as she crouched down to retrieve them from the puddle they had landed in.

She shook them off, straightening up. The rush of footsteps from behind came too fast. She didn't have time to react. A sudden shove in the small of her back knocked her off balance. She tumbled forwards, banging her temple on the driver's side window with a horrendous thud, dropping the keys again.

Before she could regain her composure, a hand grabbed her arm, twisting it painfully behind her. In one lightning-fast manoeuvre she was pinned against her car.

'What the–'

'Shut up,' someone hissed in her ear. 'I'm going to talk and you're going to listen, and then you're going to answer my questions. Got it?'

Vicky recognised the voice. Beth Carter.

'Get off me you psycho!'

Beth twisted Vicky's arm higher up her back. A searing pain shot through her shoulder.

'Don't push me. I've lost my job. My family. I haven't got anything left to lose. Do you understand?'

Vicky nodded.

'Tell me about Michael Noakes.'

Vicky laughed.

Beth grabbed Vicky's hair, screwing it up in her hand.

She winced, letting out a slight whimper.

'I'm guessing you didn't go to school with him like he told me?'

'No. I met him when I was at uni. I wrote my dissertation on the Billy Noakes case, and I interviewed him and his mother a few times. I knew he was... *keen* to find you. We exchanged details and kept in touch. I studied that case in great detail. Spent hours staring at your face. I knew who you were as soon as I saw you, so I called him but he didn't seem surprised. I got the impression he already knew. He asked if I could introduce you.'

'And you brought him along to Chloe's birthday drinks like a good little puppy.'

'Yeah. You should have seen your face. Thought all your Christmases had come at once.'

Beth twisted Vicky's wet hair tighter in her hand.

'What does he want?'

'How do you mean?'

'Why is he here? Does he want to hurt me? My family?'

'I don't know. I guess he wants to make you suffer. Make you pay. It's no more than you deserve.'

'I didn't do anything. I'm innocent!' Beth spat into her ear. Vicky sniggered sarcastically.

Beth shoved Vicky's head, banging it against the car window again.

'You keep telling yourself that, love,' she snarled, writhing under Beth's weight.

Blood mixed with the rain running down Vicky's face, dripping down her front.

'Why would you do this to me? What have I ever done to you?' Beth pleaded.

She let go of Vicky's arm. Vicky turned and slid down the car until she was sitting on the soaking concrete. Beth crouched, so she was looking directly at her.

'To me?' Vicky shrugged. 'Nothing. But you got away with what you did to that little boy. You never had to pay.'

'You think I haven't paid for my part in that? You think I don't suffer every damn day of my life?'

Vicky smirked, spitting blood out onto the floor.

'Do I think you've suffered? No. I don't. Not *nearly* enough. You have your perfect husband, your beautiful family, lovely big house in the country. Tell me, *Kitty*, what is so terrible about your life?'

'Nobody knows what I have to endure. It took me a long time to get to where I am mentally.'

'Oh boo-fucking-hoo. At least you're alive! You had the chance to live a life. Billy Noakes never got that luxury.'

'I'm not going to justify myself to you. I don't have to. What involvement have *you* had with all the crap that's been happening to us? Did he have you delivering the notes? Scratching our car? How much of it was *you*?'

Vicky frowned.

'What?'

'The notes. To our house. To Charlie's work. Sneaking into my house and taking photos of me in the bath! Did you kill my dog? And what about my son's girlfriend? Who did that?'

'You really are crazy, aren't you? I honestly have no idea what you're talking about.'

'Stop lying!' Beth slapped Vicky in the face as hard as she could. Vicky looked defiant as she licked blood from her split bottom lip.

'As far as I knew he was only going to mess with you. Seduce you, then tell your husband. Send him photos of the two of you in the sack or something. I don't know anything about notes. He clearly has his own agenda. He doesn't report to me.'

Beth straightened up.

'How can I find him?'

Vicky looked confused for a moment.

'Michael Noakes. Where is he?'

Vicky stared at Beth, smirking. Beth crouched down again. Taking the sides of Vicky's head in her hands, she gripped her hair, balling it tight into her fists.

Vicky winced again.

'I won't ask again. If you believe that I'm so guilty, do you really want to take the chance of pissing me off? If you think I'm capable of... that.'

Terror flashed in Vicky's eyes.

'He's staying in a flat down on Broad Street in town, near the gay strip. Yellow front door. I've not been inside, but that's where he is.'

Beth let go of Vicky's hair, standing up. She looked down at her, damp, huddled against the car, like a pathetic, wounded creature. She resisted the overwhelming urge to kick her in the ribs.

'You will never understand what you have done. What you have destroyed. I hope you're happy.'

'He'd already found you. I sped up the part where he got to meet you, that's all. You can't blame me for any of this. You brought it all on yourself. You're finally getting what you deserve.'

There was *no way* Michael could have found her. She'd been so careful. More bullshit, probably to ease her own conscience over all this.

Beth turned and walked away, leaving Vicky to lick her wounds.

51

Beth sat in her Range Rover, parked down one end of the street. She stared at the sunshine-yellow front door. Bin bags piled up outside. Broken glass on the pavement. This was *not* what she expected.

Nothing could be less aligned with the handsome, well-groomed, charming man she had spent time with. She shook her head, pulling her phone from her pocket and typed out a quick message to Mikey.

Let's meet. My house. ASAP. x

A few seconds later a reply appeared on Beth's screen.

Ok! On my way x

She smiled, sliding her mobile away. A few minutes later, Mikey emerged from the front door. He pulled it shut behind him, locking it. Glancing at the broken glass outside his door, he kicked it towards the road sending it rattling across the pavement. He hurried away, disappearing around the corner.

She waited a few minutes to make sure he didn't return. Climbing out of her car, she glanced nervously about for a traffic warden. With nobody in sight, she risked it.

Michael Noakes was heading to her house in Falmer. A good thirty-minute drive each way from town. That gave her at least an hour. Beth approached the flat. She pushed the handle, thinking it was worth a try. It didn't budge. A sign on the door said *basement flat*. A black door to the left, had a notice which said *upper flat*.

She scoured the front of the building. To the right of the steps leading up to the doors was a drop to the lower part of the property. Below her, beneath some railings, an open basement window attracted her attention.

Silly boy, she thought.

She looked around again. A few punters stood smoking outside a pub at the other end of the street. They were deep in conversation and hadn't seemed to notice her.

Apart from that, the road was deserted. No pedestrians. No nosey neighbours. She took the chance. She heaved herself up over the black, cast-iron railings, then lowered herself down into the chasm, dropping onto the damp concrete below. With one last look up over her shoulder into the street above her, she slid the sash wide open, climbing inside. She had to push her way through some tatty curtains, drawn closed.

The room was pitch black.

She opened the curtains a crack, just enough to let in a little light. The place reeked of stale sweat and cigarettes. As her eyes grew more accustomed, she took in her surroundings. Seeing a switch on the wall opposite her, she flicked it on, filling the space in bright light.

Discarded beer bottles littered the floor beside an unmade bed. A bare duvet sat crumpled at the end of the mattress, which had no sheet on it. Spotted with yellow stains.

On a small side table sat a dog-eared photo of Wendy Noakes, with her husband, and Billy, on a beach somewhere. Billy was younger than when Beth had... found him.

A normal, carefree family. A family that Michael Noakes had never known. Beth felt a pang of sadness for him. Then she remembered what he had done to her and sympathy turned to rage.

In the photo, Wendy threw her head back in laughter. She was beautiful. Happy.

Doug Noakes ruffled Billy's hair, staring down at him adoringly. Billy licked a Mr Whippy, splodges of ice cream all over his face. All three of them oblivious to the horror that lay ahead of them. Beth screwed her eyes up tight and shook away the dark thoughts that crept into her mind.

That was another life. That was not *her*.

She stepped out of the bedroom into a narrow hallway. The light spilled out, illuminating the laminated floor. At one end of the corridor was a spiral staircase. Daylight fell from upstairs, spilling into a mottled pattern of shadows across the walls.

She climbed the steps, her feet clunking on metal, blinking as the change in light dazzled her.

She found herself standing in a small dual-aspect kitchen which doubled up as a sitting room. The room ran the entire width of the property. One enormous bay window to the left of the front door looked out to the street, with privacy from a voile. The back end was entirely taken up by floor-to-ceiling glass, with bi-fold doors leading out to a tiny enclosed courtyard. A solitary deckchair sat in the centre of the yard, an overflowing ashtray beside it.

The kitchen was mostly pristine. Takeaway containers littered the worktop, but the appliances were unused. Mikey wasn't one for cooking, it would appear. In fact, it didn't look like he was one for anything. There was nothing in the room. Only a chair and a small table. No papers. No books. No handwritten *evil plan*. Beth didn't know what she'd expected to find, but it wasn't... this.

She sidestepped some containers on the floor, heading towards a door in the opposite wall. She reached for the handle, opening it. Stepping into the darkness, she pushed the door open further to allow more light inside. She flicked a switch beside her; bright white light flooded down from a fluorescent tube above her. She saw now it wasn't a room at all. It was more like a cupboard.

Beth took in a sharp breath, as a feeling of horror washed over her. An old wooden chair sat in the middle, facing the back wall. But this wasn't what alarmed Beth. The wall beyond it was covered with newspaper clippings. Hand-scrawled, angry notes. Photographs.

Photographs of Beth.

Of women who looked like Beth, question marks scribbled beside them, and names crossed out. Pictures of Charlie, Peter and Daisy. Cooper. Their house. Every single aspect of Beth's life. Her Range Rover, her office.

Beth stepped closer to the wall, surveying the documentation of her life, playing out in front of her like a macabre comic strip. One photo showed her collecting Daisy from school, crouching down to envelope her in a hug. In another, the family were walking the dog in the field behind their house. Taken with a telephoto lens. Beth bit her lip as she tried to figure out where the person would have been standing. She concluded it had been snapped from the farm track at the end of the field.

As Beth's eyes darted around the wall, taking in the photos, something occurred to her. Some of these pictures were old. *Years* old.

Taken long before Vicky or Mikey arrived on the scene. How the hell did he have these? It made no sense. Then it hit her.

He had been watching her for years.

Vicky hadn't been lying. Michael Noakes had found her on his own. But how? Beth's mind raced as she tried to figure it out. She had no social media, no pictures online. Nothing alluding to her actual identity anywhere. So how did Mikey manage to track her down?

She couldn't think of any plausible explanation. She slammed her hand against the wall, cursing under her breath. Something caught her eye. A photo she hadn't noticed earlier.

Daisy, Peter and Charlie. Coming out from Derek's flat in town.

He had found them.

He knew where her kids were. She felt sick as the realisation set in.

Her family weren't safe.

A muffled sound drew Beth's attention away from her wall of fame. A cough. Close by. She poked her head out of the room, peering to her left down towards the front door. A key in the lock set her heart racing. Her eyes darted in panic around the room. The stairs were too far. She couldn't risk getting caught. Instead, she stepped back into the cupboard, pulling the door behind her, flicking off the light. She heard someone enter the flat.

Footsteps on the wooden floor grew closer. Hurried.

He'd forgotten something.

Beth held her breath as she heard him opening cupboards, closing them again and swearing under his breath. There was nothing in this room, so Beth hoped she was safe for now. She hadn't shut the door entirely and prayed that Mikey wouldn't notice. Would he remember that it had been closed when he left? Beth would. But her paranoia about being discovered had trained her brain to pick up these tiny details over the years.

She heard him rush down the cast-iron stairs. As he grew quieter, she realised she had left the bedroom light on. She'd also left the window wide open. Most people would notice that.

Sweat formed on her brow, her heart rate increased. Her only option was to make a run for it out of the flat. She pushed the door slowly open, taking a step out into the kitchen, allowing herself to let out a long breath. Before she had a chance to get anywhere, she heard a footstep on the bottom rung of the spiral stairs.

'Hello?' she heard Mikey's voice call almost playfully from down below.

She stepped back into the cupboard, pulling the door to.

'Kitty? Is that you?' The Birmingham accent he had clearly been hiding, now laced every word.

The clunk of another foot on the next step.

'I know you're here.'

The voice that Beth had once found so attractive now filled her with terror and loathing. Hearing him call *that* name. She shivered.

Another thud on the steps.

'I'm guessing Vicky spilled the beans. That poor cow. I think she believed I might actually be interested in her.'

One more clunk.

'But then again. So did *you*.' He laughed.

It crushed Beth to hear him say it. As much as she wished it didn't.

A few more steps.

'Where – are – you?' A sing-song voice. He was toying with her.

The sick bastard was enjoying this. A final clunk, and then the sound of his feet on the laminate.

He'd reached the top.

Beth held her breath. The sweat ran down her face, down the back of her neck. She gripped on to the door handle with clammy hands. Fear permeated through her entire body. She wanted to run, but she couldn't make her legs move. They felt like slabs of concrete, bolted to the floor.

'Kitty... you going to come out and play?'

She shuddered. She had worked so hard to leave that person behind. Nobody had the right to call her that.

'Are you scared, Kitty?'

She heard two tentative steps across the kitchen floor. Mikey paused again. He was taking his time. Relishing the game.

'Are you scared like my brother would have been when you took him away from our mother?'

A couple more steps towards the cupboard.

'Was he scared? Or did he think it was a game? At what point do you think he stopped smiling?'

Beth glanced around the cupboard, searching for something she could use as a weapon. The only object was the chair. And there wasn't enough space to swing it. She clutched the handle.

Another couple of footsteps across the wooden floor.

'Do you think a kid Billy's age would have known he was going to die? I can't imagine it from his perspective. I don't think any of us can. He must have been... terrified.'

The footsteps stopped. He was standing right outside the door. Beth could hear him breathing he was so close.

'Are you terrified now, Kitty?' Mikey whispered through the door.

Beth's fight-or-flight instinct kicked in. She pushed the door as hard as she could. There was a loud whack and a crunching sound as it connected with Mikey's nose. He let out a shriek, and Beth heard him collapse to the ground.

She pushed again, and the door collided with his skull. She

slipped through, glancing down at him. He was writhing around, blood pooling on the floor by his head. More had spattered over the wall.

Beth turned and hurried towards the front, but a powerful hand grabbed at her ankle. She turned, kicking out with her free foot. It collided with his arm, then his face. She kicked again, her foot connecting hard with the side of his head this time, and he let go. She took the chance and ran.

As she reached the door, he shouted after her.

'Come back here, you bitch! I know where you live! You hear me? I know where your fucking family are hiding!'

She fumbled with the latch, her hands shaking. The adrenaline surged through her as the door swung open and she fell out onto the concrete steps, tumbling down them onto the path. She grazed her palms, but she was grateful to be outside. She gulped down air, greedily filling her lungs.

Mikey was still yelling from inside the flat. She looked back over her shoulder and saw he was getting up from the floor.

She climbed to her feet before Mikey had a chance to catch her, and bolted towards her car. As she unlocked it and threw the door open, Mikey barrelled outside, still howling after her.

The punters outside the pub stopped their conversation, staring at Beth in bewilderment, then back down the street at Mikey.

'Call the police!' she screamed at them. 'He's trying to kill me. He's got a gun!' The threat of a firearm would hopefully convince them to get help.

She clambered into the driver's seat and started the engine. As she screeched away, she saw Mikey running down the middle of the road after her. One of the guys outside the pub had his phone pressed to his ear, a panicked expression on his face.

Beth's heart pounded as she drove.

52

The buzz of the phone woke Charlie from a brief nap on the sofa. His eyes darted around Derek's flat, momentarily forgetting where he was.

The confusion faded as he recalled what had become of his perfect life.

He grabbed his mobile. He didn't recognise the number on the screen.

'Hello?' he grunted.

'Mr Carter?'

'Who's this?'

'It's DI Burns from Sussex Police. We spoke the other day regarding the incident at your office.'

'Oh, yes, hi.' Charlie's register altered immediately.

'Further to our discussion I wanted to let you know that we did manage to lift a partial print from the perfume bottle.'

Charlie held his breath. He felt his heart speed up.

'Okay.'

'Can you come into the station, please? It might be best if you bring your wife and family in too.'

'It's not convenient right now.'

'Mr Carter, given what you told me about your wife's identity, I think it's important that you and your family get somewhere safe. In light of our new information, I really think you need to come in.'

'And were you thinking about my wife and family's safety when the information was leaked?'

'Excuse me?'

'It's out. Everyone knows. Our kids know. This has torn us apart.'

The line was quiet for a moment. Charlie could hear DI Burns breathing down the phone.

'Mr Carter, I have behaved with complete discretion. Any number of staff at the station would have been privy to that information. If there has indeed been a leak as you suggest, I can assure you that it did not come from myself.'

She said *myself* instead of *me*, the way people did because they thought it made them sound more intelligent. Charlie resisted the temptation to correct her.

'If you say so. I'd be having a word with your officers if I were you.'

Another pause.

'We can discuss this when you come in. If you and your *wife* would like to make a complaint, then I can certainly put you in touch with the right people.'

The way she said *wife*, Charlie could tell she didn't give a shit. She was glad Beth was suffering.

'Yeah, and I'm sure Beth would be treated totally fairly.'

Charlie heard a sigh.

'Mr Carter will you come to the station or not?'

'Why? Who did the print belong to?'

'It was Kieran Taylor's.'

53

Happy families, strolling on the promenade in the early-evening sun, whizzed past Beth's passenger-side window. Children with balloons. Fathers carrying laughing toddlers on their shoulders. Adoring mothers dawdling behind with prams. Each snapshot a reminder of what Beth had lost; what she must now try to protect.

She had to get to Charlie. Had to warn him. She'd tried to ring him twice, but it had gone straight to voicemail. She approached a pedestrian crossing, and the light turned red. Slamming her foot down, she sped through, much to the disgust of an elderly lady with a Zimmer frame.

A siren drew her attention. A police car was following behind and wanted her to pull in.

'Shit!' she cursed under her breath.

For a moment she considered driving away, but she knew that wasn't wise. Reluctantly she pulled over to the side of the road. As the car parked up behind her, she dialled Margot's number.

'Hello, darling!' Margot's dulcet tones seeped into Beth's ear like warm treacle.

'Margot, I don't have time to explain, but can you to do me a favour. It's an emergency,' Beth exclaimed down the phone.

'Okay. What is it?'

'I need you to get to Charlie and the kids. They're staying at his boss's flat. Can you get there immediately and get them away? Take them somewhere safe. Take them to your place, anywhere. And make sure you aren't followed.'

'Beth, what on earth is going on?'

'I'll explain when I see you, but for now can you do this for me right away, please?'

'Of course, sweetie.'

'Thank you. I'll text you the address as soon as I hang up.'

She pressed the end-call button and hammered out the address into a message, as a surly-looking police officer, who appeared adolescent, rapped on the window with his knuckle.

Beth opened it, eyeing his name badge, which identified him as Constable Drake.

'Hello, madam. Can I ask if you know what the speed limit is along this road?'

Beth hesitated. 'Yes.'

'And can I ask what speed you were doing?'

'I... I think I was...' she stuttered. It didn't really matter what she replied, whatever she said she was screwed.

'And are you also aware that you ran a red light back there, narrowly missing pedestrians who had started to cross the road?'

'Yes, I'm sorry about that.'

'May I have your driving licence, please?'

She pulled her purse from her bag and handed the constable her photocard.

'Beth Carter?' Something about his tone set her on edge. Her heart pounded.

'Mrs Carter, would you get out of the car for me?'

'Why?'

'Because I'm asking you to. And I'm a police officer.'

'Look, I'm in a bit of a rush. Could you give me the ticket and let's get this over with?'

'Can you step out of the vehicle, now.' His tone was curt. Beth decided it was pointless arguing. She climbed out. He pulled something from his belt.

'Have you been drinking, Mrs Carter?'

'No, of course I haven't.'

'I'm pretty sure I can smell alcohol from you, so I'm going to ask you to provide a breath sample.'

'You are wasting both of our time. You know as well as I do that you can't smell anything. You're picking on me because... because of my name.'

'I don't know what you mean, madam. I'm simply doing my job. Are you refusing to provide me with a sample?'

Beth's shoulders slumped.

'No. I'm not.'

Constable Drake slowly performed the charade, breathalysing Beth. Passers-by smirked as they stared at her. She felt ashamed, which was ridiculous, as she knew she was completely sober. The officer held out the apparatus, and Beth blew into the tube, while he smiled at her, knowingly.

The test was negative. No surprises.

'Can I go now?' Beth said impatiently.

Drake eyed her, then looked at her Range Rover.

'Nice car,' he drawled. 'No, you can't go yet. I need to radio in and get a check on your vehicle.'

Beth tutted as the officer turned his back to her and walked away.

'This is harassment,' she shouted after him.

He stopped, turning back to face Beth.

'Really? And why would I be harassing you?'

'Because you know who I am.'

Drake laughed but said nothing. He turned and continued walking to his car. He pulled his radio from his belt and said something quietly so Beth couldn't hear. There was a crackled reply. Beth craned her head a little to hear. But it was no use, he was too far away. The officer frowned as he listened, then returned to Beth.

'Mrs Carter, one of my superiors has asked if you can accompany me to the station.'

'I have done nothing wrong.'

'That's not entirely true, is it? You were speeding, and you ran a red light. But that's neither here nor there. This is unrelated. Apparently, they need to talk to you about something else.'

Beth's mind raced as she wondered what it could be. Constable Drake must have seen the panic on her face.

'You can take your own car and follow me. You are not under arrest. I'll give you your ticket at the station.'

'Okay.'

Drake returned to his vehicle, starting the engine. Beth climbed into her front seat, briefly checking her phone before doing the same. There was nothing from Margot. The police car pulled away and overtook her, and Beth pulled out behind him, driving exemplarily.

Her phone buzzed as the cars approached the station. Officer Drake parked up and got out, walking in through the main doors. Beth pulled in, grabbing her mobile quickly.

Margot.

'Hello.'

'Beth, I'm at the apartment. But...'

'What's wrong?'

'It could be nothing, but I'm outside, and the front door is wide open. I've pressed the buzzer but there doesn't seem to be anyone in.'

A wave of fear washed over Beth, so strong that she felt physically sick.

'I didn't want to just walk in. I thought it would be best to call you first.'

'Can you go in?'

'Sure, no problem.'

'Be careful.'

Beth heard the sound of Margot's stilettos on concrete.

'I'm going to buzz again, in case they didn't hear.'

Beth heard the doorbell echo down the phone, as Margot called out, 'Hello, Charlie?'

There were muffled noises, and Beth pictured Margot pushing the door and stepping inside the property. More footsteps.

'Oh my God!' Margot's voice sounded panicked. Afraid.

'What is it?'

No reply.

'Margot? What's going on?' Beth yelled into the phone.

Beth heard sounds of a scuffle, heavy breathing, then Margot screamed.

'Please, no... DON'T!'

There was a clatter, as if the handset had fallen to the floor.

The line went dead.

54

Beth sat staring at her phone. Afraid to breathe, afraid to move. Her jaw hung open in disbelief.

Her family were in grave danger. And what's more, she had put Margot, her only friend, in the path of that danger and something had happened to her. Something bad.

She glanced over to the double doors leading into the police station. She could make out the figure of Constable Drake waiting impatiently for her inside. She started her engine and pulled away, watching in her rear-view mirror as the officer rushed outside, waving his arms in frustration.

It was a short drive to the apartment. She drove quickly but nervously. Two tickets in one afternoon would not be ideal, but that was the least of her worries.

Nothing mattered anymore apart from the safety of her family, and Margot.

She screeched to a halt by the curb outside Derek's flat. Margot's silver TT sat abandoned a few spaces down, hazard lights blinking. Beth glanced at it, noting the driver's side door was ajar.

As she approached the apartment, it was as Margot had

reported. The front door was open. Beth climbed the concrete steps. 'Hello,' she called, her voice catching in her throat, the resulting sound being rather pathetic.

Silence.

She pushed and the door creaked slowly as it opened inwards. Everything appeared normal. No overturned furniture. No bloodied note pinned to the wall.

If the door hadn't been open, you would be forgiven for thinking things were fine. She stepped inside, calling out again, more confident this time. Her footsteps sounded like hammer blows as she made her way towards the living room. She reached the corner and gasped, as she was met with a substantial amount of blood.

Margot's phone lay on the wooden boards beside the puddle. A mass of dark crimson was pooled on the ground inside the doorway and spattered across the white furniture and walls.

Arterial spray? Beth tried not to think about that. Her eyes widened as she surveyed the room. Took it all in. There were signs of a struggle. Shattered glass strewn across the floor. Messy red handprints smeared the wallpaper and sofa. Cushions lay scattered on the floor.

Beth began to hyperventilate.

Feeling dizzy, she steadied herself against the wall, putting her hand in a sticky wet patch. She recoiled in horror, wiping it on her leg, leaving pink streaks on her jeans. She rushed around the flat, calling for Daisy. The property was deserted. Beth collapsed onto the settee in tears, holding her head. As she sat sobbing, her phone buzzed to life. A message.

If you want to see your family again come and find them. I'll be waiting where it all began. Come alone. No police or they die.

Beth read it again, her heart pounding. Her mouth was dry,

hands shaking. She took a few deep breaths, trying to regain her composure. But her mind kept racing through what might have happened in this room. What had her children witnessed? Whose blood was decorating the walls? She thought of Charlie. Had he been taken by surprise, caught off guard? Had he put up a fight?

It certainly looked like it. Charlie was a big man. It wouldn't have been easy to overpower him. She pictured Mikey. He was toned, but slim. And much shorter than her husband. How had he managed to get the upper hand?

Beth felt another wave of nausea flow up from the pit of her stomach. She ran her hands through her hair, breathing out slowly. With a calm head, she reread the text message.

I'll be waiting where it all began.

Until recently, when she visited Wendy Noakes, Beth had not returned to Birmingham since the day she left. When she was seven. Her family had been driven from their home. They didn't even have time to gather their belongings.

When the newspaper ran her name and picture, her parents knew. They had to leave, and fast. They had never looked back. Beth had no desire to return.

The scene of the crime, as it were. It held nothing but terrible memories for her. It was all part of a life she had tried so hard to forget. And from the outside, it appeared that she had succeeded. But the horrors that had unfolded in her childhood had never left her. They lived with her every day. Every night when she closed her eyes. They hounded her while awake and haunted her dreams.

She had vowed she would never go back. No good could possibly come from it. And yet here she found herself having to return for the second time in the space of a week. It had taken every bit of strength Beth could muster to do it once. To look Wendy Noakes in the eye and confront her.

She didn't want to, but she had no choice. Her family's lives were at risk. Assuming it wasn't a trick. They could already be dead.

Beth shook the thought from her head. She couldn't allow herself to entertain that idea.

Worse than having to return to Birmingham. Worse than having to see Wendy Noakes. Beth had to go *there*. To the hotel.

And for the first time in years, Beth was Kitty Briscoe again.

Scared, pathetic Kitty Briscoe. Who did a bad thing and got caught.

When Beth had rewritten her past, her identity, she had vowed she would never allow herself to feel like this again. She had found safety with Charlie. And she'd stopped running; created a new family, who brought her comfort.

She made a life for herself that she knew she didn't deserve.

But it felt good. And as she pictured them there, in that place of horror and wicked secrets, she imagined Daisy, confused, terrified. She saw Charlie, hurt and bleeding. She thought of Peter, wondered if he was afraid, or if he was putting up a fight. Her poor, beautiful family.

They needed her, and she had to save them.

She didn't deserve them, but she had them none the less, and she had to do what she could to help them. A sudden strength and resolution surged up from within her. She stood from the sofa and walked out of the apartment, pulling the door closed behind her. Climbing into her car, she held down a rush of nausea. She was returning to Birmingham, hopefully for the last time.

Whatever awaited her in that damp, dark hotel, whether she survived it or not, there was one thing she was sure of. Nothing would ever be the same for her... for any of them again.

55

Charlie opened his eyes slowly. His head throbbed; he'd been hit from behind with something heavy. A great deal of blood was still flowing from what he guessed was a fairly deep wound on his scalp. He inhaled deeply; his nostrils filled with a musty smell. The air felt cool, damp.

His vision adjusted to the darkness as he tried to make sense of what had happened. His arms were tied behind his back painfully, tethering him to a pillar as he lay on the dirty ground. The space was vast, but about twenty feet above his head was a small section of ceiling, like a mezzanine, or a large balcony jutting out from the wall. It looked unstable. Dangerous. Parts of it had caved, so you could see right up to the roof.

Somewhere off in the darkness he could hear Daisy. She was sobbing.

'Daisy!' he shouted as loud as he could.

'Daddy! Where are you?' Her voice was quiet, not in the same room... if *room* was the correct word. Most of the walls were crumbling. Shafts of dim evening light seeped in through cracks and holes in the roof, but not enough to illuminate the space. They threw dappled shadows onto small areas, falling across piles of bricks and twisted, rusty metal girders.

'I'm right here, honey. Are you okay?'

'I'm scared, Daddy. It's dark!'

'I know, sweetheart. Can you see Peter?'

There was a pause.

'Yes. He's here... but he's sleeping.'

Charlie's heart pounded. He hoped Peter *was* only asleep.

'Okay love, try to stay calm. I'm going to get us out of here, I promise.'

In reality, Charlie had no idea *how* he would escape this situation. He scanned the room.

'Daisy, can you move? Can you run away?'

'No, Daddy. I can't. We're both stuck.'

Charlie pictured his children, alone in the dark. Terrified.

A surge of adrenaline rushed through him, and he let out a loud cry, wriggling, trying to break free from his bonds. Pain coursed through his body. Although his head had the most obvious injury, the rest of him had taken quite a pummelling too. He twisted from side to side. As he did so, dust and debris crumbled down onto his face from high above him. The pillar wobbled precariously.

Perhaps he would be able to dislodge the structure and escape. He sat up, bracing his back against the bricks. Digging his heels into the dirt, he pushed backwards. More crap fell down from above.

Without warning, a large piece of masonry came loose, falling down and narrowly missing Charlie's head.

It crashed to the ground with a loud thud beside him, as he was showered with dust and bits of concrete. Caution kicked in. If this went wrong, the entire thing looked like it could come down on top of him. One false move and it could be game over. Not worth the risk.

He would need to keep very still. He couldn't remember a time in his life when he had ever felt as useless... as helpless.

Something wet and furry scurried over his arm. He writhed around, bringing more debris down on him.

A rat emerged in front of his face. Its nose wiggled as it sniffed the air. It seemed to stare straight at Charlie, fearless. In the surrounding darkness, Charlie sensed more movement.

The rodent was not alone.

Charlie screwed his eyes shut and hoped with all he could muster that this was not the last place he and his children would ever see.

56

It was dark by the time Beth arrived in Birmingham. She had stopped at a hardware shop so she could arm herself. After assessing the rows of tools, she had chosen a heavy claw hammer. It was easy enough to carry, swing, and could deliver an impressive amount of damage to a human skull. She had also picked up a small silver Stanley knife as a backup. You could never be too sure when dealing with a psychopath.

She didn't intend on letting Michael Noakes leave Birmingham alive. She couldn't risk a repeat of this. Whether her family made it through this and stayed together or not, she wouldn't let someone come after her kids ever again.

Driving through the city streets, Beth was aware that none of it was familiar to her. She was so young when she left. It hadn't occurred to her last time, when she visited Wendy Noakes.

But tonight, she could have been anywhere. It was as if she had never been there before. Her brain had blocked it out. The pain. The horror.

Her mind would wander now and then. She would think of Daisy. She hoped her daughter wasn't afraid, unlikely as that was. Beth's mood fluctuated between extreme anger, to desperate terror, and a plethora of emotions in between. She thought of Michael Noakes again and slammed her fist hard onto the steering wheel.

He had humiliated her, yes. That was one thing. In a funny way she could see his justification for that. But to take her family. Her children. That was a step too far.

Knowing that he had killed Zoe left no doubt in Beth's mind that he would hurt them too. But she wouldn't allow that to happen.

As she headed away from the city centre towards the outskirts, where the derelict hotel was situated, a sinking feeling consumed her.

The Marshall Hotel had burned down in the late seventies. Several guests had died in the fire, the Marshall family were billionaires and so had cut their losses, deciding not to reopen it. The back half, where the kitchens were located, was completely destroyed. This was where the blaze had started. Beth would never forget the first time Kieran Taylor had taken her to the hotel.

The day they killed the stray cat.

That was where the seed had been sown. When they had joked about killing her father. Of course, it had begun as a laugh. Beth had never imagined that they would actually do anything.

But Kieran Taylor was unhinged.

Childish banter had led to something far worse. Two sad, broken children, egging each other on. Beth wouldn't let her thoughts go there. This was not the time for that.

She drove along what was little more than an overgrown grassy footpath. Her Range Rover bumped and toppled over uneven ground. And there it was, looming before her.

The imposing silhouette of the once opulent Marshall Hotel now reduced to a relic.

Suddenly it felt as if she had been there only yesterday. The two parts of Beth's life came crashing together.

In the moonlight, the hotel had the same eerie quality she remembered. Even without Kieran's ridiculous ghost stories she had found the place terrifying. Something about it; she could never put her finger on it, but it felt wrong.

Sheets of perished plastic, which used to cover windows and doorways, blew in the wind. Catching the moonlight sporadically, they looked like ghostly figures dancing in the breeze. Beth imagined they were the spirits of the dead guests, writhing in agony as they burned eternally.

She shivered.

Parking up, she surveyed the scene ahead of her. This was where it had all begun. The dark path her life would take. Beth shook her head, cursing. She had often wondered how differently things would have turned out if she had not visited the hotel with Kieran that first time. If she had only gone home to her mother, like she had wanted to.

But she didn't. And nobody can change the past, as much as they might yearn to.

Beth had made her choices. All she could do was try to live the best life possible. And she had. But now it was all crumbling around her, like chalk from a weathered cliff. Much the same as the hotel she sat in front of, afraid to enter.

She slid the silver Stanley knife into her sock, the cold metal against her skin made her body tingle. Gripping the hammer tightly in her lap, she sat for a moment, looking at the derelict building. She scraped her hair back into a tight ponytail, securing it in place with an elastic band.

She was ready.

Climbing out of her car, she trudged through the waist-high grass towards the skeletal remains. Weeds tangled round her ankles, almost tripping her. Her foot sank into a bog-like patch of mud. She grimaced, shaking off the excess muck.

Reaching the perimeter, she raised her head, looking up at the roof. The place was in a far worse state than when she had last been here. Over thirty years had passed. But it still felt the same.

Beth was amazed at how the scene was opening up old wounds. Tearing scabs from long-healed scratches. Bringing back memories she had tried so hard to keep buried.

She eased herself around the wall with her free hand, edging around the wreck of the Marshall Hotel. Eventually she came to a way in. When she was a child, they had entered through an actual doorway where the chipboard covering had come loose. She blinked, remembering how Kieran had pushed the board and slipped through, out of sight. She had followed obligingly, as she always did. No comprehension of what danger may be lurking on the other side.

Now, an entire wall had collapsed, leaving a gaping space large enough for an adult to fit through easily.

With one final glance around her, Beth slipped through the gap, into the darkness.

57

The interior of the hotel was far from what Beth remembered; what she could see of it, at least. When she was last there, it had seemed much grander. Wooden panelling had still been visible. Traces of bookshelves, even some tattered old books. Now it was little more than a pile of rubble. Impossible to tell where each room had originally finished. Walls had tumbled. Ceilings had caved.

Over thirty years of the elements had taken their toll on the place.

A memory of Billy Noakes running away down a corridor ahead of her flashed into her mind's eye. His pale-blond hair caught a beam of moonlight which shone through a large gap in the roof. His curls bounced around as he darted away into the darkness.

Billy, come back here! she remembered shouting after him, but he'd ignored her.

Had he been playing, or trying to escape?

Beth couldn't remember.

Don't, she thought. Just don't. She wouldn't allow those black thoughts to cloud her mind. What was done was done. She shook the image away and crept deeper into the belly of the building. Shafts of patchy white moonlight illuminated her path. It felt like a scene from some teen horror flick. And here she was, the stupid girl, heading straight towards the danger.

Now and then she would trip on some bricks. The stench of this place was horrendous. Damp. Mould. And dead things. But beneath the smell of decay, something else.

Something familiar. But Beth couldn't place it.

She passed the remnants of a campfire. Discarded beer cans and a wine bottle lay strewn around. A used condom beside the charred remains. Obviously a popular hang-out for delinquents. Beth wondered sadly to herself how many girls had lost their virginity in this awful place. She wondered if things had been different, would she have done the same? Perhaps with Kieran?

She had been infatuated with him. Looked up to him. She had often been attracted to the wrong kind of men. Charlie was the first truly *good* man she had been with. That's why she had stayed. Against her better judgement.

He was the reason she had broken *all* of her own rules.

The hotel was eerily quiet. Beth could hear her own breathing, her footsteps crunching across the dirty floor. She glanced around, making sure she wasn't being followed. She considered texting the number, telling him she had arrived. But she had to imagine that for the time being, she had the element of surprise in her favour.

Unless he had been watching. Waiting for her to arrive.

Mikey's face flashed into her mind. Grinning his stupid boyish grin on the night they first met, at Chloe's birthday drinks. Beth wished so much that he was standing in front of her right now, so she could smash him over the head with the hammer. She was surprised by the level of animosity that she felt. The violence. She didn't simply want to stop him.

She wanted to *kill* him.

The knife concealed in her sock dug uncomfortably into her ankle, serving as a reassuring reminder that it was there.

She heard a cough close by. She stopped, holding her breath. Silence. She continued around a corner, and the space opened up. She recognised it. The ballroom. Or at least that's what she had imagined it was when she was little.

This is where they had brought Billy.

She glanced across the floor. Standing in the doorway, she felt afraid to move forwards. Paralysed with fear and sorrow all rolled into one. Another cough, from the direction of the mezzanine.

'Hello, is somebody there?' Charlie's hoarse voice called out from the darkness.

'Charlie?' Beth replied in a half whisper.

'Beth?'

She ran towards the structure. As she grew nearer and her eyes adjusted, she could make out his shape, huddled on the ground. He was tied to one of the corner supports of the balcony. She crouched down in front of him, cradling his head in her hands. He winced.

'Charlie, my God, are you okay?'

In the dim light, Beth could vaguely distinguish his face, crusted with blood, and bruised.

'What has he done to you? Are the kids all right?'

'Don't worry about me, I'm fine. They're in another room, I don't know where, but if you call out Daisy will reply. Peter is... I think he's... unconscious.'

Beth moved round behind Charlie. Dropping the hammer on the ground, she fumbled with the cord that was tied round his wrists. A shower of dust and loose stones fell down from above.

'Careful, it's really unstable. If you move me too much, you'll bring the whole thing down on top of us. Just leave me. Go make sure the kids are okay. I'm fine.'

'But–'

'Go, Beth!'

The sound of a slow clap echoed around the space. Beth stood up quickly, pivoting.

'How touching!' a voice called out from the darkness.

A figure walked slowly towards them from the shadows. A beam of light hit his face. Michael Noakes stood before them.

'If only someone had shown this much compassion to my brother he might still be alive.'

'Michael, you don't have to do this. I understand you're angry, and you want to hurt me, and that's fine. But please... let my family go. They don't deserve any of this.'

Mikey frowned, continuing towards Beth.

'Who the hell is this guy?' Charlie shouted, his voice full of hatred.

'Why don't you ask your wife?'

'Michael, please... don't,' Beth begged.

'Oh that is beautiful, that right there. *You* pleading with me for mercy.' Noakes laughed.

'I will do whatever you want... I deserve it. But let my family go,' Beth continued.

'I don't want to hurt them. If I'd wanted to do anything to your kids, I'd have done it when I spoke to your daughter in town that day... gave her the lollipop. I simply wanted to mess with you, flirt with you... seduce you. Then tell your husband here what had happened. Destroy your perfect little family like you destroyed mine. And God, you should have seen your face that night when I kissed you. You pathetic old slapper. You actually thought I was interested in you.'

Beth's eyes shot down towards Charlie. She felt her cheeks flush. The look on his face was heartbreaking.

'Oh yeah. That's right. Your pretty little wife here… she threw herself at me. She was gagging for it. I took her out to a gig and she couldn't get down my throat fast enough.'

'Shut up!' Beth hissed at him. But the damage was already done. Charlie sagged, his shoulders dropped, face crumpled. Noakes took a few more steps towards them.

'And what about Zoe? She didn't deserve to die. She did nothing to you.'

'Who the fuck is Zoe?'

'My son's girlfriend.'

Noakes frowned again and shrugged.

'What are you talking about?' He took a step closer to Beth. She crouched down, retrieving the hammer from where she'd dropped it when she was attempting to untie Charlie. Springing up, she waved it wildly in front of her, gripping it with both hands.

'Woah…' Noakes held up his palms towards Beth. 'What are you doing?'

Beth continued to swing the hammer back and forth.

'Get back!' she screamed. 'I will hit you with this if you come any closer.'

Noakes backed off a little, lowering his hands, eyes fixed firmly on the weapon.

'Can you put that down? Didn't you do enough damage to my face already? I could have quite easily gone to the police, but I didn't.'

'*You* could have? Is that a joke? After everything you've done, I'm the one who should be going to the police.'

'I'm pretty sure I haven't done anything illegal… apart from keying your husband's car… I couldn't resist. But I'm guessing you didn't report that anyway.'

Beth was astounded by his arrogance. The man was clearly unhinged if he thought he had been behaving within the limits of the law.

'Look, *Beth*, I don't know what you're playing at, but I came in good faith when you asked me to meet you here. Why don't you calm down, stop waving that hammer around like a lunatic, before you hurt someone, and tell me what it is you want?'

Beth paused momentarily, confused by the statement.

'What do you mean when *I* asked you to meet *me*?'

Noakes pulled out his phone. He tapped on the screen, reading aloud.

'Mikey, I think this has all got a bit out of hand. We need to talk. Meet me at the Marshall Hotel. I'll wait for you inside.'

Beth glared at the handset.

'I didn't send that.'

Noakes turned the screen, holding it out towards Beth, taking a few steps towards her. She flailed the hammer between them as a warning, then took a step closer for a better view of the phone. The message appeared beside her name.

But she hadn't sent it.

Letting go of the hammer with one hand, she pulled her phone out, scrolling through her messages. She found Mikey's name, turning it to show him.

'I didn't send it,' she said firmly.

Noakes's brow furrowed as he tried to make sense of the situation.

'Well somebody did,' he replied sarcastically.

Cogs began to whir inside Beth's head. A rush of information swam around, and she felt suddenly dizzy.

'How did you find me?' she shouted.

'Huh?' Noakes still seemed to be trying to figure out if Beth was lying or not.

'In Brighton... how did you find me? I was *so* careful. I always thought it was Vicky who had told you. But when I was in your flat and I saw your little shrine to me, some of the photos you had there predated Vicky working with me. You must have tracked me down before that. How?'

Noakes smiled.

'Oh right, yeah. I got an anonymous tip-off. A handwritten note delivered through my door one night. It had your name, your address, and a photo of you. I knew it was you as soon as I saw it. I showed my mum, to make sure. She was adamant.'

'But that doesn't make any sense. Who would have done that?'

'It could have been anyone. You haven't changed that much... not really. Your eyes are the same. Anyone could have recognised you.'

Beth considered this for a moment. She noticed Noakes eyeing the hammer in her hand, which she had lowered down to her side by now. He edged forwards slightly. She swung her arm up towards him.

'Don't!'

Noakes stopped. His eyes wide. He looked confused. Beth swung her arm again, but he appeared to be looking through her. He was trying to trick her, and she wasn't going to fall for it.

A shove from behind sent Beth falling onto her hands and knees. She glanced up to see a dark figure dressed in black motorcycle leathers and helmet stride past her towards Noakes. His eyes widened further in terror, as an arm swung up, holding a knife.

'Look out!' Charlie yelled, but it was too late.

The blade plunged deep into the side of Noakes' neck. As the biker pulled it out, a plume of red rocketed out, showering the floor around him, splattering across the biker's jacket and trousers.

Beth screamed.

Mikey made a gurgling sound. Raising his hand to the wound, he held it there, trying to stem the blood flow. A look of confusion and disbelief fell across his face as he realised what was happening. He stumbled backwards a few paces, before steadying himself slightly.

Without warning the biker thrust the knife forwards, plunging the blade deep into the front of Noakes' throat. He fell to his knees slowly. The biker pulled the knife out, and Mikey's body slumped face forward into the dirt, blood mixing with dust.

Beth watched in horror, as his life ebbed away.

The biker turned towards her, unzipping his jacket. He slid the knife into an inside pocket, then began fiddling with his chinstrap.

Beth glanced down at Charlie. He looked broken; eyes fixed in horror on the corpse on the ground. They both returned their attention to the biker, who grasped the sides of the helmet with his hands, then slowly lifted it off, the moonlight glistening off the iridescent visor.

And what was left of Beth's world crumbled into confusion.

58

An abundance of deep auburn curls tumbled from beneath the helmet, as Margot pulled it off her head.

Beth and Charlie both stared, dumbfounded. Suddenly Beth was able to place the smell.

Margot's perfume.

'Margot... I thought you were hurt... I don't understand.'

Margot looked down at Beth on the floor. Her face devoid of its usual friendly smile.

'Oh you mean my little scream down the phone? You're not the only actress here, my dear!'

Beth looked across to her husband, who was staring in disbelief at what was unfolding before him.

'Please... this wasn't all you?'

Beth stood up slowly, hammer in hand, looking back at her friend. Margot returned her stare with the hint of a grin.

'Oh, Kitty, you really are quite stupid, aren't you?' she said mockingly.

'My God... that night... it was you! You rammed my car off the road?'

Margot nodded proudly.

'But why, Margot? I don't understand why you would do this to us. I thought we were friends.'

'So did I!' Margot spat, her voice laced with venom.

She pulled the knife out from her jacket, pointing it towards Beth.

'You're not the only one who can change your accent you know, Kitty.'

A trace of Brummie crept in beneath the perfect pronunciation.

'I started taking puberty blockers pretty early on while I was inside. A man I was... *friendly* with, shall we say, had them smuggled in for me. It was a mutually beneficial arrangement. I knew from an early age that I had been... born into the wrong body. You can't imagine how terrible that is for a child. Knowing your anatomy is all wrong. Living a life that isn't your own.'

Beth glanced at her husband as what Margot was saying sank in.

'By the time I got out, I should have been through puberty, but the drugs delayed that. At the first opportunity I went abroad and had the operation. And I became the person I had always wanted to be.'

'Kieran? You're Kieran Taylor?' Beth whispered, wondering if she should laugh or cry.

Margot's face changed instantly. A look of pure disgust.

'Don't call me that. I'm no more *Kieran Taylor* than you are Kitty Briscoe. Why should you be the only one who gets to rewrite her past?'

Margot stepped forwards. Beth swung the hammer towards her.

'Eight years, Kitty. You robbed me of my childhood. I thought we were friends. We *agreed* neither of us would say a word. You promised. I stuck to it. I didn't tell them anything. I kept my mouth shut! But you... you spilled your guts to the police as soon as you got into that room with them.'

Margot's eyes were fixed firmly on Beth's own.

'And you lied, Kitty... you *lied*!'

'I didn't lie. I told them what happened. I told them what you did.'

Margot laughed loudly, but there was no humour.

'No, Kitty... what *we* did.'

'Stop calling me that... that's not who I am anymore.'

'Yes... you managed to walk free from court, get a new identity, start again. You got to have a new life. But you will *always* be Kitty Briscoe. You'll never be able to escape what you did.'

'I didn't do anything!'

Margot took a few steps to her side, edging closer to Charlie. Beth swung the hammer, and Margot danced backwards, narrowly avoiding its claws.

'Is that what you *honestly* believe? Have you been telling yourself that rubbish for so long that you actually think it's true?'

'I was seven!'

'And I was eleven! I was a kid too.'

There was silence as Beth and Margot stared at each other. Kitty Briscoe and Kieran Taylor together again.

'I tried to start a new life. I really did. And for a *long* time it worked. My hatred for you... for what you did to me, it faded away as I accepted responsibility. Because, you see, Kitty, I did that. I accepted my responsibility for the part I played. But you never have, have you?'

Beth lowered the hammer a little. The weight was becoming hard to bear.

'I studied. I bettered myself, became a lawyer... it's easy enough to fool people if you know where to get paperwork. And

I met some *extremely* dodgy individuals inside. Some of them turned out to be quite useful to me. I decided I wanted to help children. Because that's what I felt was right. To make amends for what I had done. That was my penance. And for a long time I didn't think about *you*.'

Margot eyed the hammer, lowered down by Beth's side, and took another step towards her. Beth swung her weapon manically back and forth.

'Then one night, I was sitting eating my dinner at home, minding my own business, and there you were. On my screen. With your perfect little family, laughing in the street. The reporter was banging on about some royal visit in Brighton or something. And I knew... as soon as I saw your eyes, I knew it was you.'

And suddenly it began to fall into place.

Beth remembered the day well. The only time she let her guard down. She had been joking with the kids and hadn't noticed the news crew pointing a camera at her.

She had screeched and howled at them. She remembered vividly the fuss she had made... how terrified the children looked. The way Charlie had watched her, like he didn't know who he was looking at. The reporter had assured her they wouldn't use the footage. Clearly he had lied to appease her.

'I tried to forget about it. But all of a sudden, I knew where you were. And that knowledge ate away at me like a cancer. I went from being cheerful and bright, to obsessed and angry. You were all I could think about. You looked so... happy. I remember thinking how unfair that was.'

Beth lowered her head. Charlie watched in bewilderment as the scene played out. His eyes darted between Margot and Beth.

Beth glanced at the bloodied body of Michael Noakes, lying off in the distance. She couldn't help thinking how sad it was that both the Noakes brothers had met their demise in this dismal place.

'So Noakes...?'

'Michael was simply an all-too-willing puppet. I knew he was on some mad quest to find you, although I had no idea what he was planning to do if he ever did. I fed him enough information to help him along on his journey a little. Wound him up and watched him go, like a little clockwork soldier. I needed someone to misdirect the attention from me. You should have seen your face that night you met him. Like an excited schoolgirl. I was quite surprised... I always thought you and Charlie were solid. But I suppose you're rotten to the core... you can't help yourself, can you?'

'None of this was him? Zoe...'

'Ah yes, Zoe. I was particularly proud of that part. I saw the way Peter looked at her. Heard how you gushed about her at work. It was clear that she was special to you. So I took her away from you all. I managed to slip Peter's phone into my purse the night I babysat. I also found your spare front door key in a bowl on the kitchen worktop. That came in very handy. I had *a lot* of fun creeping around your house! Zoe was a lovely girl... she deserved so much more than your family. I did her a favour, really. You should have seen the terror in her eyes as I tightened that scarf around her throat. She didn't understand. She died afraid and alone. And that, my dear, is *all* on you.'

'Why, Margot... why, if you were doing so well, why throw it all away to come and get revenge? Is it worth it?'

'YES!' Margot screamed. The level of her fury made Beth jump.

'Yes, it was... because I realised you had got away with what you did, with not even so much as a slap on the wrist. I *paid*. I went to prison. And can you imagine what happened to a slim young effeminate boy in there? I'll tell you... I was fair game for everyone. They thought all their Christmases had come at once. And do you know what? I even told myself I deserved it. Because what we did to that little boy, it was horrendous, Kitty. Horrendous!'

'Margot, I'm sorry, okay. Is that what you want to hear? I'm sorry. But you did what you did!'

'No! WE! It was us. You know that as well as I do. It was *your* idea. You wanted to take him! Not me. I wanted to impress you. All I ever wanted was to impress you. Perfect little Kitty Briscoe. With her pretty blonde hair, and big blue eyes.'

'I didn't... it wasn't me! I would never–'

'Yes, Kitty, you did! We were at the fair and you saw him. You said *let's take him.*'

'But I only wanted to play with him... I didn't want to hurt him. I wouldn't!'

'Is that what you tell yourself so you can sleep at night? My family disowned me. And it was all because of you! When I got out of prison, my father wouldn't even let me go home. He gave me one hundred grand and told me he and my mother never wanted to see me again. Can you imagine what that feels like for a young person? To be... abandoned by the people who should support you through anything? Although, with enough funds behind you, it's scarily easy to disappear. I suppose I should be grateful to my parents for that at least.' Margot paused, a smile creeping onto her face.

'Talking of families... How is your mother, Kitty?' Margot's voice had a playful edge to it.

Beth said nothing.

'I managed to track her down. You hid her well, I'll give you that. But I found her eventually.'

Beth heard a gasp from beside her. She looked towards Charlie on the floor.

'Beth, what's she talking about? I thought your parents were dead?'

'Oh, Charlie, you poor deluded fool. Haven't you figured out yet that everything she told you was a pack of lies? Her father is dead, yes. But her mother is alive. Well, she was... not so much anymore.'

Beth's head whipped round towards Margot.

'What?'

'I looked her in the eye and I slit her throat. I made sure she knew who I was too... so she knew she deserved it. I wish I could tell you that she didn't feel a thing, that she didn't suffer... but—'

Beth screamed, hurtling towards Margot, keeping her shoulders low. Margot was caught off guard and didn't have time to move out of the way. Beth's head connected with Margot's stomach, and they both tumbled to the ground. Margot wheezed as the air was knocked from her lungs, her knife clattering across the ground.

Beth had dropped the hammer, but she straddled Margot, holding her arms down, pinning them tightly. Margot writhed, trying to throw Beth from her, but Beth had the advantage. She reached to her side, but she couldn't quite get the hammer. She lifted her hips into the air slightly, trying to extend her body further. Margot brought her knee up hard, throwing Beth into a heap beside her.

Beth scrambled on the floor, but Margot was faster. She sprang to her feet, kicking the hammer. It scuttled across the ground. She spun towards Beth, and a heavy black motorbike boot connected with the side of her jaw.

Stunned, she fell, and Margot quickly moved closer, stamping on her wrist. There was a crunch, a hideous cracking sound. Beth screamed in agony, and Margot kicked her in the kidneys with such force, Beth thought she was going to be sick.

'Is that all you've got, Kitty? You used to be much tougher.'

Beth pushed herself up onto her knees, her head slumped. Her hair had come loose and hung down in front of her face. Her hands either side of her feet. She breathed heavily, slowly.

Margot retrieved the knife, taking a step forwards, pointing it down close to Beth's head. She traced the blade across Beth's cheek, digging the point into her flesh. Beth winced, as a trickle of blood ran down the side of her face.

'How fitting that it should all end here, like this. Where it all began. It's kind of poetic, don't you think?'

Beth's head fell lower. Margot took this as a sign of defeat.

'I'd like to say that your family will be fine. I did consider letting them live. But I can't. I'm going to kill them one by one. Little Daisy will be last... so she has time to realise what is coming...'

Beth sprung upwards, swinging the Stanley knife she had slipped out from her sock towards Margot's head. The blade sliced through her cheek, sending blood spurting through the air towards Beth. Margot screamed, throwing her hands up to her face. The blade she was holding fell to the floor.

Beth didn't give her time to recover. She slashed hard again from the other direction, narrowly missing Margot's eye, slicing a deep gash across her forehead.

'This face cost me a fortune, you fucking bitch!' Margot screeched, holding her hand to her wounds. Beth swiped at her again. Margot weaved backwards, and the steel sliced down through the thick black leather of her jacket.

'That's more like it. That's the Kitty I knew. I wondered if she was still in there. And there she is!' Margot hissed.

She glared at Beth through her gloved hands, lowering her arms to her sides. She charged towards Beth, sending her hurtling backwards. She hit the ground hard, a wave of pain shooting up from her coccyx.

She sprang up, hurling herself at Beth once more, grabbing

Beth's hair in her hands, yanking her head from side to side. This way, then that. Searing pain radiated from Beth's scalp. She thought Margot might actually tear the hair from her head.

Beth reached her hands up to Margot's own hair, grabbing two handfuls, pulling as hard as she could in retaliation. The women rolled around on the floor. For a moment, Margot had the upper hand, the next Beth was winning. They screamed, heaving each other about in the dirt. Somehow Margot managed to flip Beth onto her back and straddle her. With Margot's full weight on top of her, Beth struggled to breathe.

She placed her hands around Beth's neck and began to squeeze. Beth writhed, trying to throw Margot off, but she was too strong. Her head felt hot, her vision blurred. From somewhere in the distance, she heard Charlie's voice cry out.

'Beth! The hammer!'

She turned from side to side, as droplets of spittle dripped down from Margot's mouth, hitting Beth in the face. To her left, a foot or so from where they lay, was the discarded claw hammer. Throwing her arm out to the side awkwardly, she grappled frantically on the floor.

Margot squeezed harder, and Beth felt as though her head would explode. She felt something hard and smooth beneath her hand.

The handle.

Closing her fingers around it, she gripped it tightly, as she arced her arm up as hard as she could, screaming. The head of the hammer connected with Margot's temple with a satisfying thud.

Margot's hands loosened on Beth's throat, a stunned expression on her face. She was looking at Beth, but it was suddenly as if she wasn't seeing her.

Beth swung the hammer again, this time striking the back of Margot's head hard with the claws, gouging into her flesh.

Margot fell forwards, landing on top of Beth, who rolled, escaping from underneath the dead weight.

She stood, unsteady, a little dazed. She edged around Margot's body, prodding it with her foot. Margot didn't move. Beth turned, hurrying to Charlie, dropping the hammer.

'Are you okay?' he called to her, as she limped towards him.

'I think so. You?'

She was close to Charlie, about two or three feet. Suddenly his eyes widened, his mouth contorted into a scream.

'Behind you, watch out!'

But Beth didn't have time to react. Margot's full weight bowled into the back of her. She flew forwards, slamming into the beam which Charlie was tethered to. Her face smashed into brick. She screamed as the pillar gave way before her. She landed on Charlie, Margot tripping on the two of them, flying over them and landing a few feet behind.

Chunks of masonry and rubble showered down from above. Charlie looked up. Beth tried to get to her feet, but before she could, the balcony came crashing down around them all.

And everything stopped.

59

Dust. And darkness.

Beth's ears were ringing. She coughed, her throat dry and raspy, full of dirt. She slowly turned her neck, it was painful but she could move. Just.

Charlie's face was a few inches from hers. His eyes closed. She was unsure if he was breathing. His head and arm were the only parts of his body not covered by the rubble surrounding them. Beth couldn't see Margot. Couldn't hear her.

She blinked a few times. As the ringing in her ears subsided, it gave way to another sound. Sobbing. Faint, but definite.

Daisy. Daisy was crying.

Beth tried to roll over. A steel girder was lying across the back of her legs. Heavy, painful. She managed to dislodge one leg from beneath the beam. The other was stuck fast, trapped between bricks, and the steel, and God knows what else. There was blood too. Thick and warm, soaking into denim. Her face throbbed from the earlier collision with the pillar. She moistened her parched lips, turning onto her side. She braced her palms against the edges of the metal and pushed. It hardly budged.

She decided to change tack. She heaved herself. Something jagged sliced into her calf. She winced, sucking in air, and shaking her head. Her daughter was scared. She needed her.

Beth pulled again, harder, trying to ignore the searing pain. Her leg came free, ripping her jeans, gouging flesh on a serrated edge. She let out a whimper. She had no time to nurse her wounds.

Tearing a strip from the bottom of her blouse, she wound a tourniquet tightly around her thigh.

'Charlie,' she whispered, as if speaking would cause further carnage.

No response.

'I'm coming back for you, Charlie, I promise. I need to find the kids.'

She had no idea if he could hear her, but she needed to say it, regardless. She kissed his dusty cheek. Turning herself to a sitting position, she glanced about the room. Dust and debris floated around. The entire structure of the mezzanine had collapsed on top of them. Margot would have taken the brunt of it, with Charlie a close second.

Beth had been lucky. Incredibly lucky.

She forced herself to stand. Her weight on her injured leg was agonising.

'Daisy,' she called out into the dark, weakly.

'Mummy?'

'Daisy, keep shouting, love, I'll come to you. I need to follow the sound of your voice!' More assertive now, the desire to find her children taking over.

'Mum!' Peter now, shaken, sobbing.

'Peter! You both okay?'

'What's going on through there?'

'Don't worry about that at the moment.'

They sounded close. Beth limped her way down what would

once have been a vast corridor, past what remained of a grand staircase. Droplets of blood trailed behind her. She rounded a corner, and the walls opened out again. This part of the hotel was much more dilapidated than the rest. This must have been where the fire had hit the worst. Beth shivered as the damp air seemed to seep into her bones.

'Daisy, Peter, I need you to shout. Where are you?'

'Mummy!'

It sounded as if Daisy was right beside her.

She scanned the room. In a black corner was one of the few remaining doors. The roof was still standing above it. Beth crossed the chasm of the room to the doorway. The handle was long gone. Beth scratched at the frame. Someone had attached a padlock onto the door, holding it closed.

'Mum, is that you?'

'Yes. I'm here. Hold on!'

Beth glanced around the floor. A large chunk of masonry sat a few feet away. She grabbed it, whacking it down on the lock. The timber crumbled, the padlock shattered. Beth heaved the door open. The smell of decay filled her nostrils as she stared into the darkness. She could just about make out two shapes in the corner.

'Mummy!' Daisy cried.

'It's okay. I'm here. Everything's okay now, I promise.'

She rushed to her children, enveloping them both in her sore, bleeding arms.

'But it's not, is it?' Peter's voice wavered on the edge of tears. Beth glanced over her shoulder, assessing the distance she had travelled, wondering how much her son had heard.

'It is, she's gone. She can't hurt us anymore.' Beth sobbed as she grappled with the ropes tethering them to their chairs.

'But the damage is done, isn't it? Zoe is...' Peter couldn't bring himself to say it out loud. He broke down, and Beth realised he'd heard more than she would have wanted.

'Where's Daddy? Is he okay?'

As Beth hugged her daughter, Peter pulled away.

'You're safe,' she whispered, avoiding answering her daughter's question.

'Are we?' She could hear bitterness in her son's voice.

'Yes. It's over.'

And Beth hoped that was true.

60

A fresh start. Hopefully, the last one, but you never know.

Beth's hair, dyed a vibrant flame red now, was cut shorter and pulled up in a bright yellow scarf, tied in a neat knot on top of her head. Two small, plastic, cherry-shaped earrings dangled playfully from her lobes, green and red projected onto her neck by a shaft of winter sunlight streaming in through the bedroom window.

She lifted a pile of books from a cardboard crate and placed them onto a shelf in the corner of the room.

Daisy was doing okay, all things considered. The kids were both finding it difficult to cope with everything. But they constantly amazed Beth with their resilience. Christmas would be challenging. But they would take each day as it came. There would be good times, and there would be bad. She was certain of that. Beth didn't expect any of this would be easy. But she was a master of making the best of a situation.

Daisy was too young. She hadn't been told the ins and outs of it all. Beth knew the day would come when she would hear the stories and make up her own mind. Until then, Beth would enjoy her time with her.

Peter was harder work. He refused to forgive her, would barely remain in the same room as her. He'd heard fragments of what unfolded at the hotel. Devastated that Beth had known about Zoe and hidden it from him. She had lost him, as she'd known she would all along. But at least he was alive. He blamed her for what had happened to Zoe.

He blamed her for Charlie's death too.

And Beth supposed he was right to. This had all started with her.

Margot had not been able to let go of the wrongs that she perceived. She had tried so hard, but ultimately, she had given in to her hatred; her desire for revenge. A basic primal instinct.

Beth hadn't changed her name this time. She didn't want to lose the last part of Charlie she had left. Couldn't do that to the kids, it wasn't fair. But they moved away. Away from Brighton, the place she had called home for longer than anywhere else in her life. The only life her children had ever known. There was no choice.

People treated them differently after the tragedy at the hotel.

They would never let Beth *just* be Beth. There was always that questioning look in their eyes. And so she had done what she did best. She had run away and started again.

She placed the last of the volumes onto a shelf, returning to the box on the floor in the middle of the room. Pulling out one of Charlie's sweaters that had been wrapped around a vase, she held it close to her face. His smell enveloped her, swirled around her head, and for a moment, she thought the grief might consume her again.

She wanted to seal that fragrance in, keep it forever. She never wanted to forget.

And a sadness and longing that she suspected would never leave her, filled her heart. She smiled wistfully. The loss of Charlie along with the death of her mother had been catastrophic. She had not seen her for years, it was too dangerous, but they spoke on the phone when they could.

So many lives lost on Beth's conscience.

Crying had never come naturally to her. She had learned to fake it over the years. It was what people expected.

Each day she tried to look for a new reason to carry on. One good thing in her world. Sometimes it was almost impossible, but then she only had to look at Daisy. Hear her giggle as she chased the new puppy around the garden. And there she found her good thing. Leaving her was not an option.

And so she went through the motions. Pretended to smile, laugh, and cry. She would chat to the neighbours, throw her head back at their jokes, eyeing them cautiously for the slightest hint of recognition. She would never allow her children to come face to face with danger again.

She acted like her life was still worthwhile for the kids' sake. Sometimes, she would think of Charlie and her smile would be genuine. But it was a rare thing.

Folding the jumper neatly, she kissed it, placing it on the foot of the bed, and glanced back down into the box. A small chunky safe-deposit tin sat in her view.

The smile faded from her lips.

Her hand unconsciously drifted up to her neck, as she fondled the tiny silver key which hung around it. Her fingertips brushed against her skin, and she drew in a breath, as her heart rate increased.

'Mummy, are you coming? We're taking the puppy out for a walk!' Daisy screeched excitedly up the stairs.

'I'll be right down!' she replied, as she padded across the carpet, pushing the bedroom door gently shut, and turning the lock. Returning to the packing carton, she lifted out the metal box, holding it tightly in both her trembling hands. She pressed it against her cheek. The cold surface sent a rush through her, making the hair on the back of her neck stand to attention.

The only thing she had taken with her through every incarnation of her life. Through every identity. The one item that linked her to Kitty Briscoe.

It was peppered with rust from where it had been buried at one point. Terrified it would be discovered when she was a child, she hadn't dared keep it in the house. She had hidden it in the stables in Brighton and gone out to look at it every now and then when she thought people wouldn't notice. She was afraid she'd been caught out by Charlie, the night after the first note arrived, when she couldn't sleep and slipped out of the bedroom. She had assumed he was deep in slumber, but he had seen her. She never knew if her story about going for a walk had convinced him.

It didn't really matter anymore, she supposed.

She unfastened the chain from her neck, and the key fell into her palm. She caressed it between her fingers, biting her bottom lip. Biting so hard she drew blood. The metallic taste filling her mouth.

Hearing footsteps galloping up the stairs, she glanced nervously towards the door. The steps passed hurriedly by, and Beth relaxed a little. Pushing the key into the lock, she turned it, opening the lid and lifting out its contents.

Smiling again, she held it up to her nose, inhaling, as she had done with Charlie's sweater, but no smell remained. Placing the package down on the carpet beside her, she drew in slow, deep breaths, trying to remain calm. She carefully unfolded the grubby blue-and-white stripy fabric, tattered, fraying at the edges.

Dark stains, almost black now, coloured the material. The paring knife she had taken from her grandmother's kitchen all those years ago glinted in the sunlight. Dry blood still dirtied the steel blade. She touched it, and it sent a shiver through her body, like a spark of electricity, the same way it always did.

Excitement? Fear? She wasn't sure anymore.

She picked up the tiny lock of blond hair, tied with a scrap of pink ribbon, stroking it softly across her cheek.

She closed her eyes, saw the metal piercing Billy's skin.

Her nipples stiffened as she felt the familiar arousal, and she blushed, ashamed of her reaction to such a thing. Even after all this time.

She knew she should have got rid of the box years ago. But she couldn't bring herself to do it. She *needed* it.

She should have left it to burn in the house, along with her father's body, after she had used the knife to slit his throat.

When she had returned home that evening; the night she'd walloped him on the head with the bronze horse. He was paralytic in his chair. He'd drunk himself into oblivion again. A cigarette sat smouldering in the ashtray beside him. She knew that there would be trouble when he was sober the following day. She had crossed a line. She'd answered back before, but she had never *dared* to strike him.

He would make her pay. Without a doubt. Her mother too.

So she had retrieved the weapon from its hiding place. Crept up behind him where he slept and finished it. There and then. It had still been sharp, which surprised her, but it sliced through his flesh like a wire through cheese. The fire had covered her tracks, leaving nothing behind but charred bones.

She had no choice. She did it to save her mother. And to save herself. But that didn't mean she hadn't relished it.

With one final glance downwards, she folded the package up again, placing it back into its casing, firmly locking it and replacing the key around her neck. She crossed to the bookcase, pushing a few of the tomes aside. She slid the box to the back of a tall shelf, replacing the books in front of it.

She needed these keepsakes. They were part of her, and she was part of them. Besides, she liked how they made her feel. The buzz. The power.

They reminded her what she was capable of.

Despite all the years she had spent denying it, there was no escaping what she had done.

She would always be the girl who got away with murder.

THE END

ACKNOWLEDGEMENTS

First of all, I'd like to thank Colin, for supporting me through this entire process, and giving me the kick I needed at times to keep going. It's a scary step taking a dream and turning it into a reality, so to have wonderful friends and family giving me the encouragement I needed to carry on has been a game changer. So to the handful of special people who have stood by me every step of the way... you know who you are, and I love you.

I'd also like to thank each and every one of my readers, who have truly given me the confidence to carry on writing. It's been a rollercoaster of a year, but for me, nothing will ever take away the feeling of releasing my debut and knowing that people enjoyed it. To those of you who took the time to let me know your thoughts, feelings and opinions, who spoke to me about my characters as if they were real people... you ROCK! Without you guys, there wouldn't be any point in me creating my stories, so I will be eternally grateful to all of you. Thank you!

A NOTE FROM THE PUBLISHER

Thank you for reading this book. If you enjoyed it please do consider leaving a review on Amazon to help others find it too.

We hate typos. All of our books have been rigorously edited and proofread, but sometimes mistakes do slip through. If you have spotted a typo, please do let us know and we can get it amended within hours.

info@bloodhoundbooks.com

Lightning Source UK Ltd.
Milton Keynes UK
UKHW011228180321
380574UK00001B/120